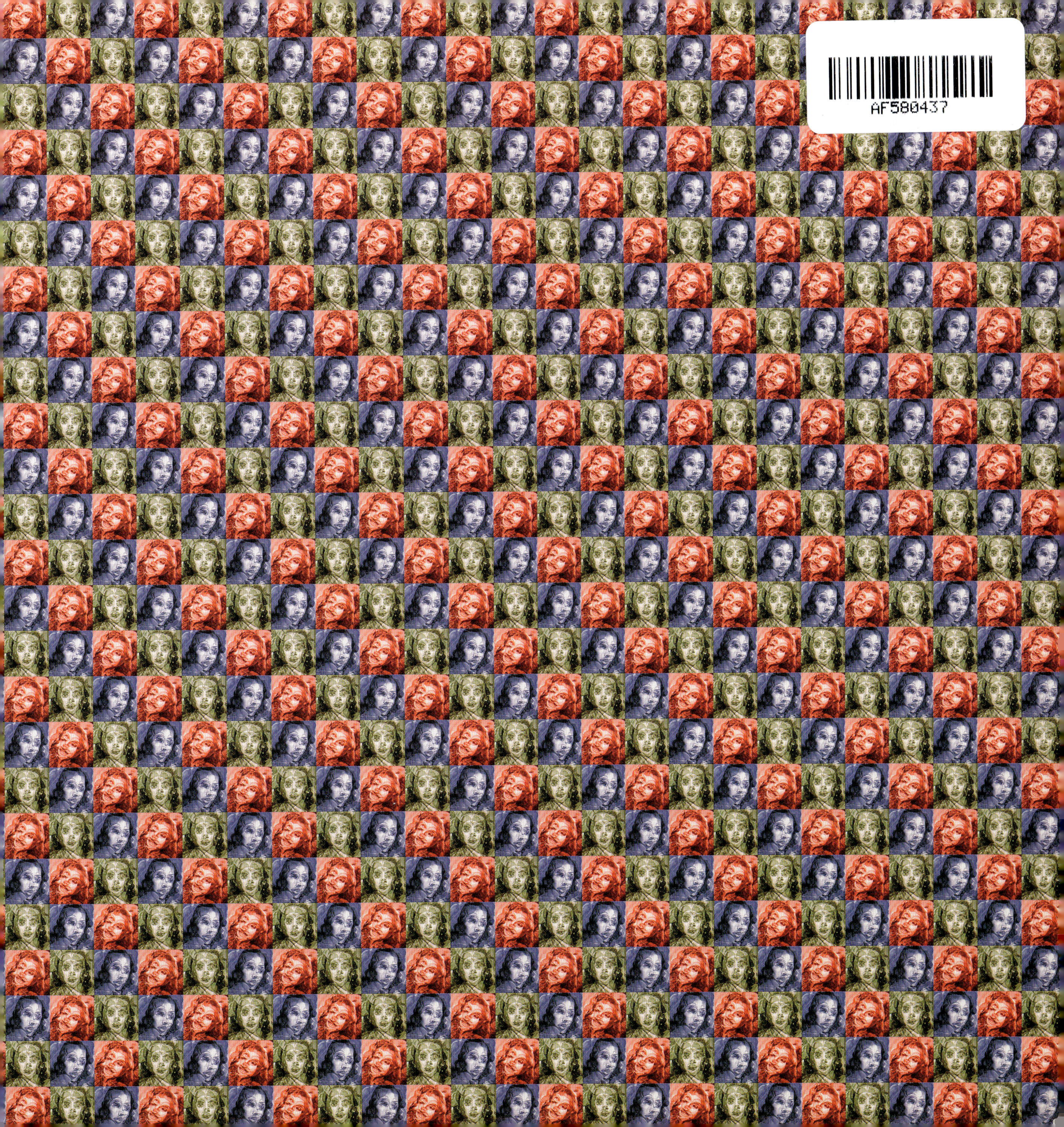
AF580437

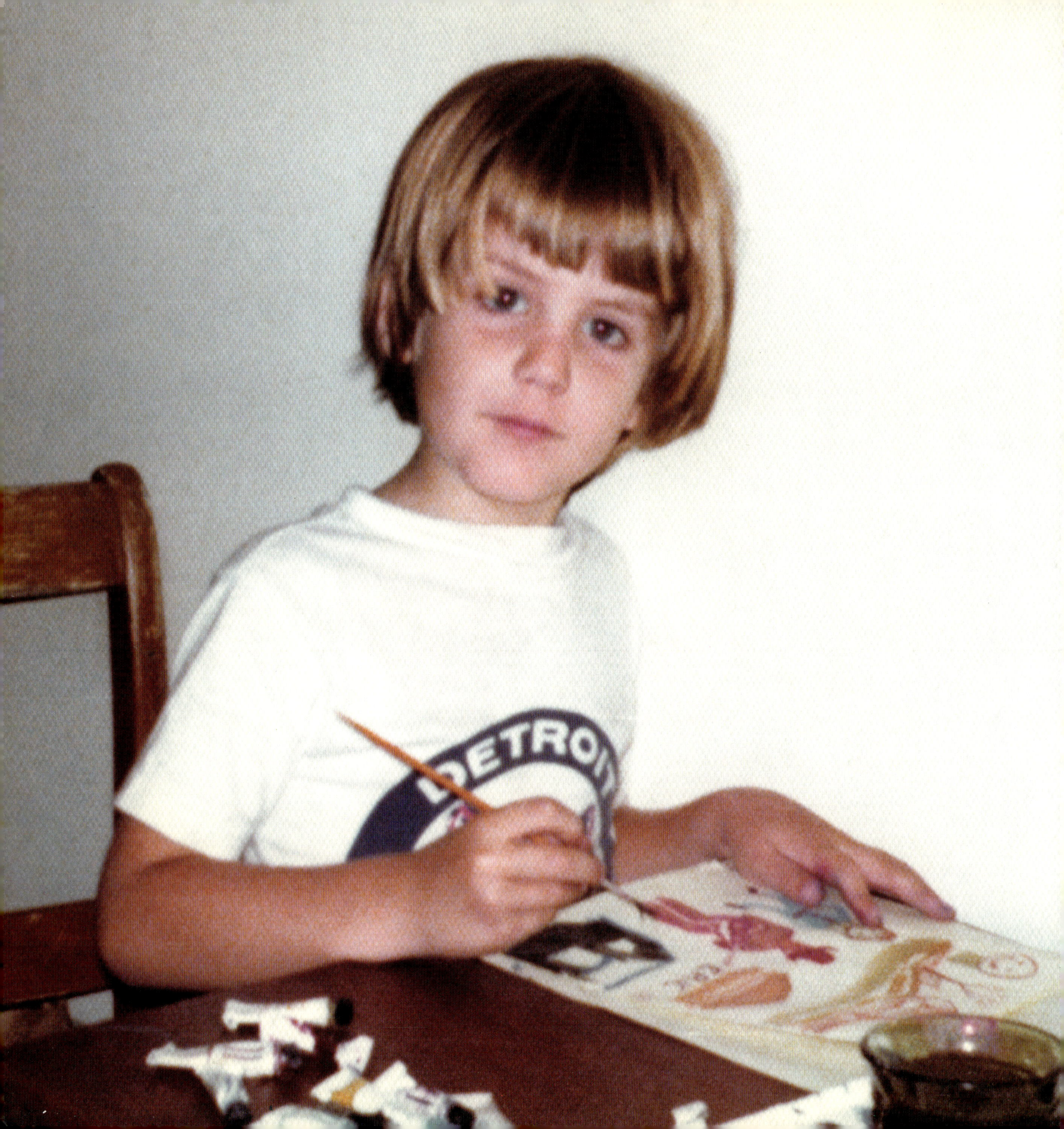
DETROIT

eric white

it feeds itself

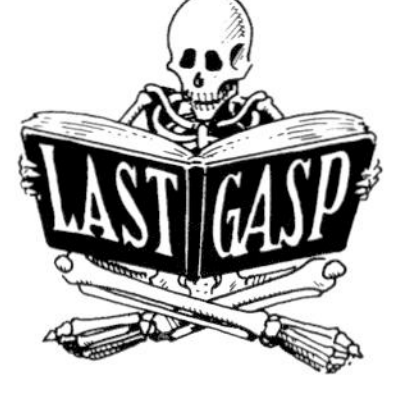

eric white: it feeds itself

First Edition Copyright © 2003 by Eric White

Published in 2003 by Last Gasp of San Francisco
777 Florida Street
San Francisco CA 94110
www.lastgasp.com

ISBN 0-86719-547-9 (hardbound)
ISBN 0-86719-483-9 (softbound)

All rights reserved. No part of this book may be reproduced or transmitted in any form or by any means electronic or mechanical including photocopying, recording, xerography, scanning, or any information storage or retrieval system now, or developed in the future, without prior permission in writing from the publisher.

"Regarding Eric White" © 2003 by Gail Zappa
"Dear Eric" © 2003 by Viggo Mortensen
"Adventures In Ulteriority" © 2003 by Carlo McCormick

Edited by Annie Tucker
Designed & Nitpicked by Eric White
All artwork photographed by Paul Felder, with the exception of
p. 34, 72, 74, 75, 87, 88, 91, 96 photographed by Steven Bates
p. 80 photographed by Tom Alexander
p. 92 photographed by Paul Kaufman
Color scans by Dana Wysocki at Raffi Imaging

Front cover: "Intermezzo" 1999

Printed & bound in Hong Kong

Text Set in Baskerville by John Baskerville 1706-1775 and DIN by Albert-Jan Pool 1960-

Contents

Dedication

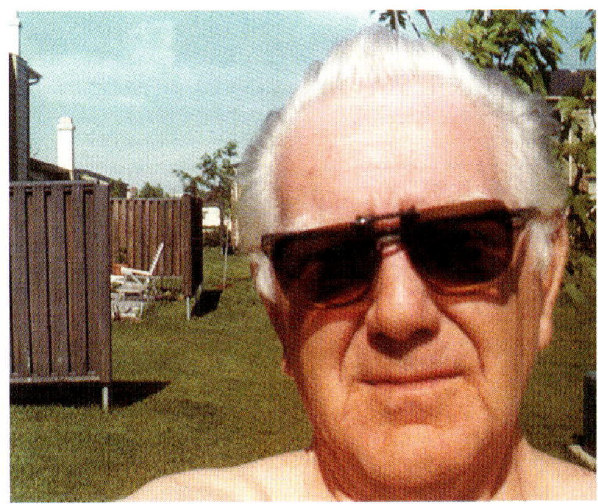

Gordon White 1901-1979
My paternal grandfather. The first painter I ever met.

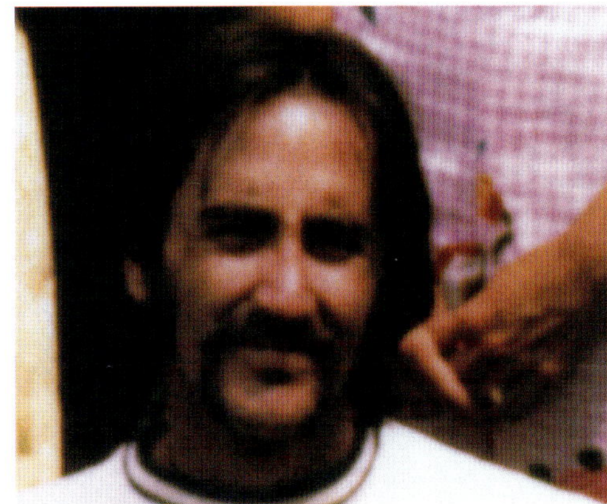

Gregory Lloyd Atkin 1946-1978
My uncle and the first person I noticed who was passionate about music.

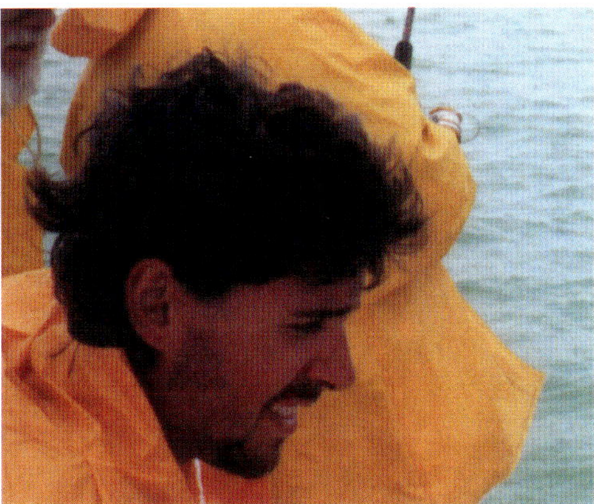

John Robert Janssen 1967-1994
My best friend from six months of age.

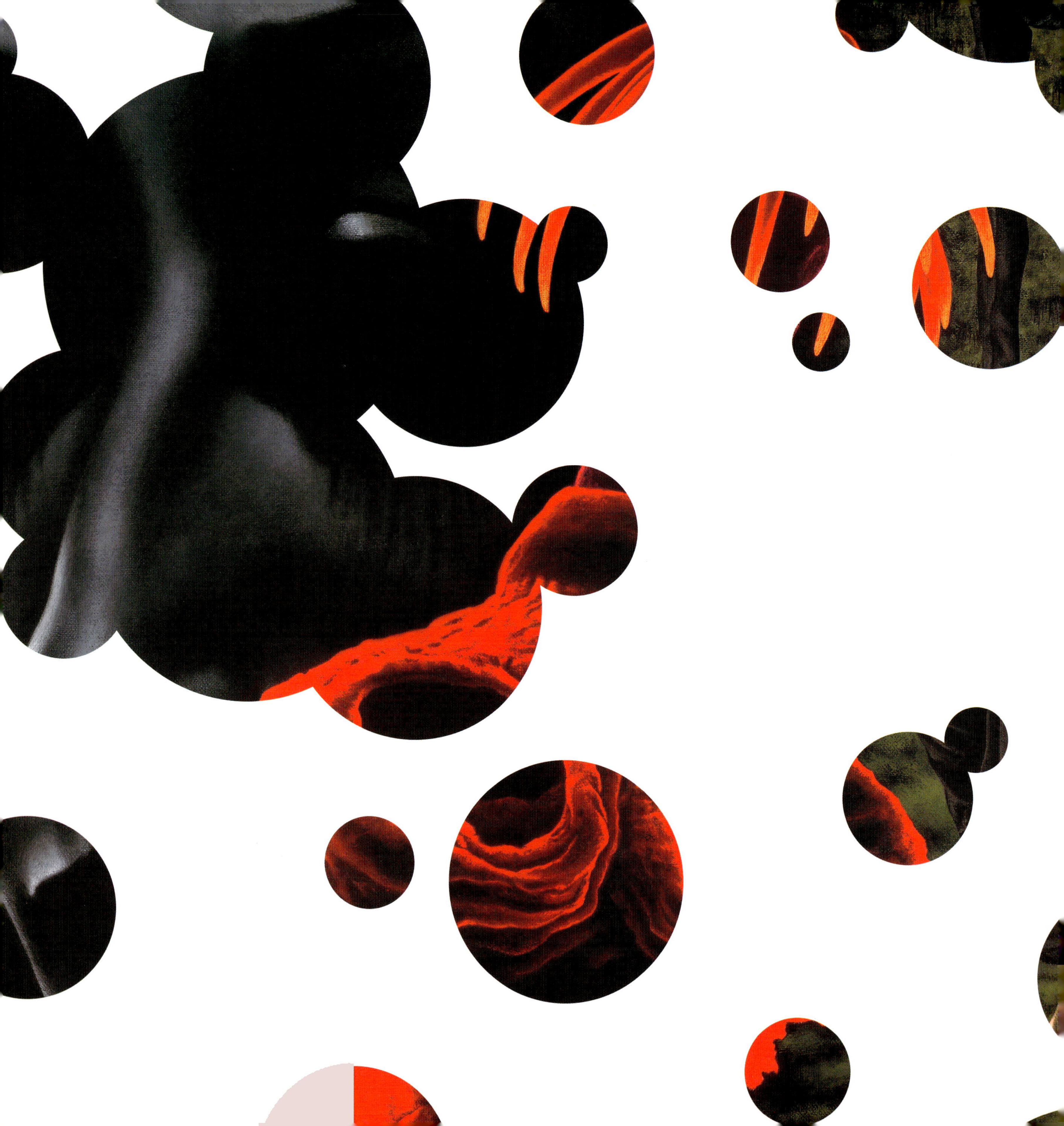

To Whom Concerns This:

When asked to write a foreword, only one word instantly pronounced itself regarding Eric White—Revelation!

I remember, in some deep reach of X-, Y-, or Z-mas past, cartoons (drawn and animated) in which the artist used a dotted line to indicate what was being viewed by a character in the strip. This line went directly from the character's eyeball (which was sometimes exaggerated for style or reaction) to the object under observation. Eric's work utilizes an excruciatingly similar technique—but with a nuclear difference. He makes *you* draw your own visceral dotted line directly from those red balloons behind your eyes to the matter at hand. Meanwhile (hold onto your little cotton socks), dontcha just have an aiiiieeeeE.S.P. from the eerie mathematics of simulcasting yourself into the actual painting, with an actual mystic dotted line from Eric's slightly exaggerated eyeball connected to you as the object under scrutiny? And dontcha feel that you just got the best seat in the theatre of the absurd? Dontcha?

When you look at a photograph of, let's say, a group of family members or dogs playing in a park, have you never been struck numb by the fact of its flatness, the images all rolled out like pastry dough, compared to the real-time experience of actually *seeing*? And when you *are*, dontcha just notice how your focus shifts all along the landscape of what is being mapped by your attention, your regard?

Regarding Eric White. It's like petting cats. Feeling bone, muscle undulating along under the 'neath, hairs growing/being high-tide texture, Fur! Feeling warmth, strangeness of creaturedom, miraculous other-dumb, the kittyness of Purr. Billions and zillions of sensational reminders waving, warping, and weaving the stuff of cosmosis.

You may see a cat's eye ten thousand times in a moment and have an intimate meld with each of her lashes, her whiskers (who got to name those!?) the stretch of her paw, a lick of her tongue, a wink; the flash in the iris takes you to Mars for several light years. But this is all happening in parsecs, and still you are seeing/reading the light coming through the window, the dust motes, the etceterae of experience, a moment! And this is what comes to me while regarding Eric White. The canvas looks right at you, loudly resonating its beakulent, tough and glyphty splendor, and it makes you Regard. Eric draws Us. In. Over. And Out. No waiting.

Regards,

Gail Zappa
Los Angeles, California, June 2003

Dear Eric,

Safely removed to the backside of the middle of where no harm spoken is heard, watching the hem of a new moon rub away the edge of a ridge that may be a roof or a bridge. Grateful for the idea of a draft that might play with unbuttoned sleeves, of end-of-summer surrenders pulling up stubborn dry roots of indecision, of polite distances bridged as heads are held and necks are allowed to collapse. There is a deer by the side of a two-lane road, lying dead in fresh-mown clover. There is also a drawing on a sheet of white paper folded three times into a neat, blank square—forgotten in a seat-back pocket of a regional commuter plane that sits idle on a Chicago runway. The drawing is the beginning of a recreation of the tragic summer snapshot, with the deer perhaps changed from a doe to a two-point buck for additional manipulative impact on imagined viewers of an intended painting. Is there a connection between roadkill and sketch? Did the artist actually see the deer? Did he merely hear about it or think the whole thing up while he was driving to the airport? Are you the artist? Is there such a drawing? Will anyone ever see it? Is it gone, disposed of by ground crew service personnel? Will it hang as is on a baggage office bulletin board or in a child's room? Will it ever be continued by your hand or any other?

Let us say that a particular painting is a glimpse of an important personal event that took place a number of years ago, say twenty-nine years ago. That would put it at 1974, at this point, complete with all the associations that year or number might carry for anyone. Or, we can assert that this painting was made very recently, entirely fabricated without any conscious emotional involvement in subject matter or imagery on the part of the artist. We are defined by our connection to other people—by connections long-standing or just made, by connections broken, never made, or never to be. We are alone, together and apart. Why is the man walking out of the room, why does the woman hold onto the table in that way, why does she smile so painfully, why are there so many solitary people on the beach? Sometimes we see or experience events in such a way that they consciously stay with us. Sometimes we make paintings to tell a story about what we've seen. When we make paintings or tell stories for no specific reason, with no particular goal or audience in mind, we choose to be alone and lonely. What was it Marilyn Monroe's character in *The Misfits* said?: "If I'm going to be lonely, I want to be alone"—or something like that. Being alone can be as much a comfort as a curse. It is where we know we belong, where we come from, and where we certainly are going. At rest, in the middle of our own quiet, blessedly immune to observation, criticism, or praise. Get lost, imitate no one, go beneath hard-won refinement and craftsmanship, let yourself destroy everything you have made. Isn't that part of what you are up to, Eric?

Viggo Mortensen

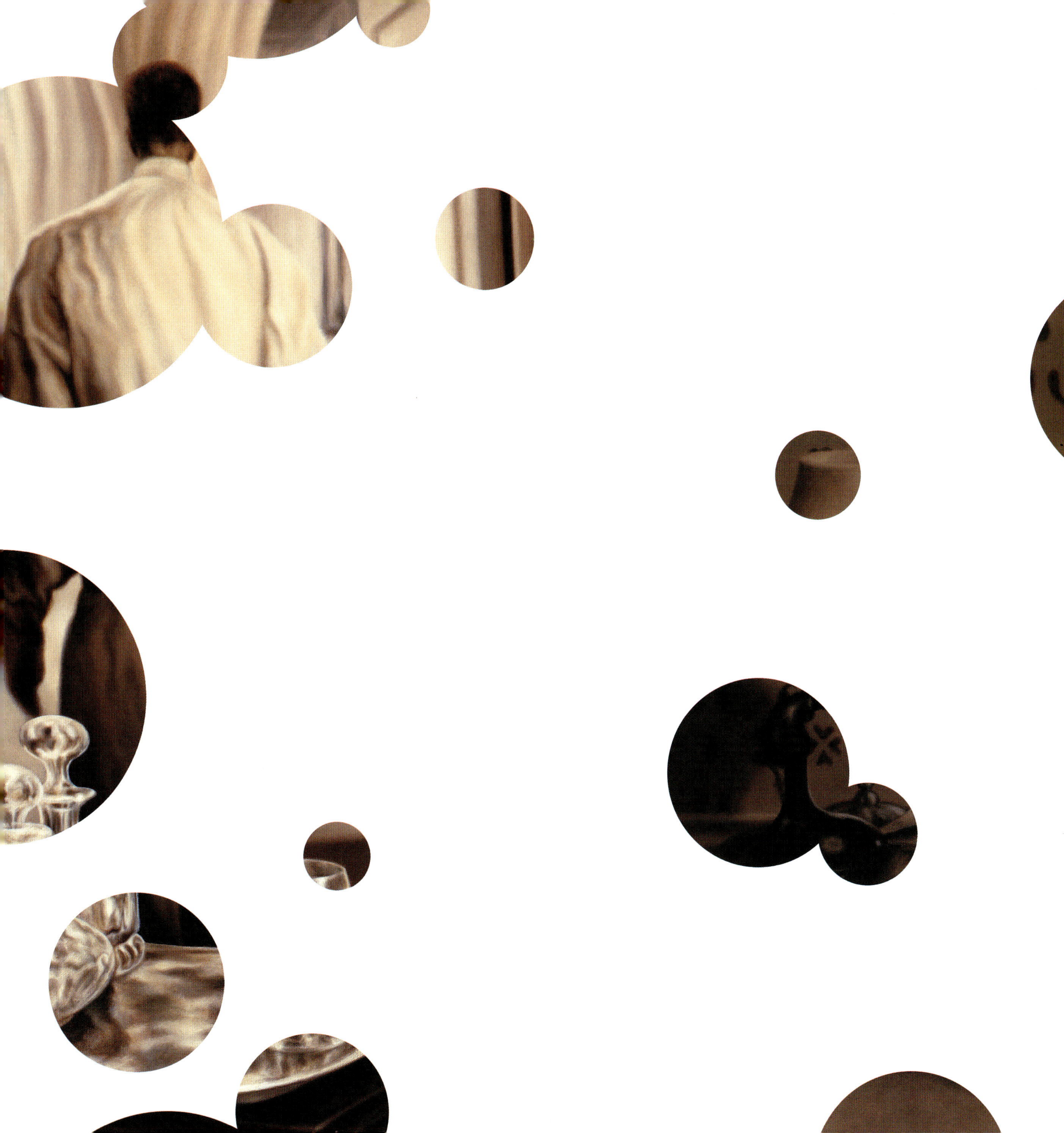

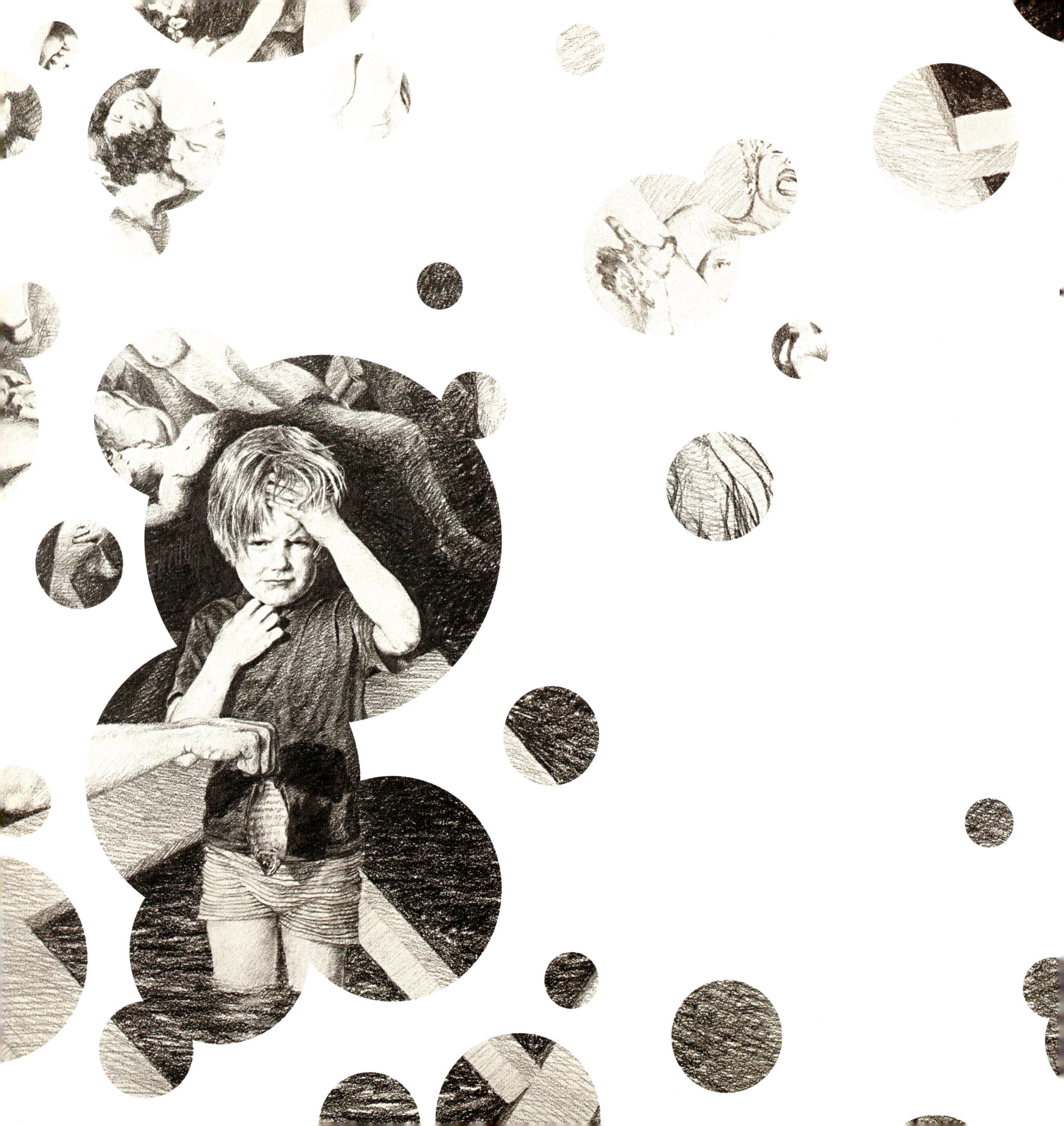

Adventures In Ulteriority

Carlo McCormick

Life as we know it is certainly a self-evident construct. Once we give up on the fallacy of knowing, however, and finally admit to ourselves that we haven't really a clue about the nature of being, well, that opens up a rich lode of alternatives. And should we happen to cede our limited perspective to a grander vision of ulterior and alternative realities, there might be no better place to look than to set our gaze within the visual dementia and representational whimsy of Eric White's paintings. White himself maintains that his art is fundamentally concerned with tapping into other dimensions of consciousness and existence that may be less evident but are there all the same. Whether one buys into the actuality of these eminently believable fictions is hardly important. Rather, the understanding they collectively impart is vital to our acknowledgment that the only thing perhaps vaster in scale than the cosmos itself is the scope of the human imagination. Unbound from the strictures of consensus reality, as it is with Eric White, there is undoubtedly no place it cannot take us.

For all its passages of radical distortion, poly-perverse morphism, and darkly subversive portraiture, Eric White's art is essentially grounded deeply in the recognizable world. This oeuvre may mark a considerable leap of imagination, but what White proposes is, at heart, much more a modulation and mediation than an outright act of invention. We must read these pictures, then, as a set of interventions, a way of cruelly undermining the crutches of normative cognition, in which the sly insinuation of an "other" preferably abstains itself from obviating the original. We see the doorways of myriad alternatives, but we consistently remain in the same hallway of an organically recognizable architecture. There's madness here, yet we remain in the general neighborhood of reason. And this is important to remember about Eric White's visionary streak. He may bend, warp, and twist reality, but he's persistent in and insistent on maintaining a fair regard for that raw stuff with which he's joyfully taking such liberties. It is as if, in the face of the common coinage of surrealism, White realizes that one way to avoid the debasedly vulgar terms of its populist proliferation is to recover the root term of this historicized hyphenate—to stress the realism as an emphatic authority to the fantasy itself.

Obsessively crafted in a digital age of endlessly reproductive domains, an unself-conscious idiosyncrasy of our rampant interconnectivity, Eric White paints for the global village idiot that is all of us today. Amidst his many contemporaries of visual samplers and appropriationists, we must admit that White chews his food very carefully. And oh, what a diet. Culled heavily from the sepia-toned glamour of what now, in our fully dawned entertainment age, must seem to be some distant arcadian past, White's investment in the imagery and imagination of '30s- and '40s-era Hollywood is for more than its aesthetic appeal alone. Much as film narrative at that time could be seen to invoke some disruption in conventional experience, the whirlwind of drama always promises its temporality and an eventual return to the norm. So, too, the engagement between what is familiar and what is alien in Eric White's paintings is one of the glancing blow, the flash or glimpse that, in its brief intensity, offers its lessons only in residual after-fact. The fearful beauty, rapture, panic, and hallucinatory revelation White offers is caught almost in fleeting, a snapshot that's steeped in recollection, a most memorable intermezzo.

If there is some nostalgia here, it is surely more for fiction than fact—for the perfection and ideal of an invented, sanitized, and airbrushed construction of reality. Be it the humor or the horror, Eric White intuitively shies away from the obvious, entering the bizarre with subtlety, taking it in and presenting it as obliquely askance. By not trying to juggle the real so much as navigate the artifice, White imagines in the conjunctive syntax of the digital ether and renders that vision in the hushed tones of photographic veracity. These paintings do not ask us to believe, but to suspend belief, to entertain the unlimited spectrum of ulteriority that lies beyond the usual field of vision. By colliding an unwieldy mass of visual information and shifts of perspective, within a very clean and bare iconographic field, density literally collapses space. Nothing can remain individuated or discrete within White's gaze, the layering always a convergence where everything seemingly infects everything else around it. The different planes of focus float the ordinary in a miasma of the uncanny, the art, like the creative process of the artist here, bringing together an esoteric catalogue of found fictions that only begin to make sense once they have been conjoined. The composition, like the ontology that directs it, is about the possibilities of coexistence and the kinds of multi-dimensionality you need to map such a non-linearity.

The metaphysics proposed by Eric White's paintings may be read in the compositional terms of their interdictions against space and surface, but the ultimate effect is more a psychological than formalist construction. Aspects of the latter bring to mind the pictorial strategies of Rauschenberg and Salle, but it is toward the former, that theater of the mindscape, where White intuitively directs his attentions and in which we find a more compelling method to the madness. By such a reading, it is hard not to find in White's hybrid representations an abiding sense of personal alienation. This is a mutant otherness that is a matter not simply of the freakishness in the figuration but of what is felt, and conveyed, by the artist. In a vernacular made all the more believable by an obsessively meticulous technique that all but makes invisible the artist's hand, a tightly rendered, seamless reality of homogenized representation unfolds ever-more-distressed anatomies of the uncanny and monstrous. This is not the world as it is, then; it is another way of seeing it. And this difference, qualitative and quantifiable, posits both the possibility of something else that we do not see, as well as the certainty that all perceptual shifts away from consensus reality are a matter of individual understanding. "Much of what is considered ordinary strikes me as grotesque," White tells us, and it is precisely in the way he weds the eerie to the everyday that we see how the commonplace can be an expression of such unmitigated horror.

By such an account, in which White's way of seeing is a reflection of his faith in the invisible and his disaffection with the apparent, these paintings are ever more fully grounded in the spiritual tradition of art's visionary lineage. The prevailing sense of mutancy, particularly here, where it is stripped of the malignancy typically associated with aberrant forms, is also quite close to this mystical form of thinking. So often, in the most utopian or apocalyptic of futurist visions, those who seek a way out of the conventional rationalist reality do so by heralding the rise of a new mutant order. Rather than proclaiming so with rhetoric, Eric White opts to simply make this transgression of the social body comprehensible to the eye. Inasmuch as White takes his cues from pre-war Hollywood's idealization of women to paint his "perfect female as quasi-religious icon," he maintains a fluid discursive relationship with time itself, arguing that if, by our attention spans, a half century constitutes ancient history, it is in fact only a blink in the eye of time. But he does something far more profound than confronting the relativity of time. What White is really after is a way to disassemble the false architecture of the self.

Deeply influenced by the works of Jane Roberts, White has, in his recent work, now come to find a visual equivalent for the parapsychological models Roberts developed in her radical theories on the nature of reality. Remembered today mostly for her claims to be acting as a channel, or medium, for the consciousness of a personality named Seth, who is "no longer focused in physical reality," it is her concept of a multi-dimensional personality that has had the greatest bearing on White's creative agenda. For White, the altered perceptions of his work are, as opposed to being mere hallucinations, embodiments of the innumerable aspects of ourselves that are living outside our own space and dimension. As for time, then, based here on the perpetually self-enfolding schematics of reincarnation, all memory has the actuality of itself being a recovery of past lives. What is important in this artist's position is that, regardless of whether or not you believe in any extra-physical source, these and other ideas be explored.

While White believes personally that Roberts channeled an entity named Seth, he does not necessarily expect the same from his audience. And the core of his beliefs—that we create our own reality as consciousness creates form; that the self is but a fragment of a greater consciousness, or multi-manifested self; and that the time/space model we live by is erroneous and incapable of acknowledging the non-linear and co-existent aspects of being—may not make the grade of high science, but they are certainly fundamental to much of the greatest art over the past century. Such ideas may have utterly changed the way Eric White perceives the world, but in the end, this artist reminds us of a truth more evident than any hypothesis whose validity he upholds: "I enjoy having my reality fucked with." That, it would seem, accounts for the poetics and passion of his art, as well as for the pleasure it affords us all.

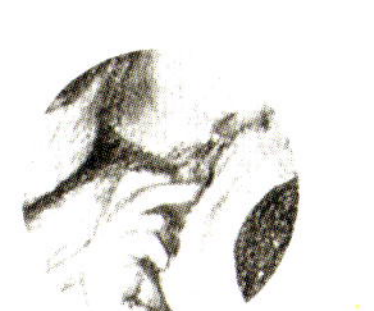

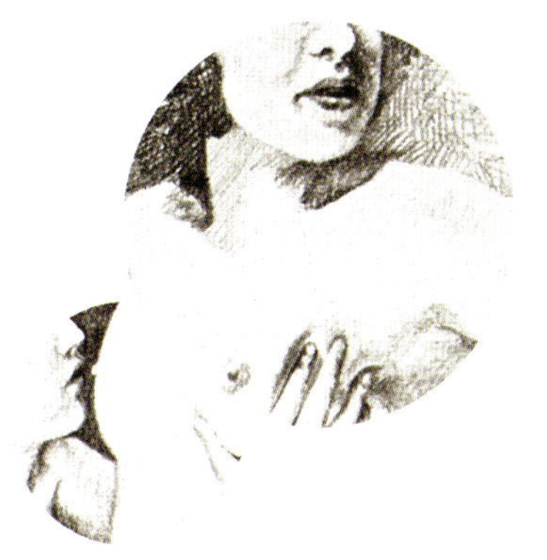

Paintings

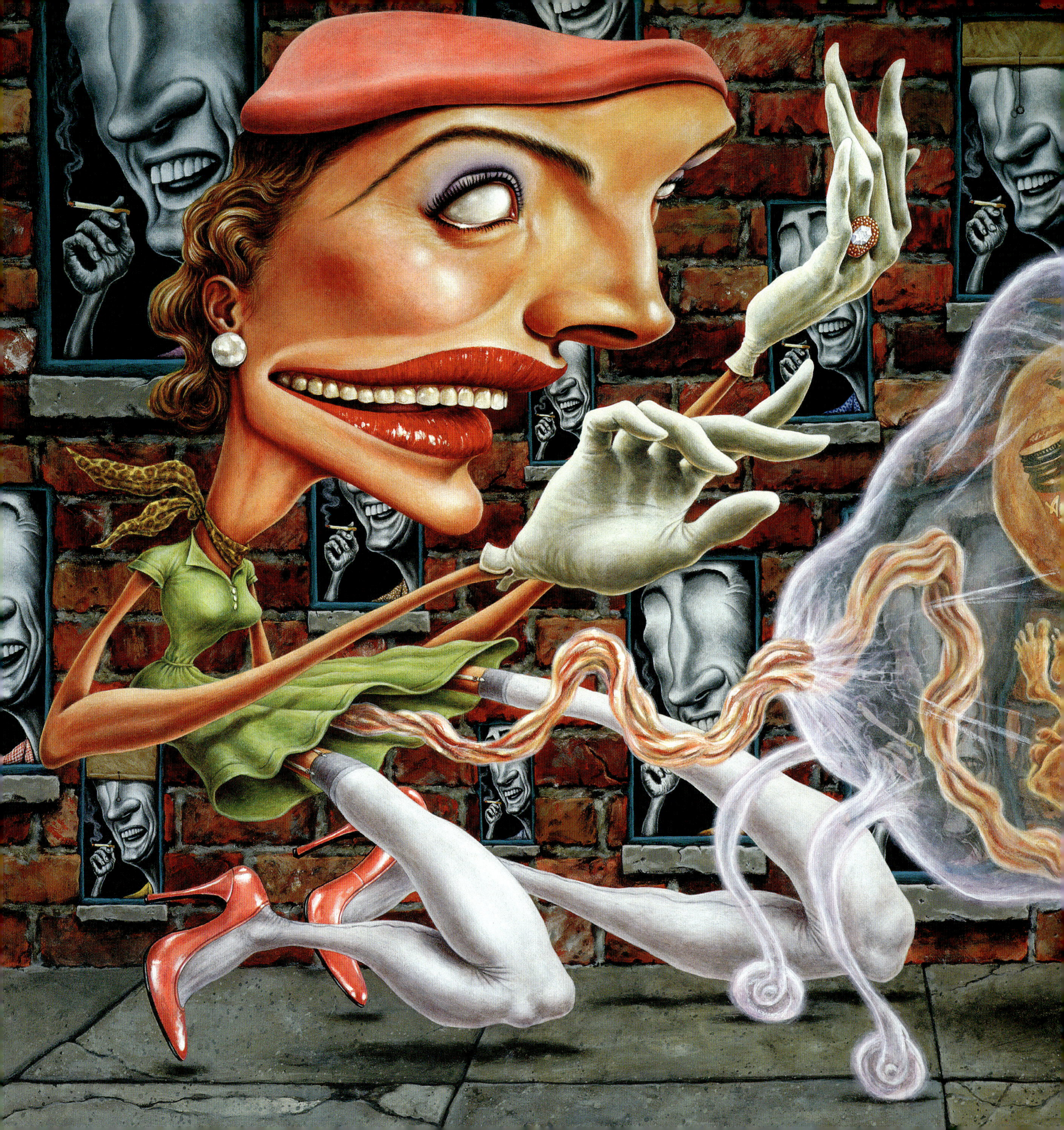

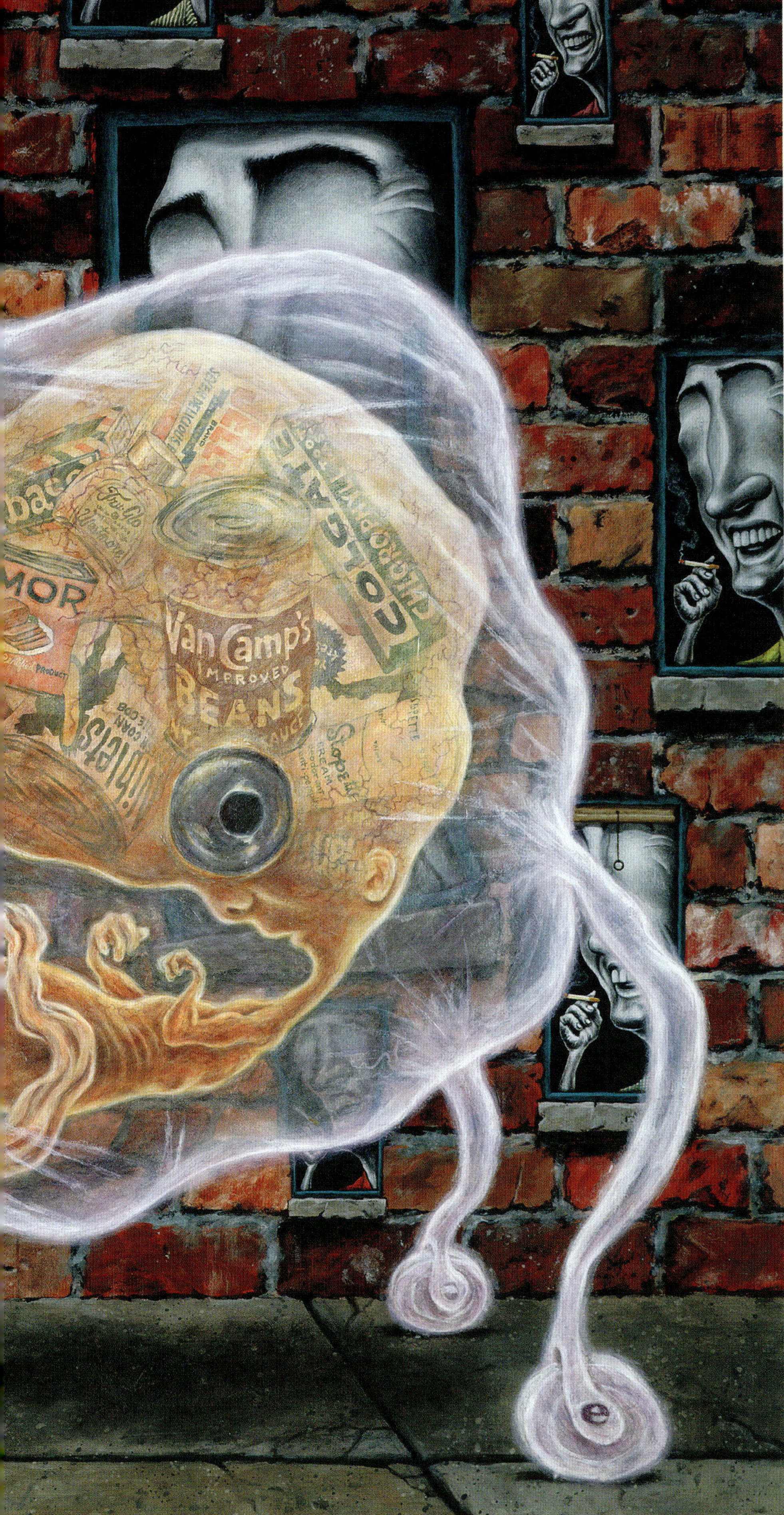

You Add Fresh Eggs 1996

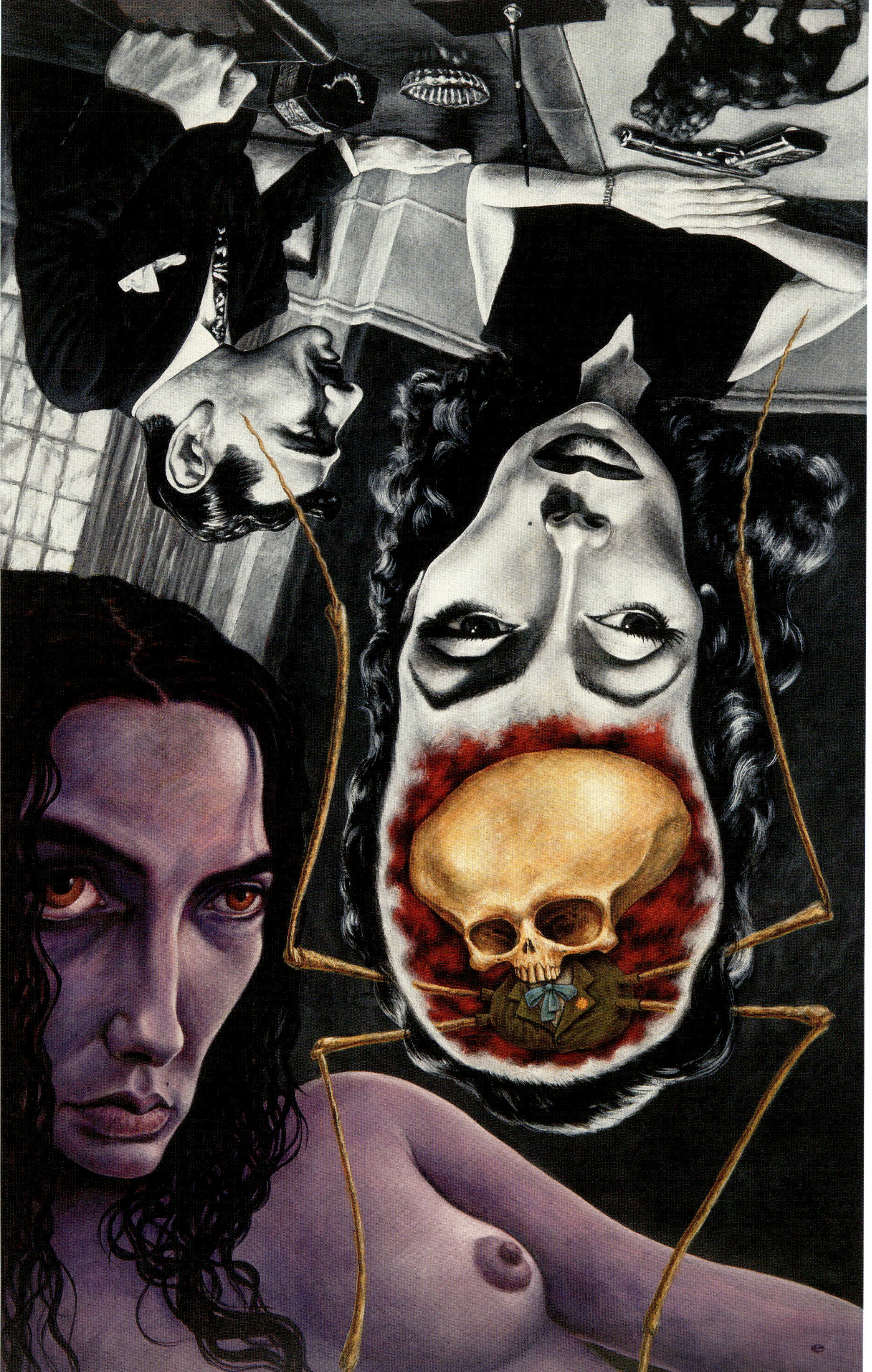

Dia de los Muertos 1995

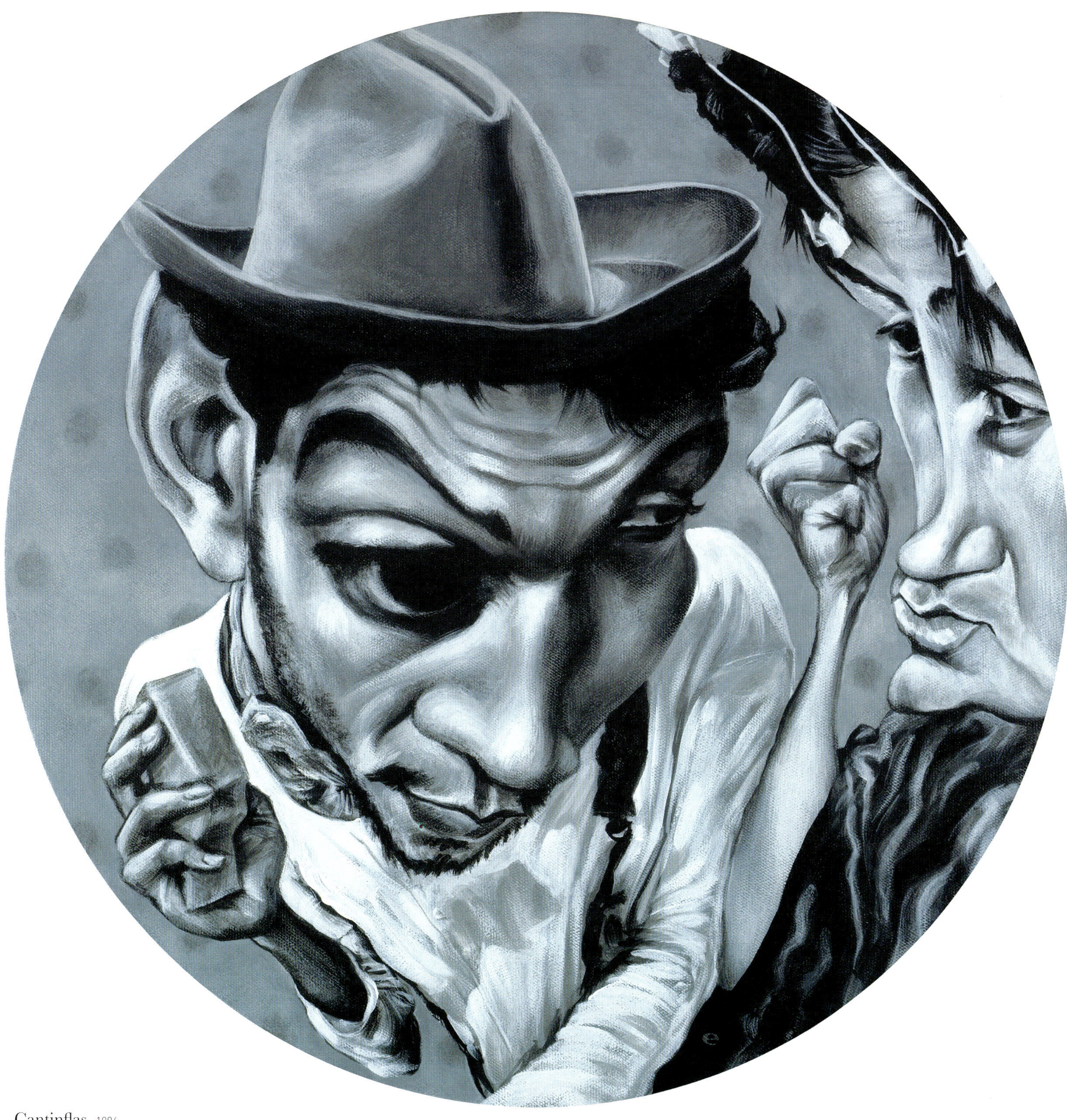

Cantinflas 1996

A Place in the Sun (Explained) 1996

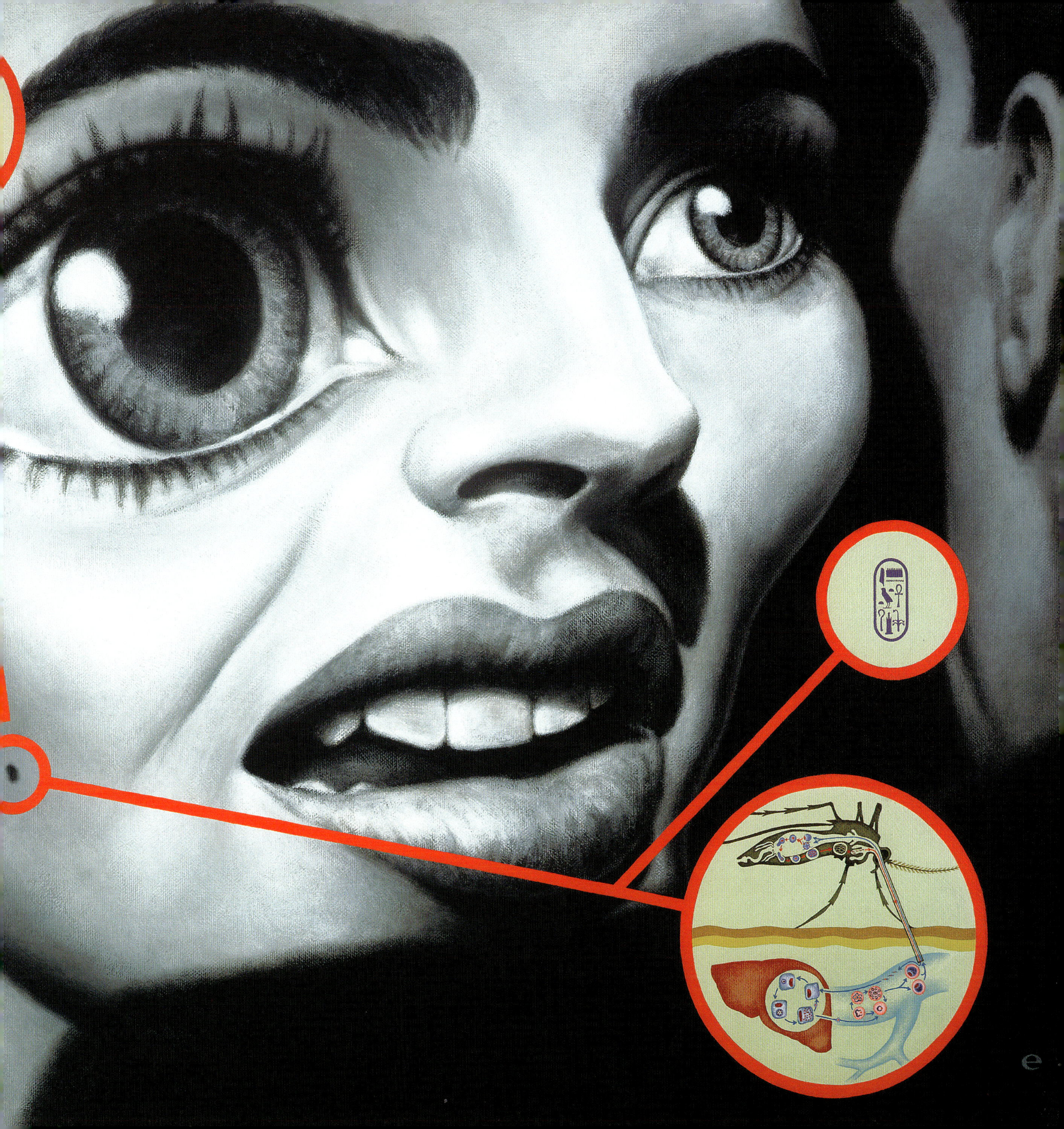

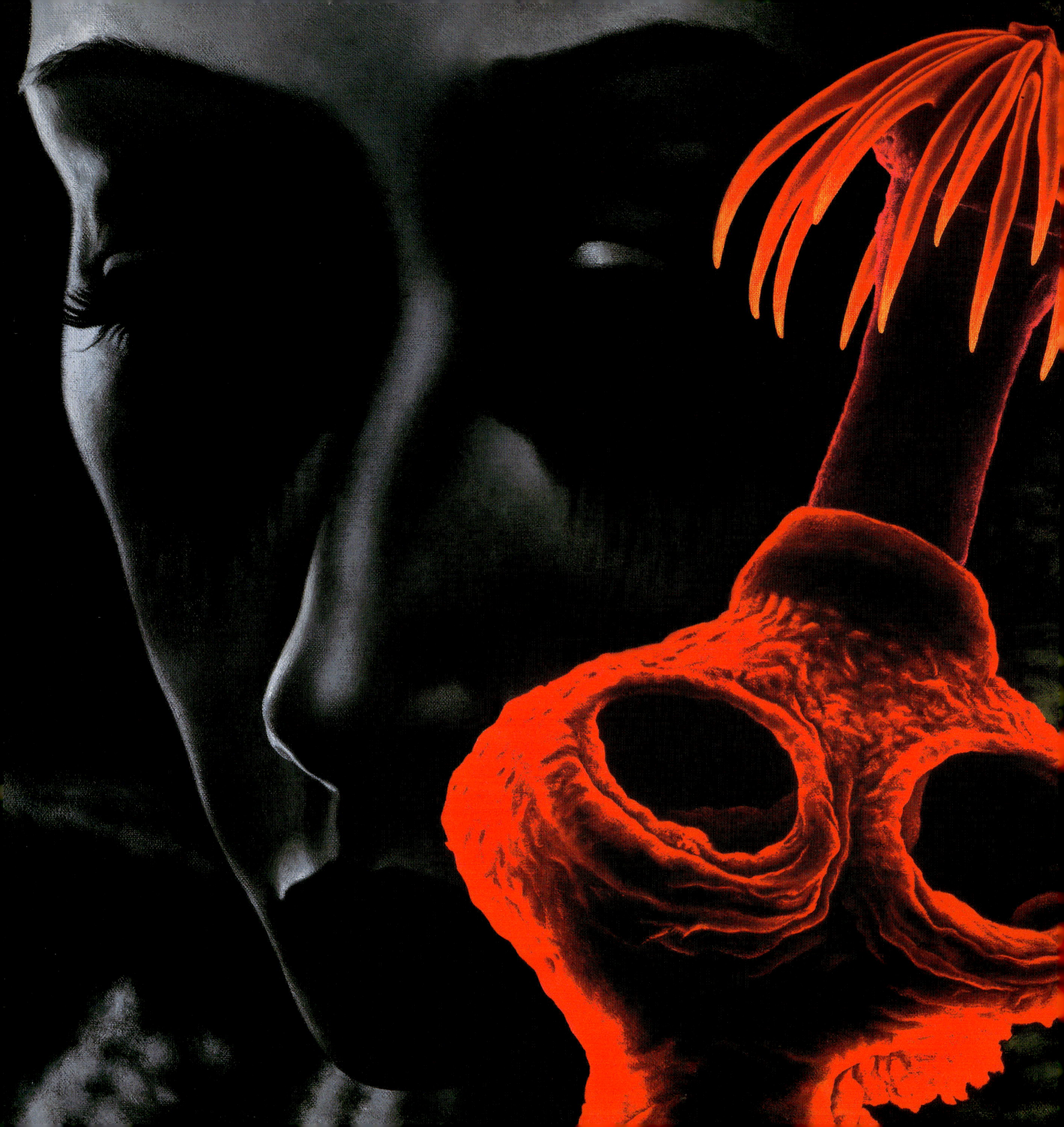

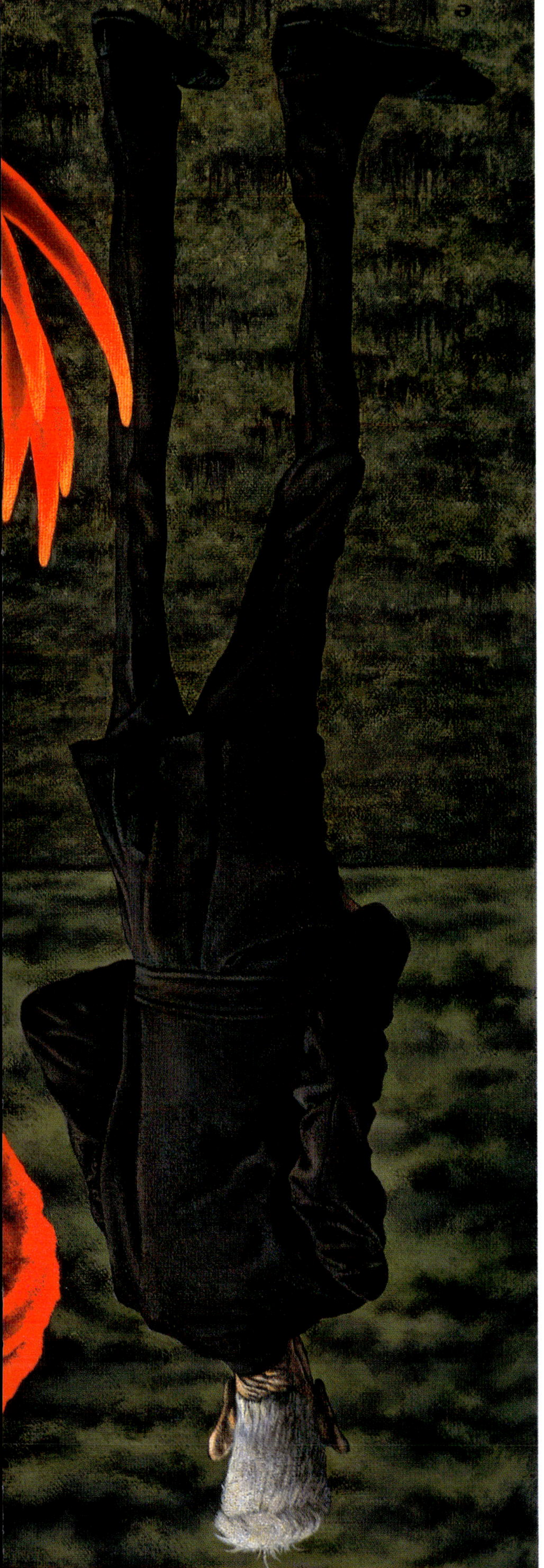

Expulsion from Paradise 1996

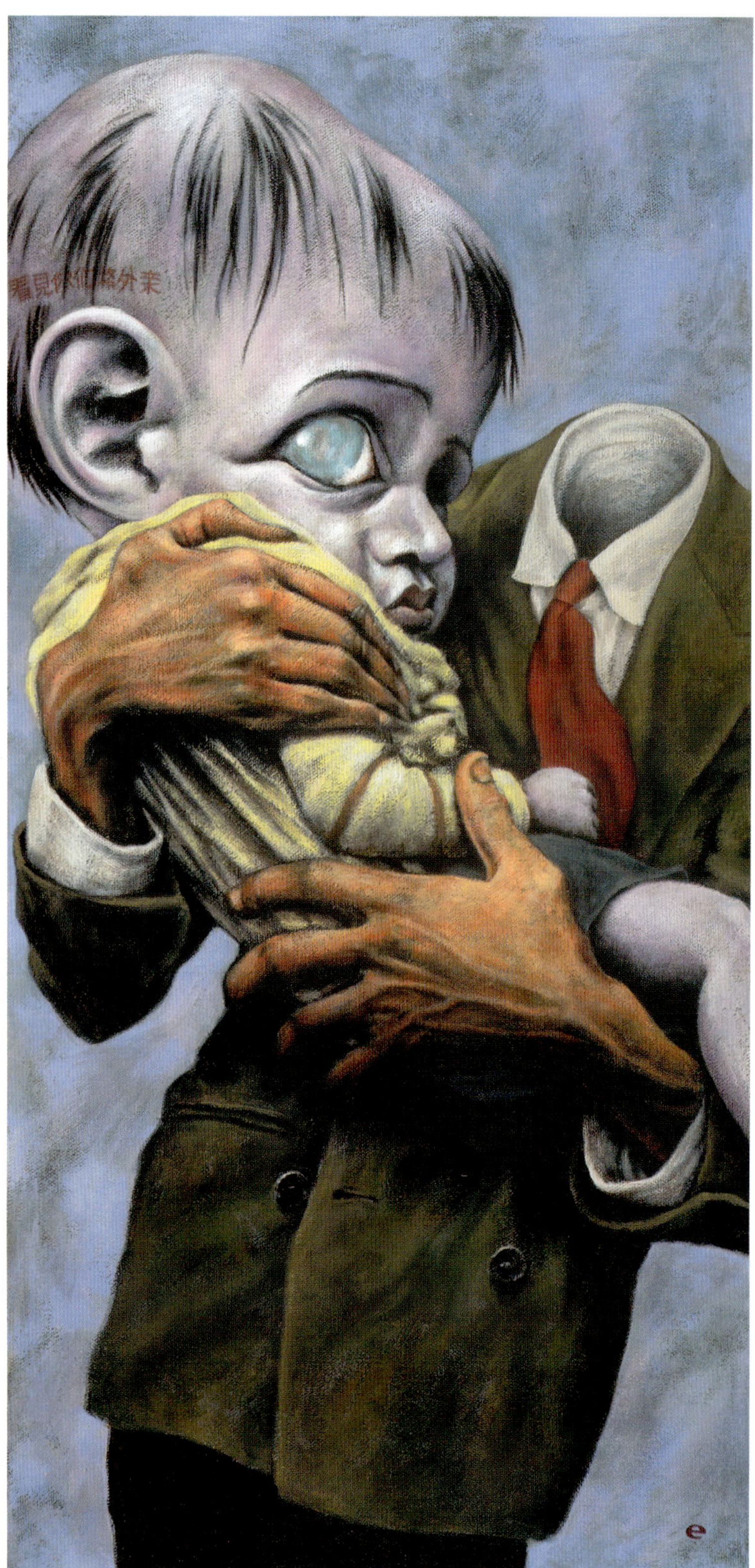

Dearer Than Ever to Us 1996

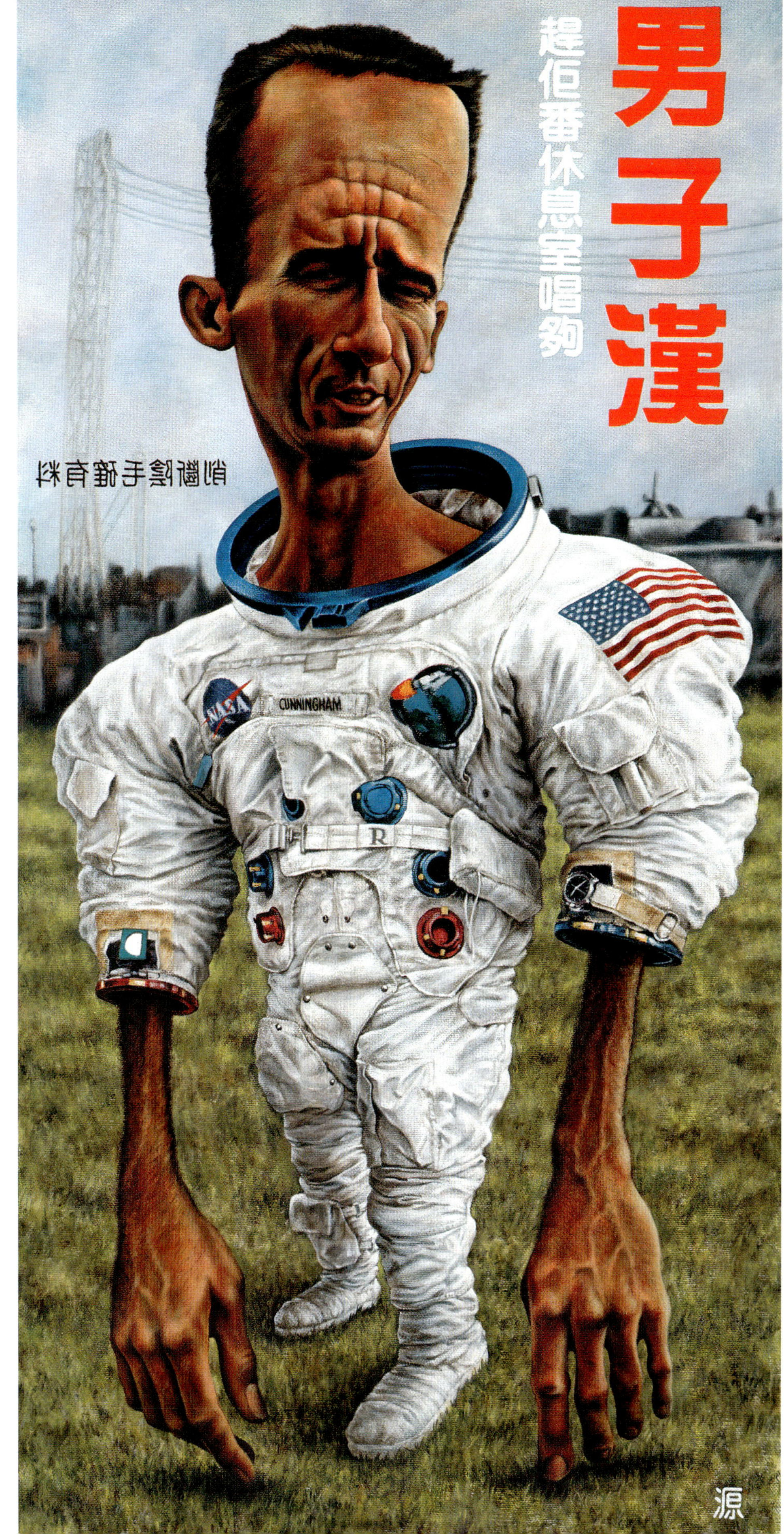

Apollo 7 1996

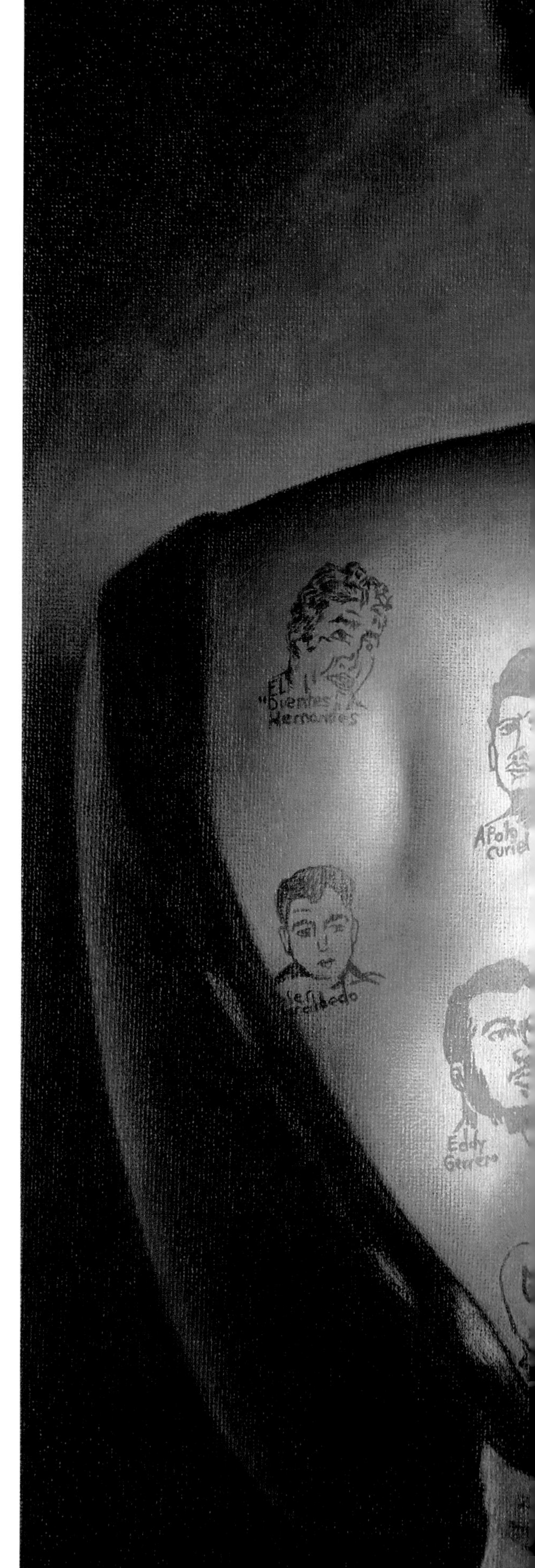

Pursuit of Happiness 1996

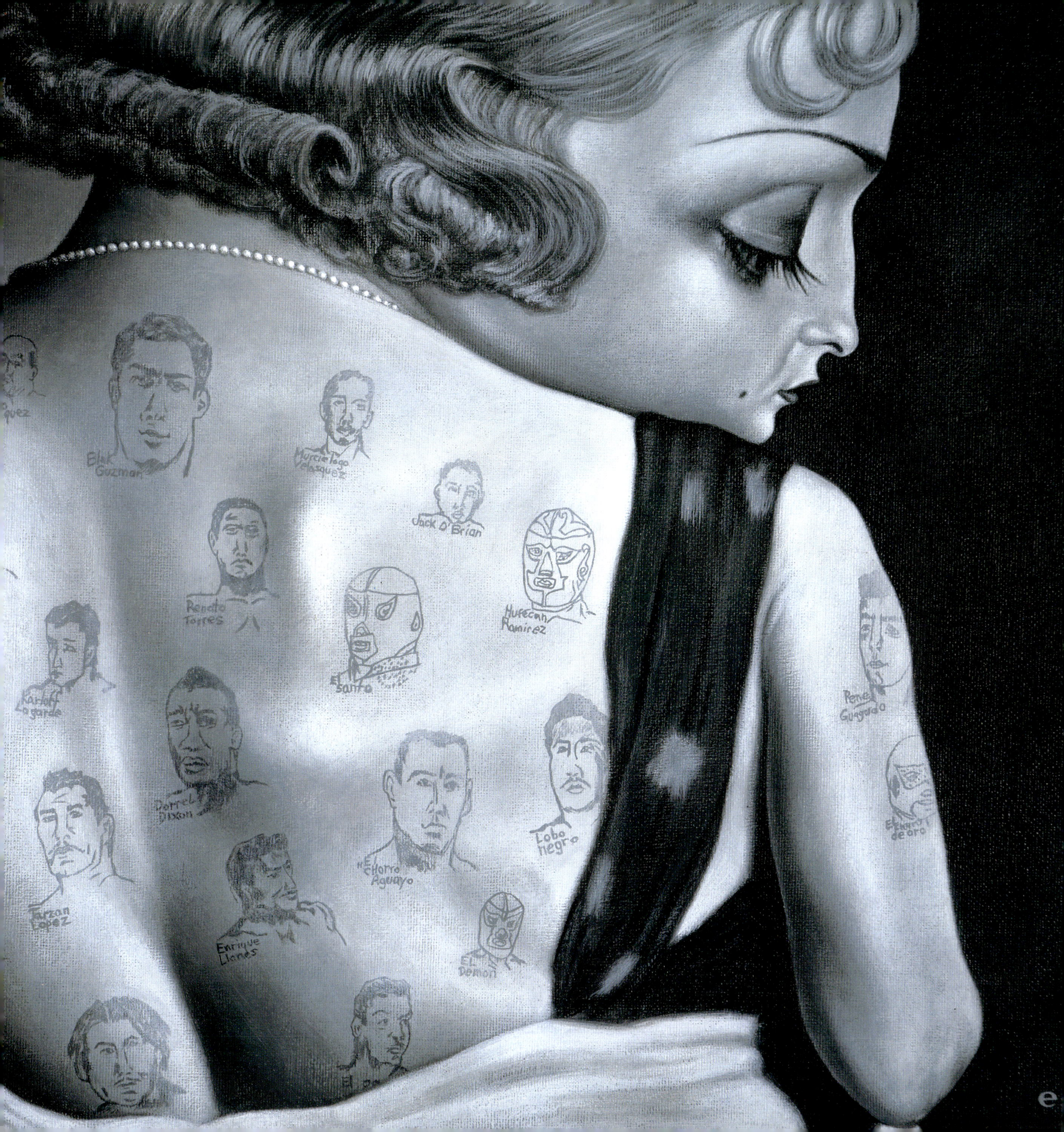
Blak Guzman
Murcielago Velasquez
Jack O'Brian
Renato Torres
Ramirez
El Santo
Karloff Lagarde
Dorrel Dixon
Lobo negro
Aguayo
Tarzan Lopez
Enrique Llanes
El Demon

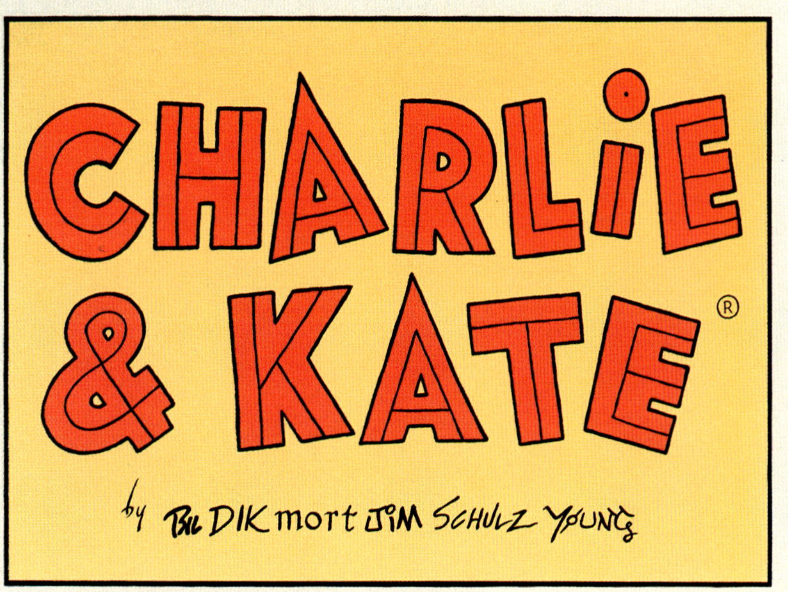
CHARLIE & KATE®
by BIL DIK mort JIM SCHULZ YOUNG

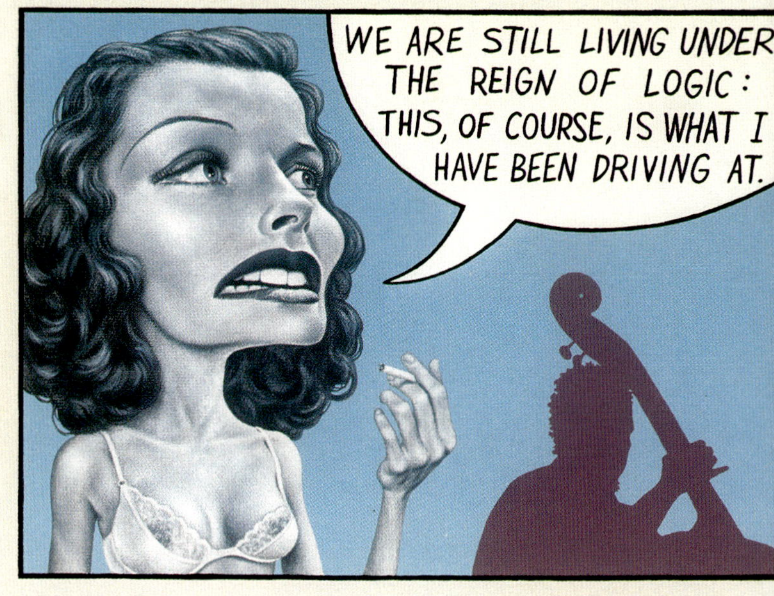
WE ARE STILL LIVING UNDER THE REIGN OF LOGIC: THIS, OF COURSE, IS WHAT I HAVE BEEN DRIVING AT.

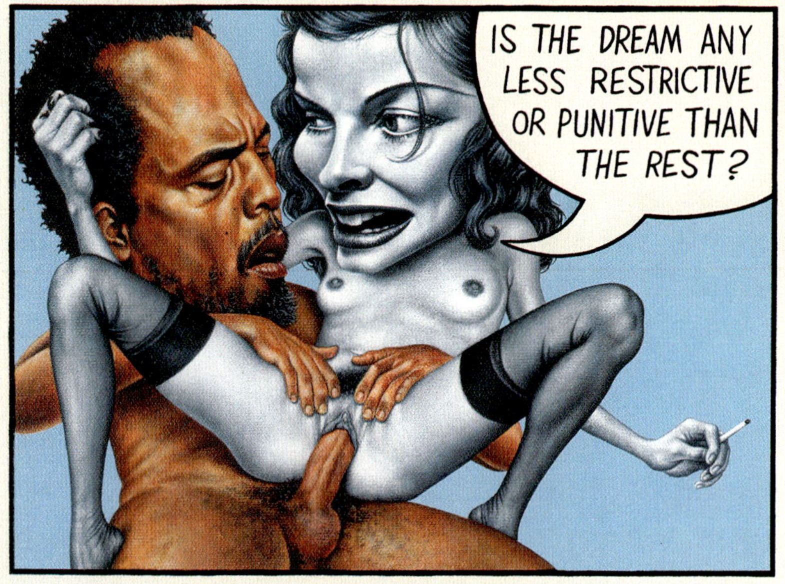
IS THE DREAM ANY LESS RESTRICTIVE OR PUNITIVE THAN THE REST?

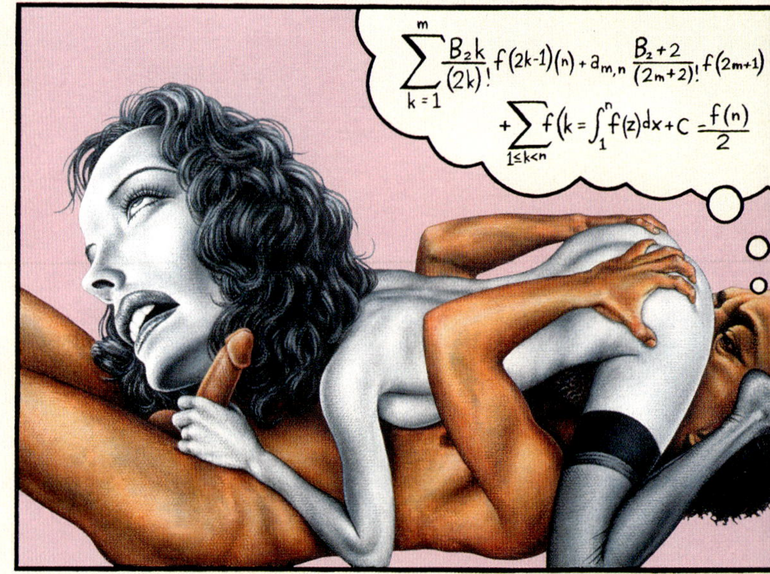
$\sum_{k=1}^{m} \frac{B_2k}{(2k)!} f(2k-1)(n) + a_{m,n} \frac{B_2+2}{(2m+2)!} f(2m+1)$
$+ \sum_{1 \leq k < n} f(k = \int_1^n f(z) dx + C = \frac{f(n)}{2}$

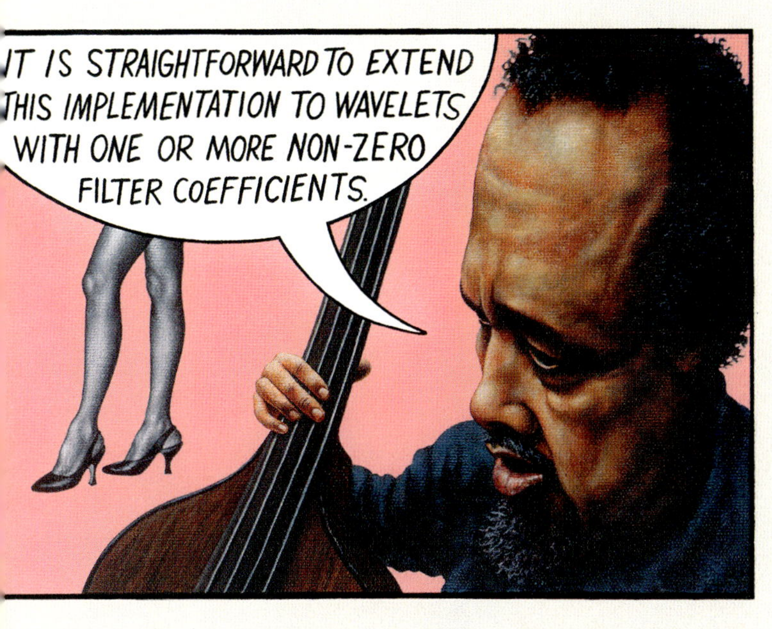
IT IS STRAIGHTFORWARD TO EXTEND THIS IMPLEMENTATION TO WAVELETS WITH ONE OR MORE NON-ZERO FILTER COEFFICIENTS.

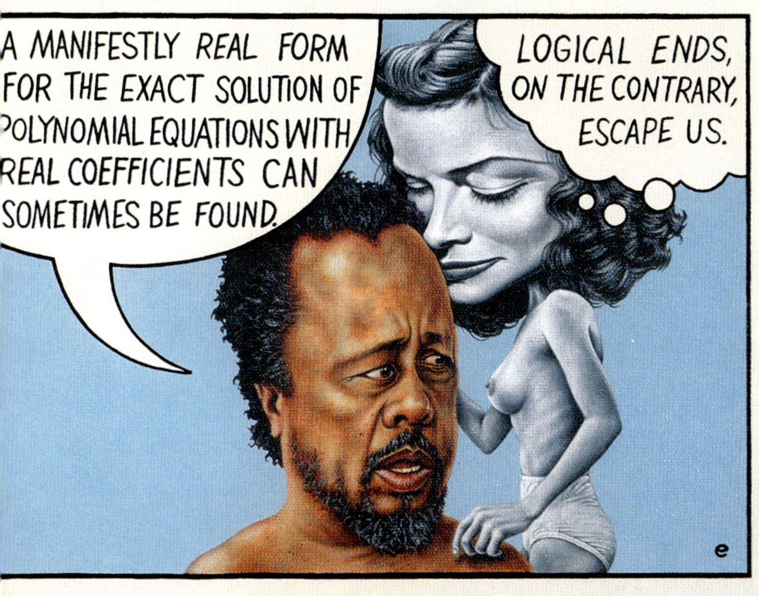
A MANIFESTLY REAL FORM FOR THE EXACT SOLUTION OF POLYNOMIAL EQUATIONS WITH REAL COEFFICIENTS CAN SOMETIMES BE FOUND.
LOGICAL ENDS, ON THE CONTRARY, ESCAPE US.

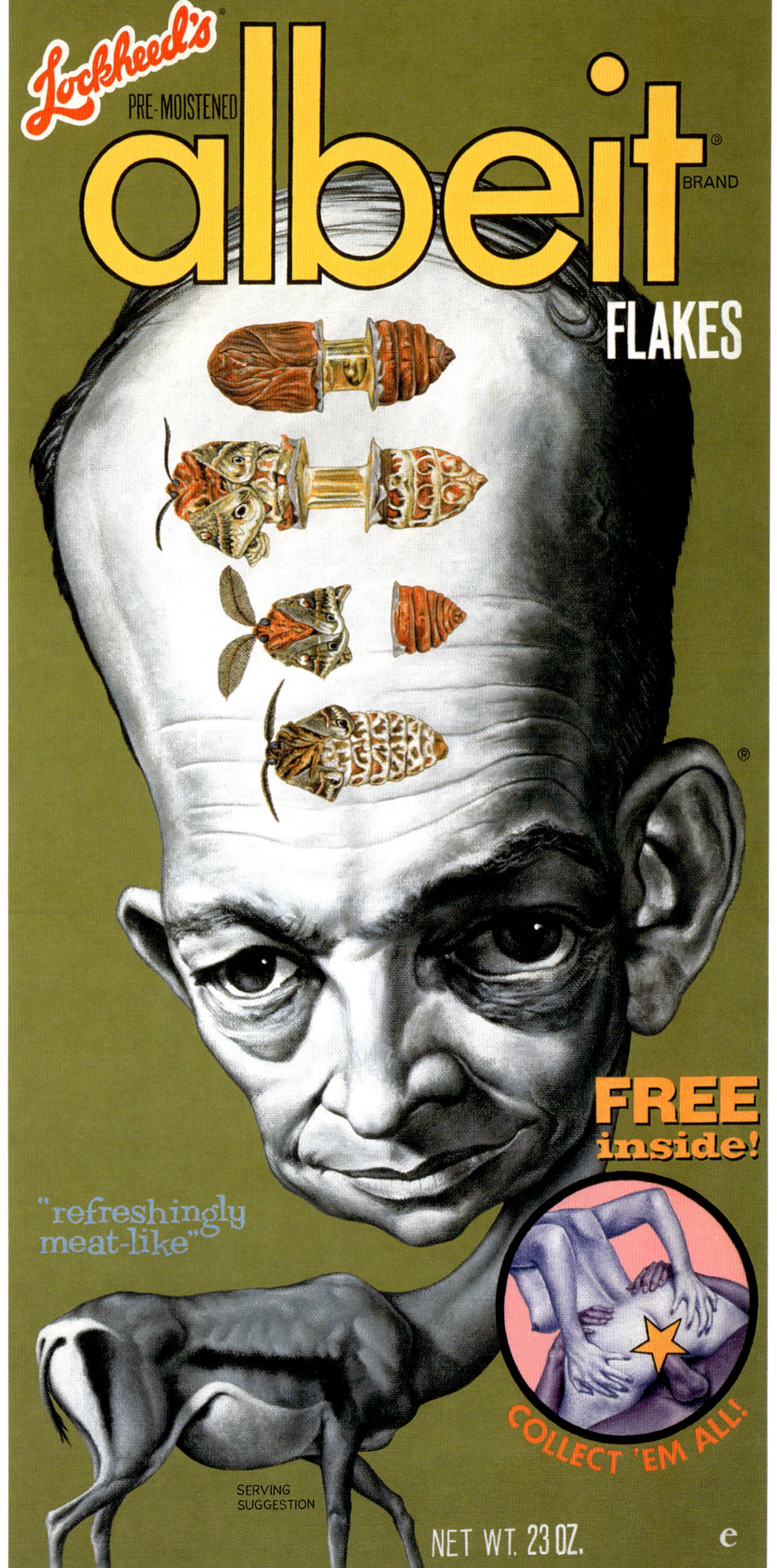

Product (Anti-Love Expurgated) 1997

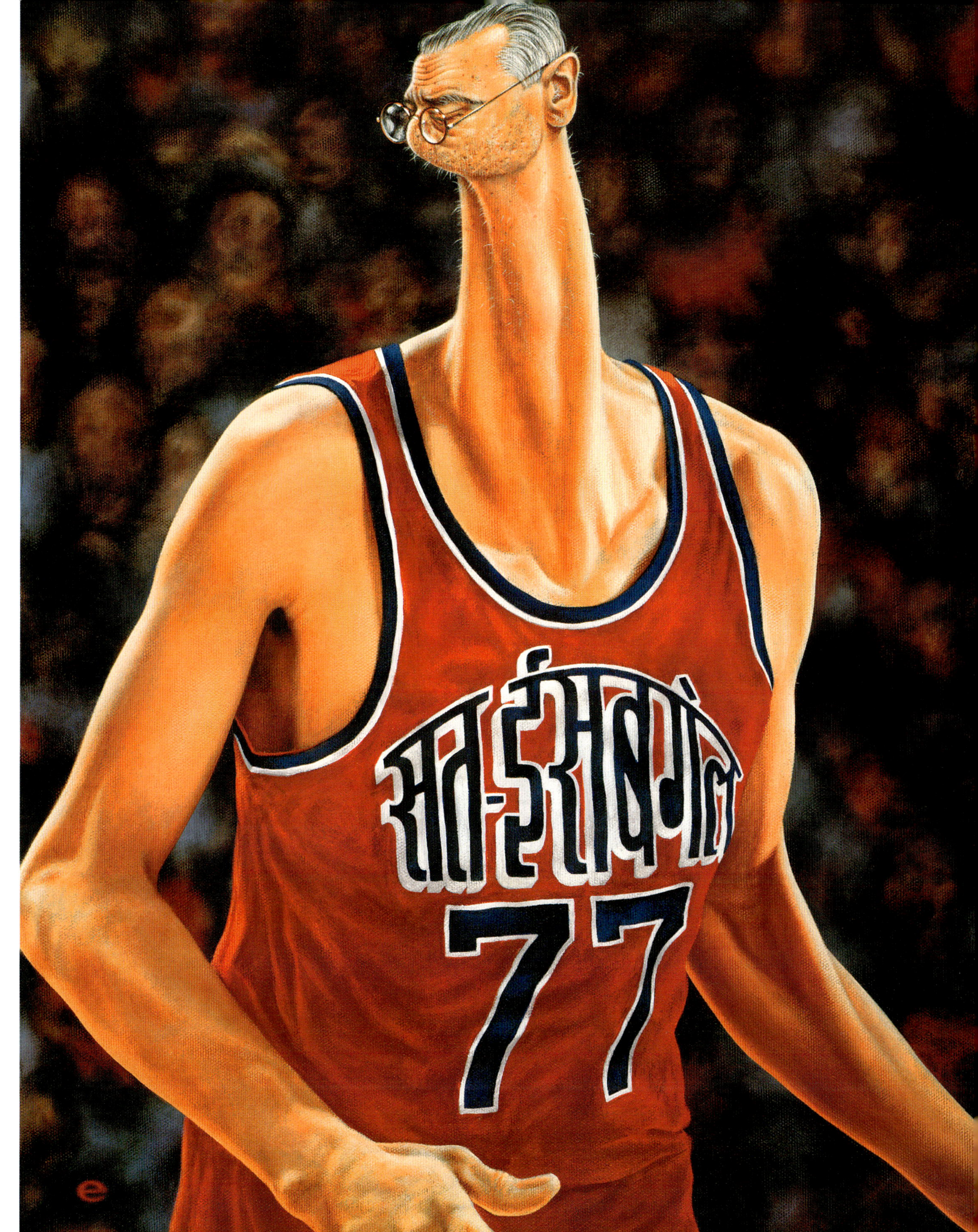

Endorsement Deal 1998

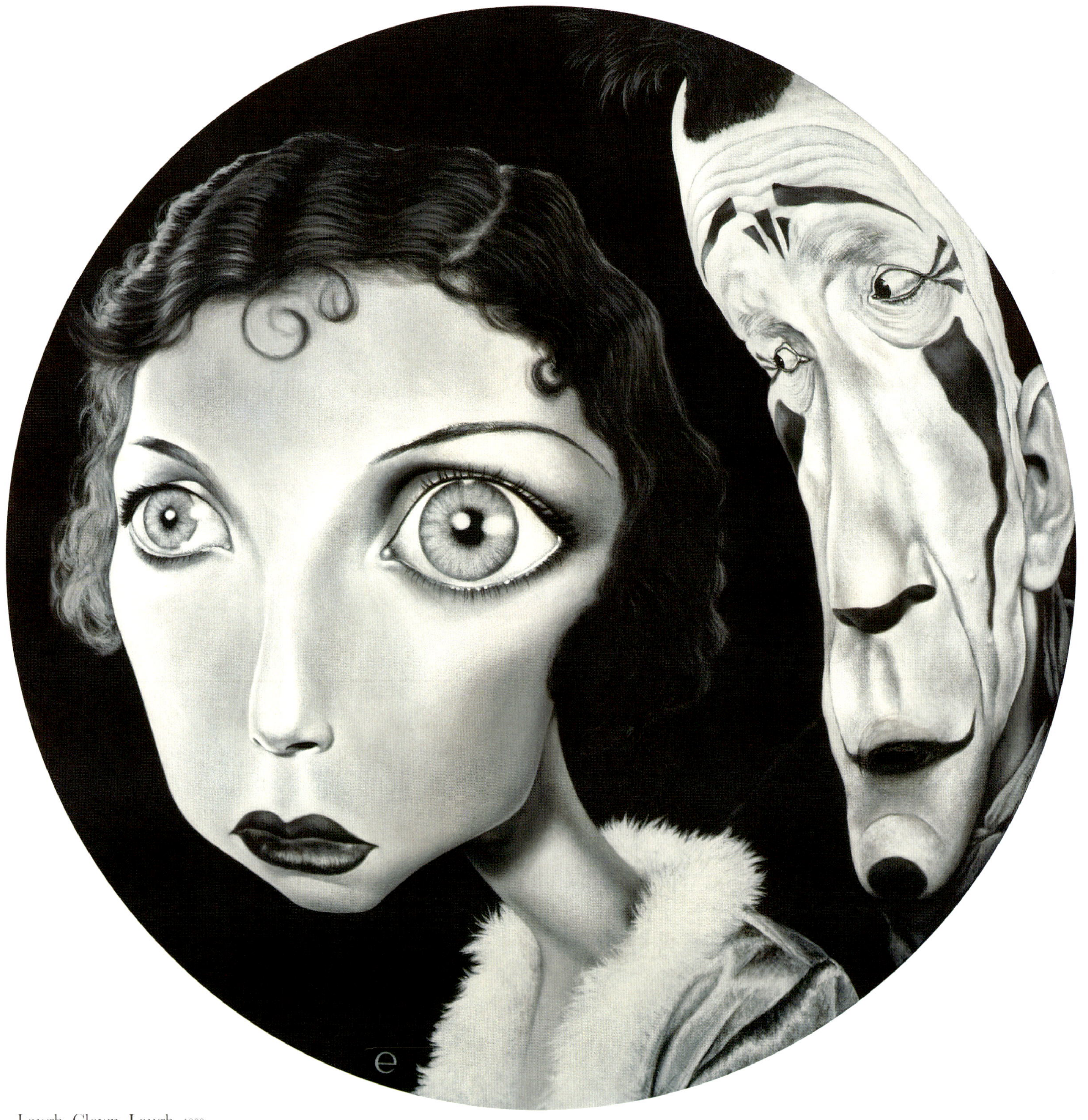

Laugh, Clown, Laugh 1998

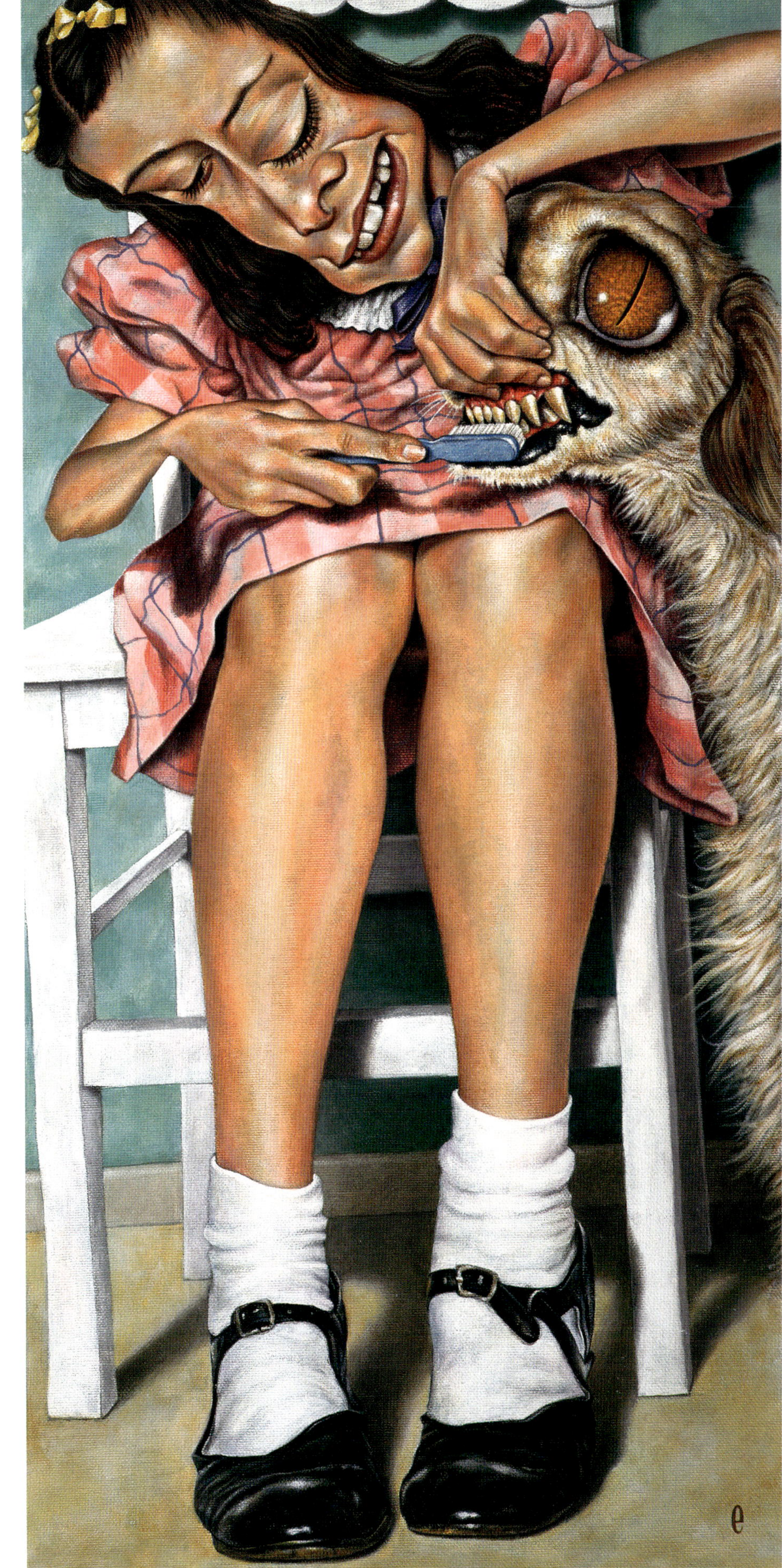

Critical Path 1997

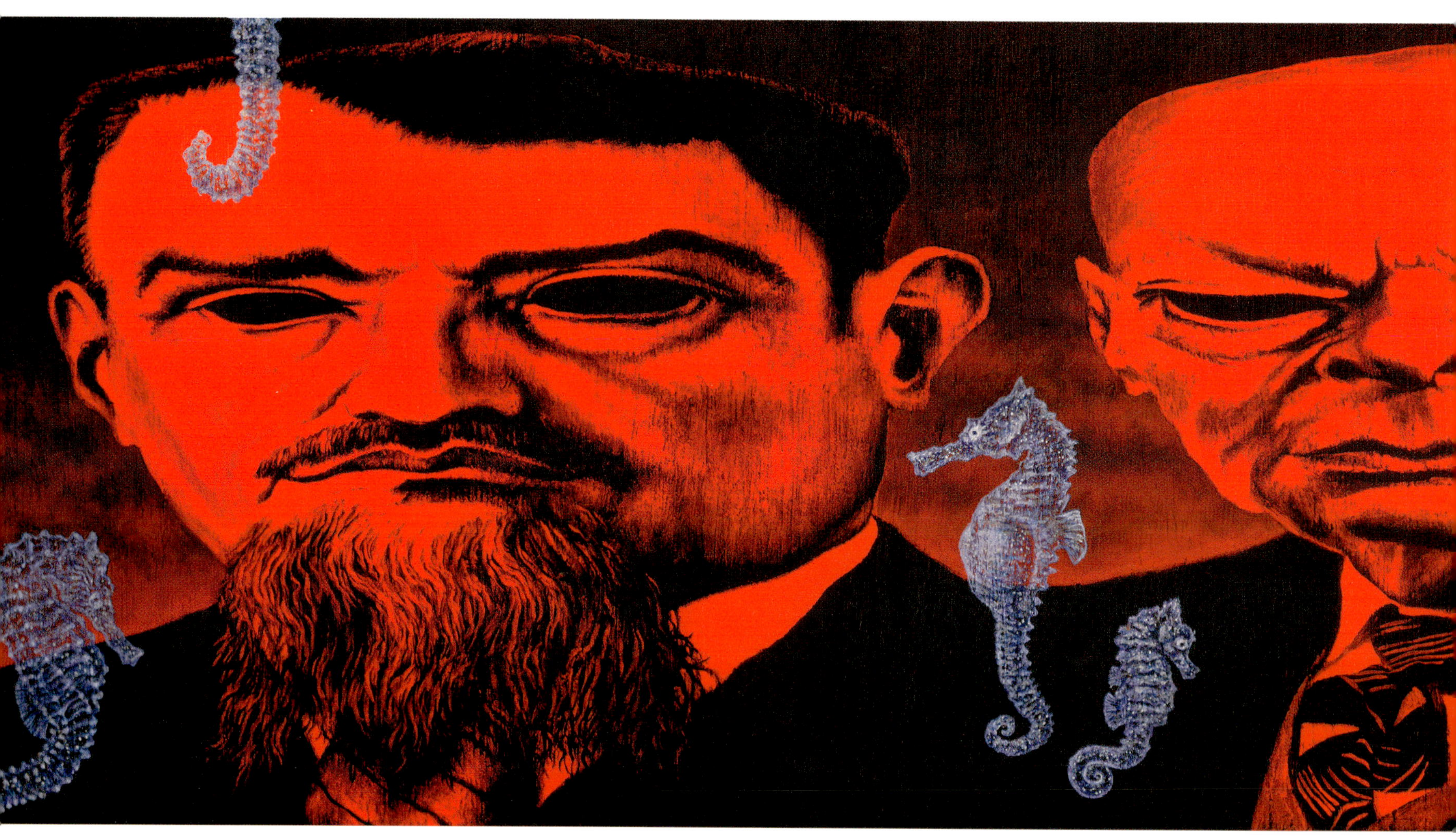

Hats Off to Fission 1998

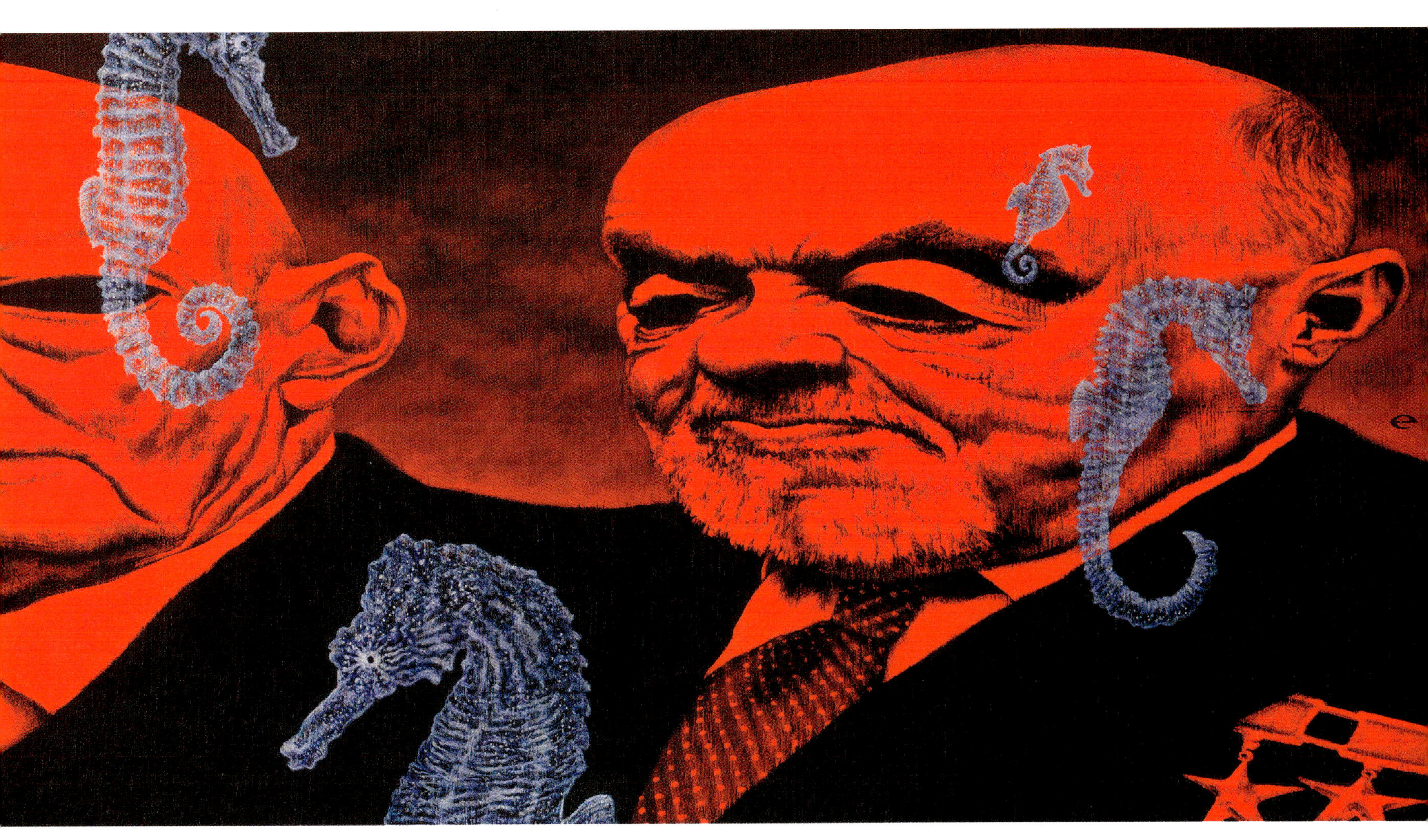

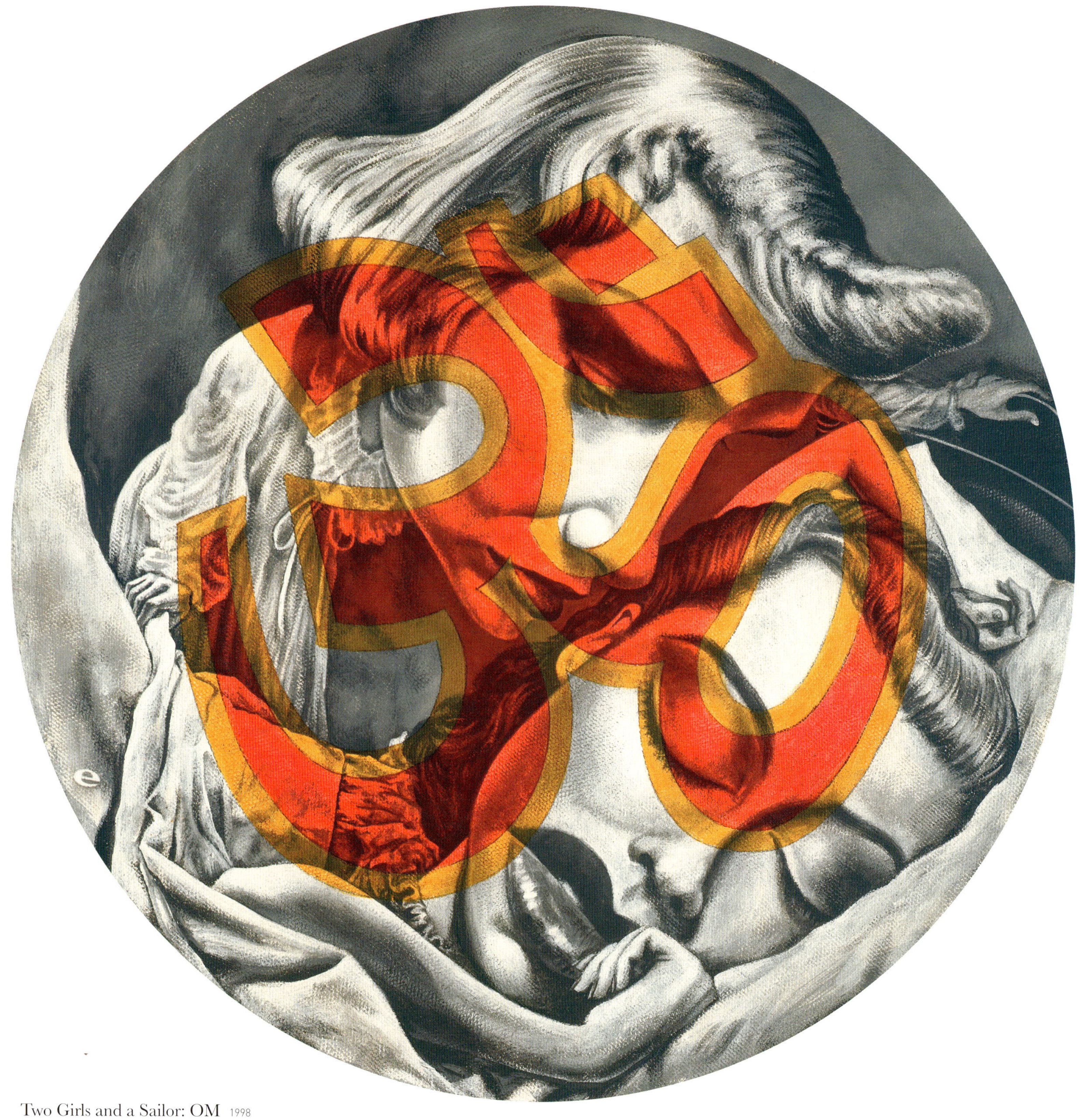

Two Girls and a Sailor: OM 1998

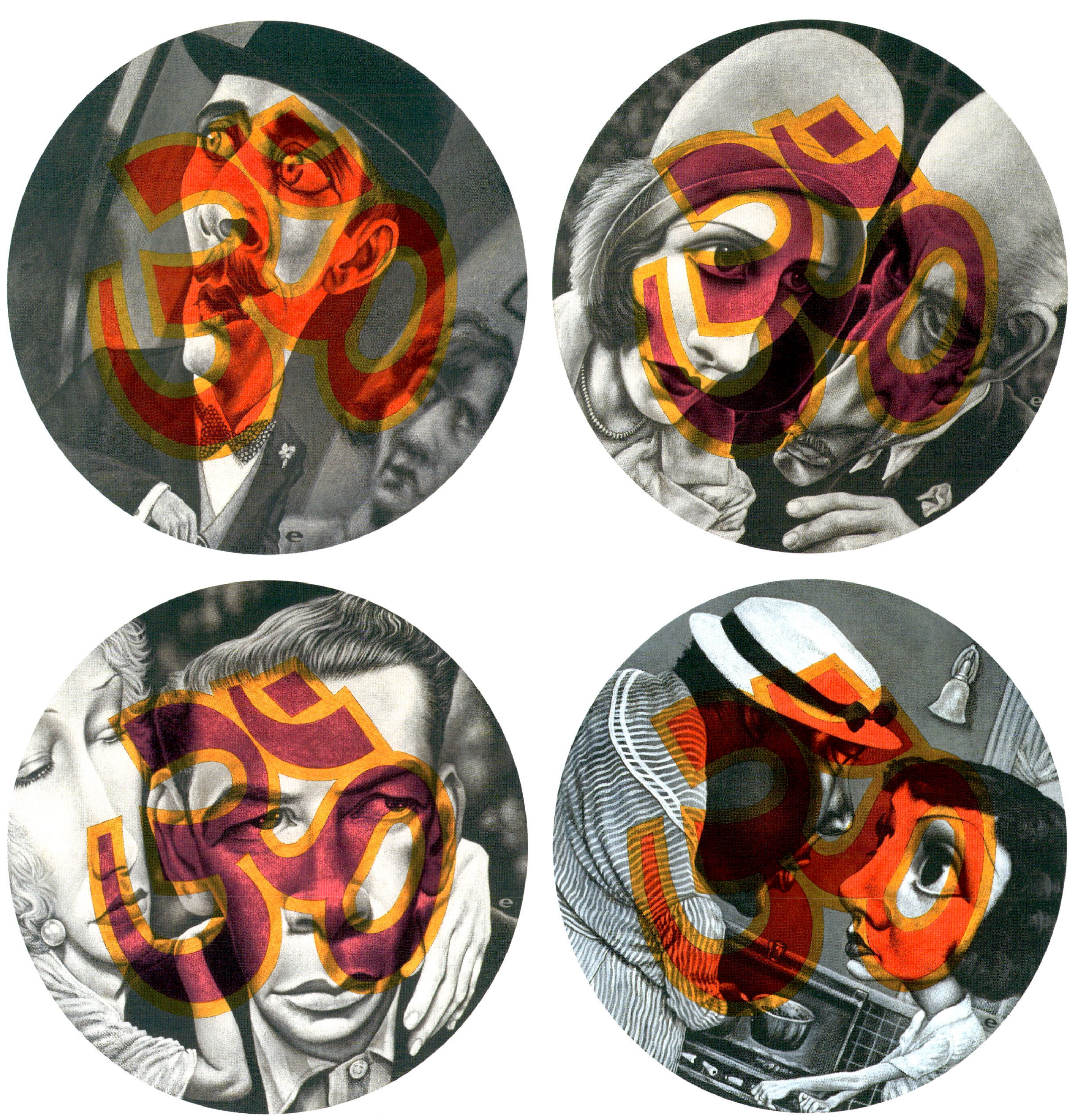

It: OM 1998

The Trial of Mary Dugan: OM 1998

I Am a Fugitive from a Chain Gang: OM 1998

Imitation of Life: OM 1998

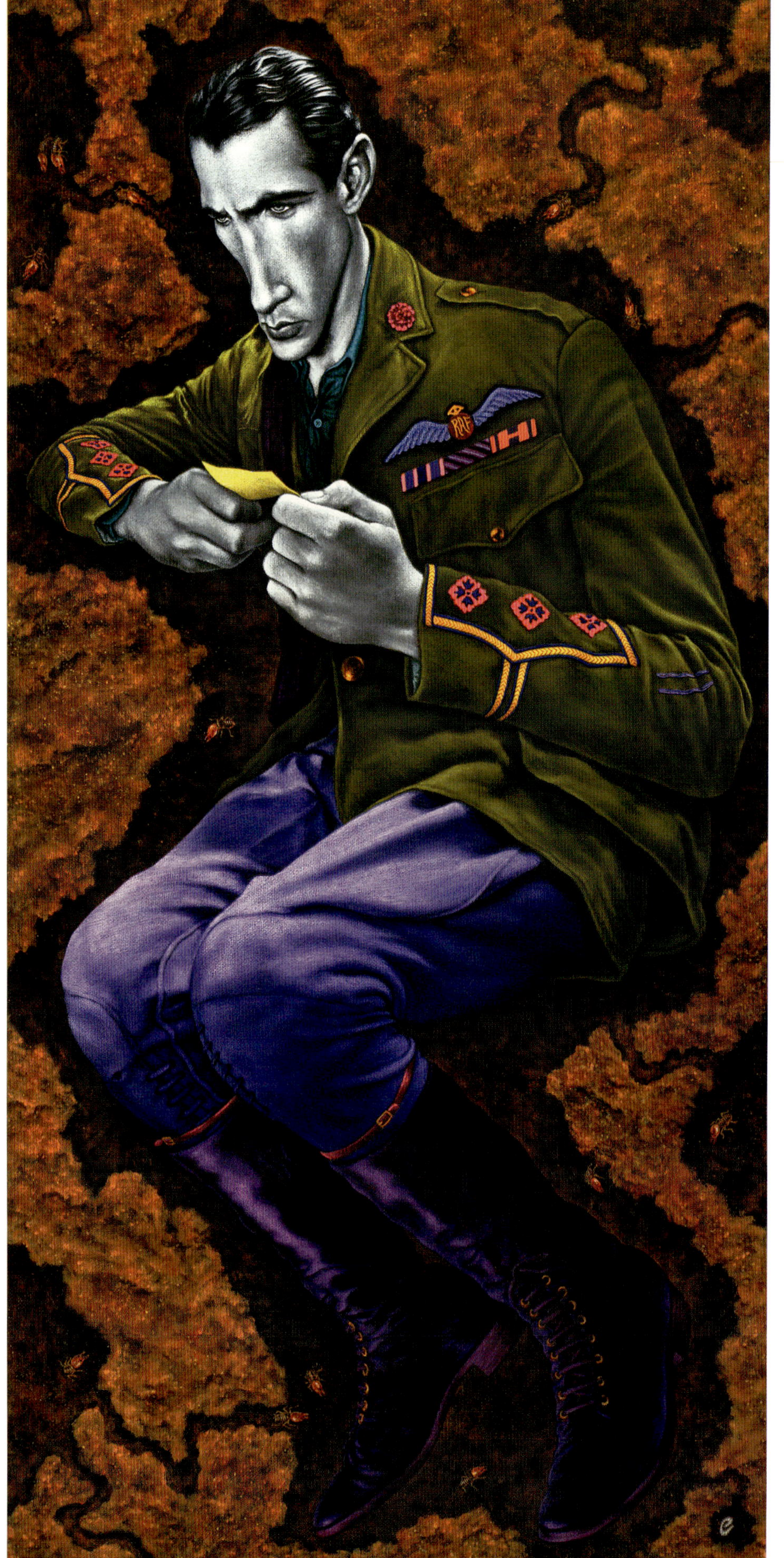

Young Gary Cooper in Termite Mound with Post-It™ 1998

Sad Pilot 1998

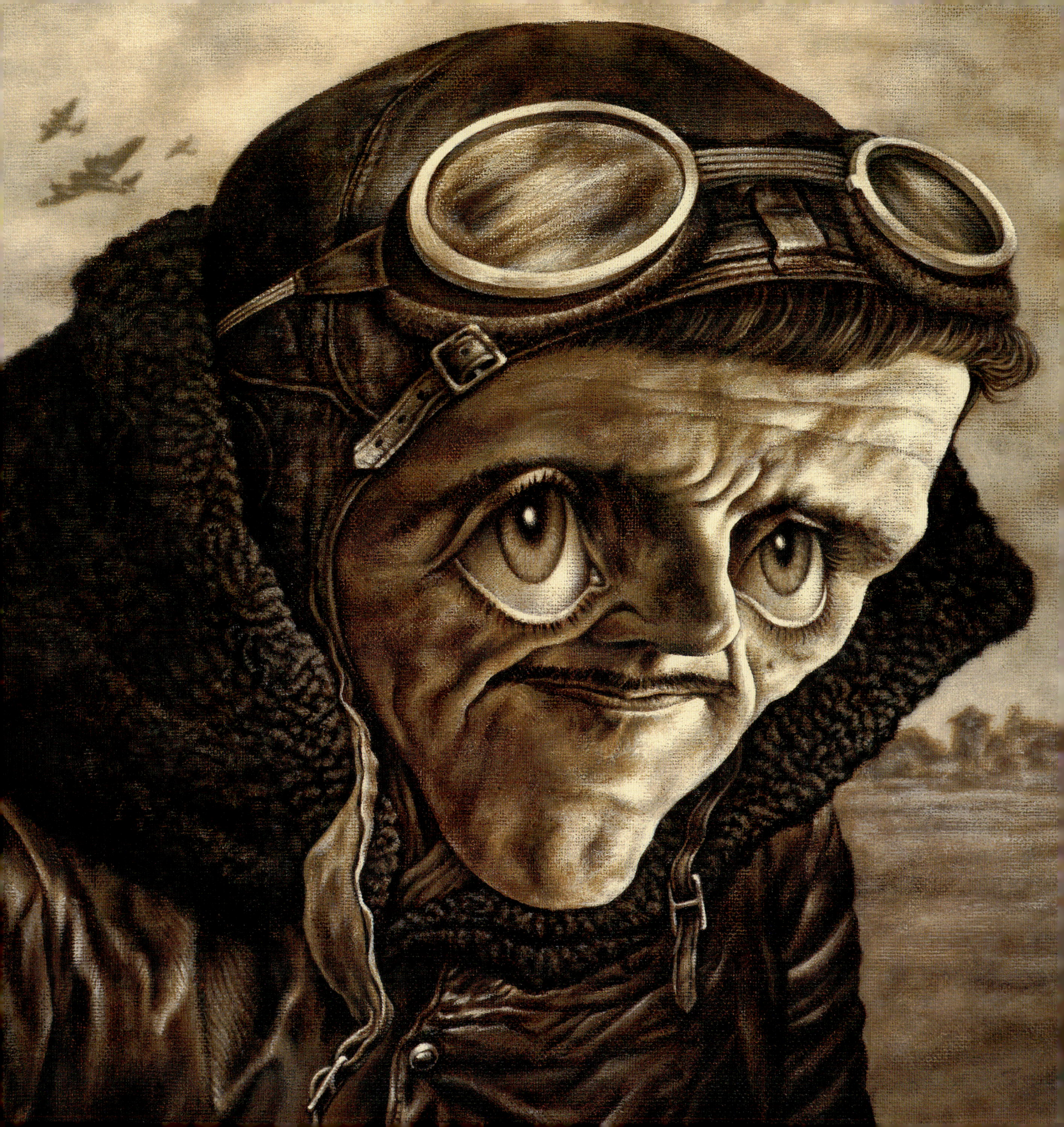

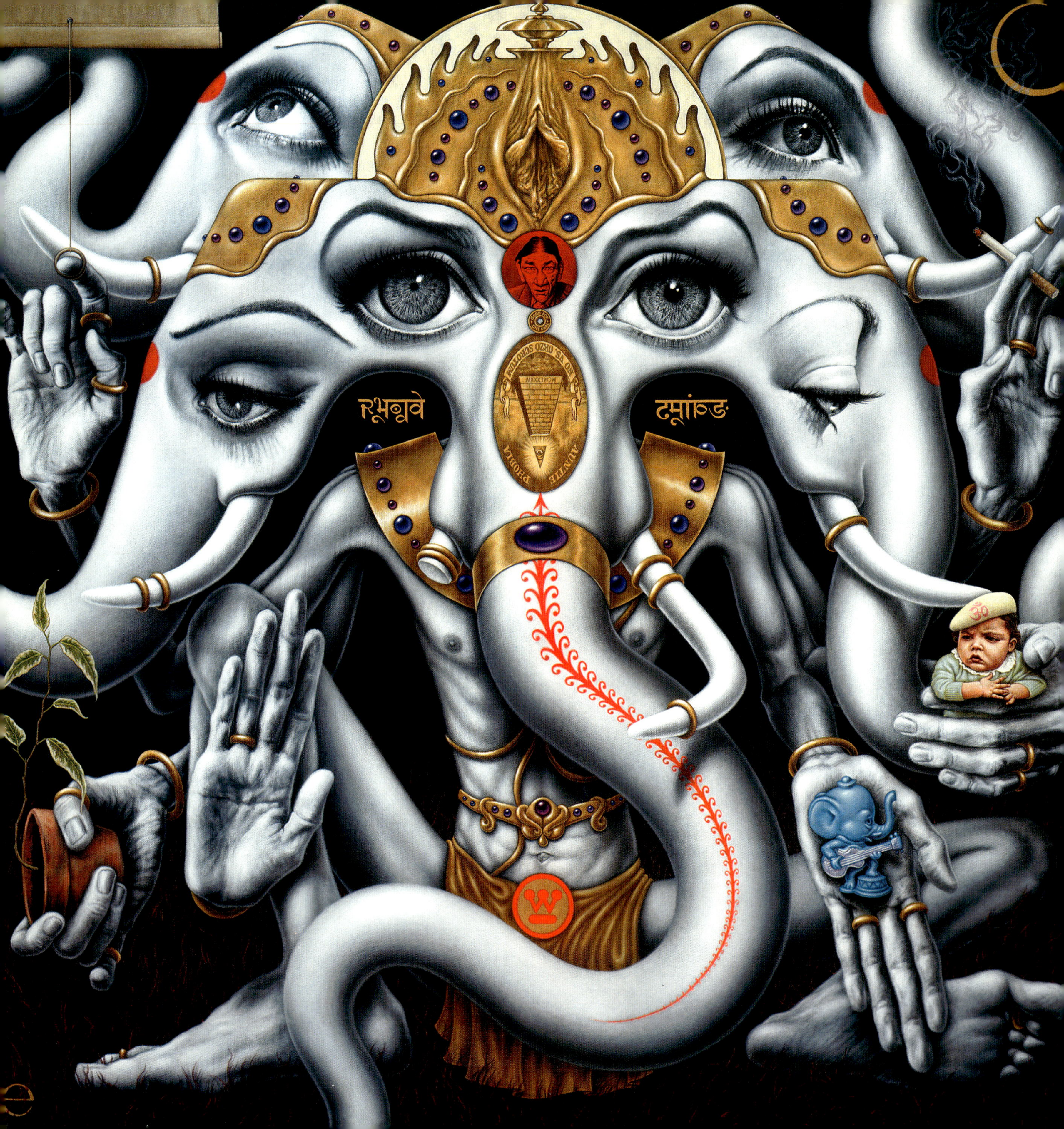
NO VS. ORZO SCROTUM
MCMLXXXIV
AUNTIE PHOBIA

Our Beloved Ganesa 1998

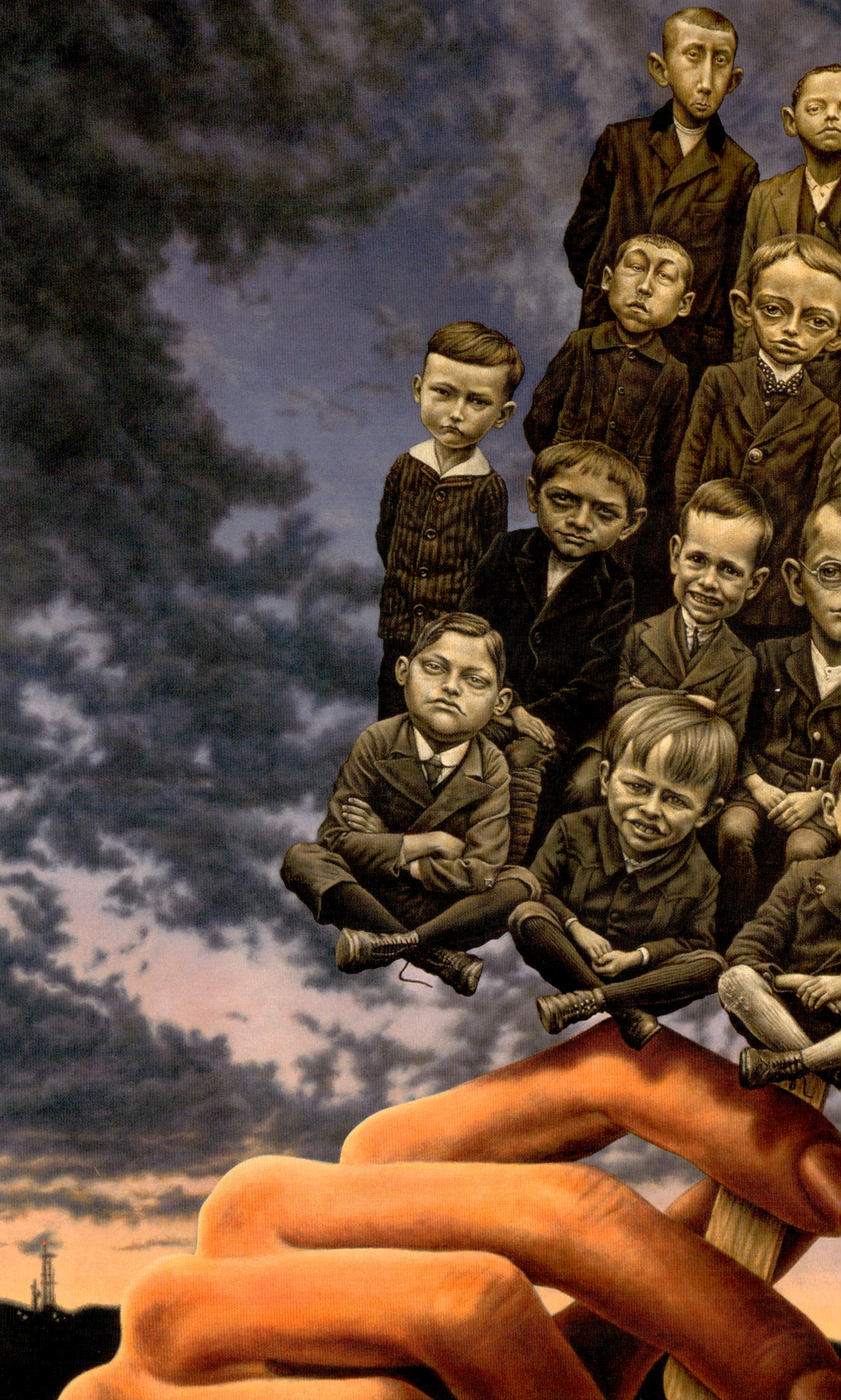

Czechsicle 1998

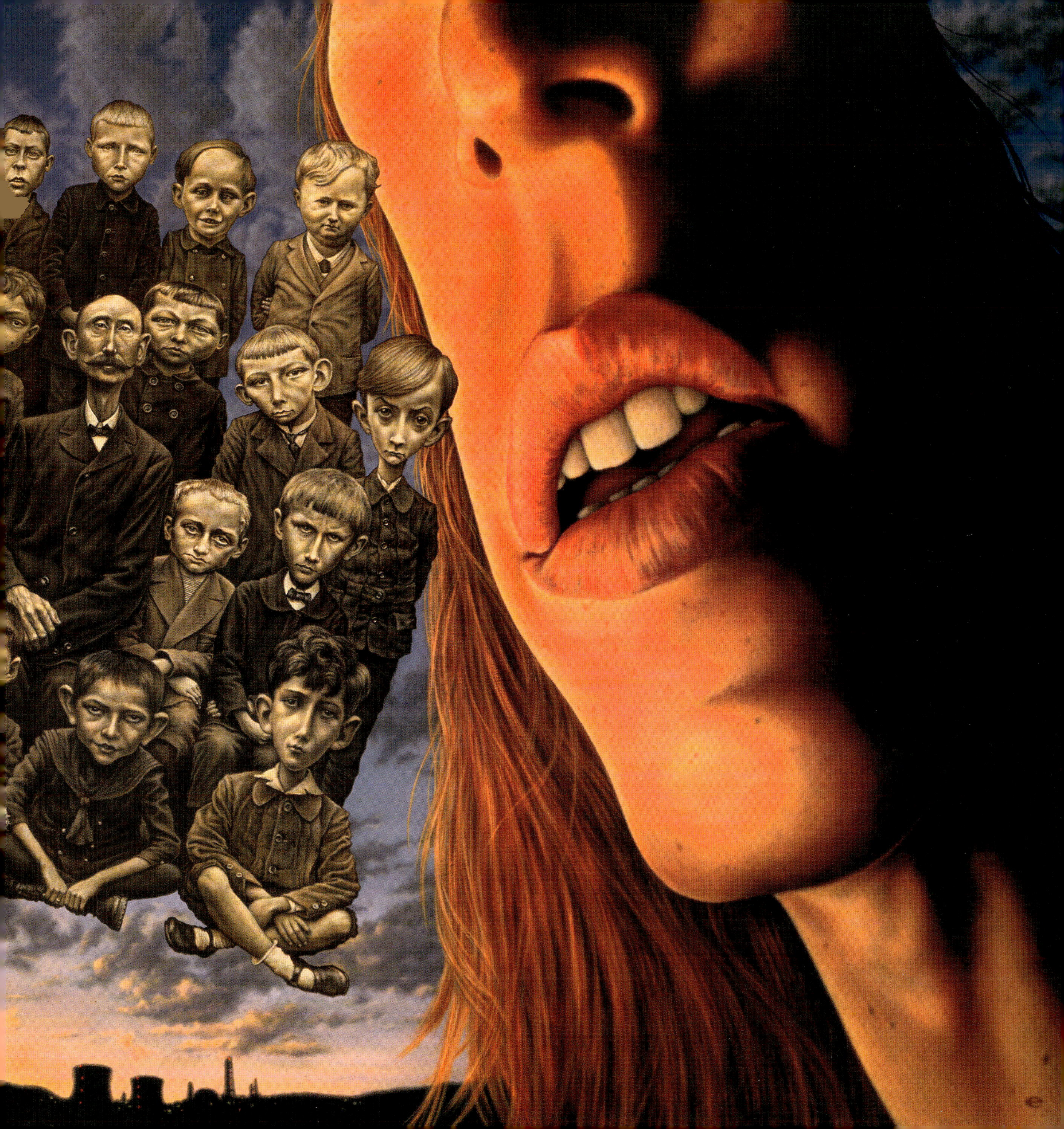

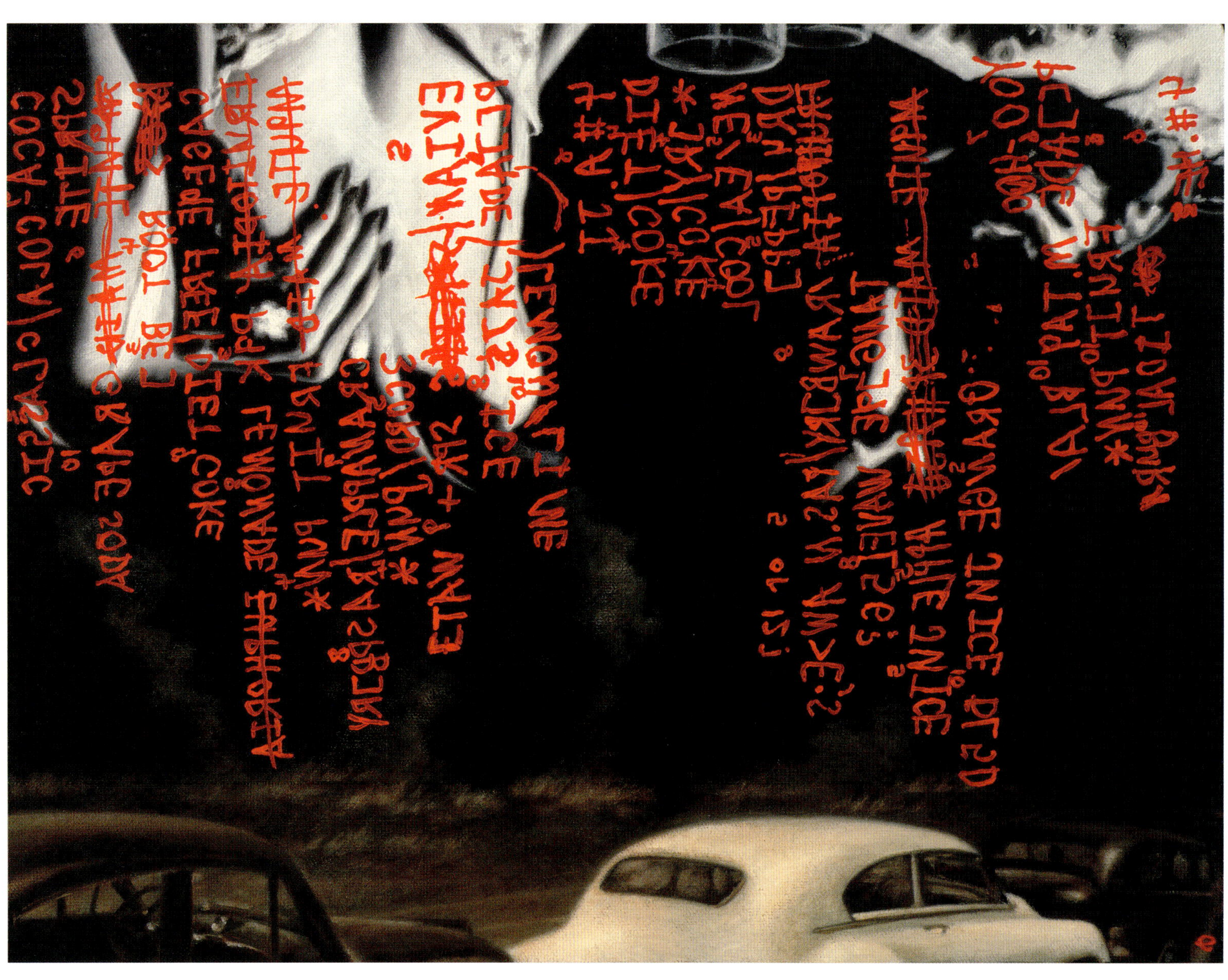

See 1999

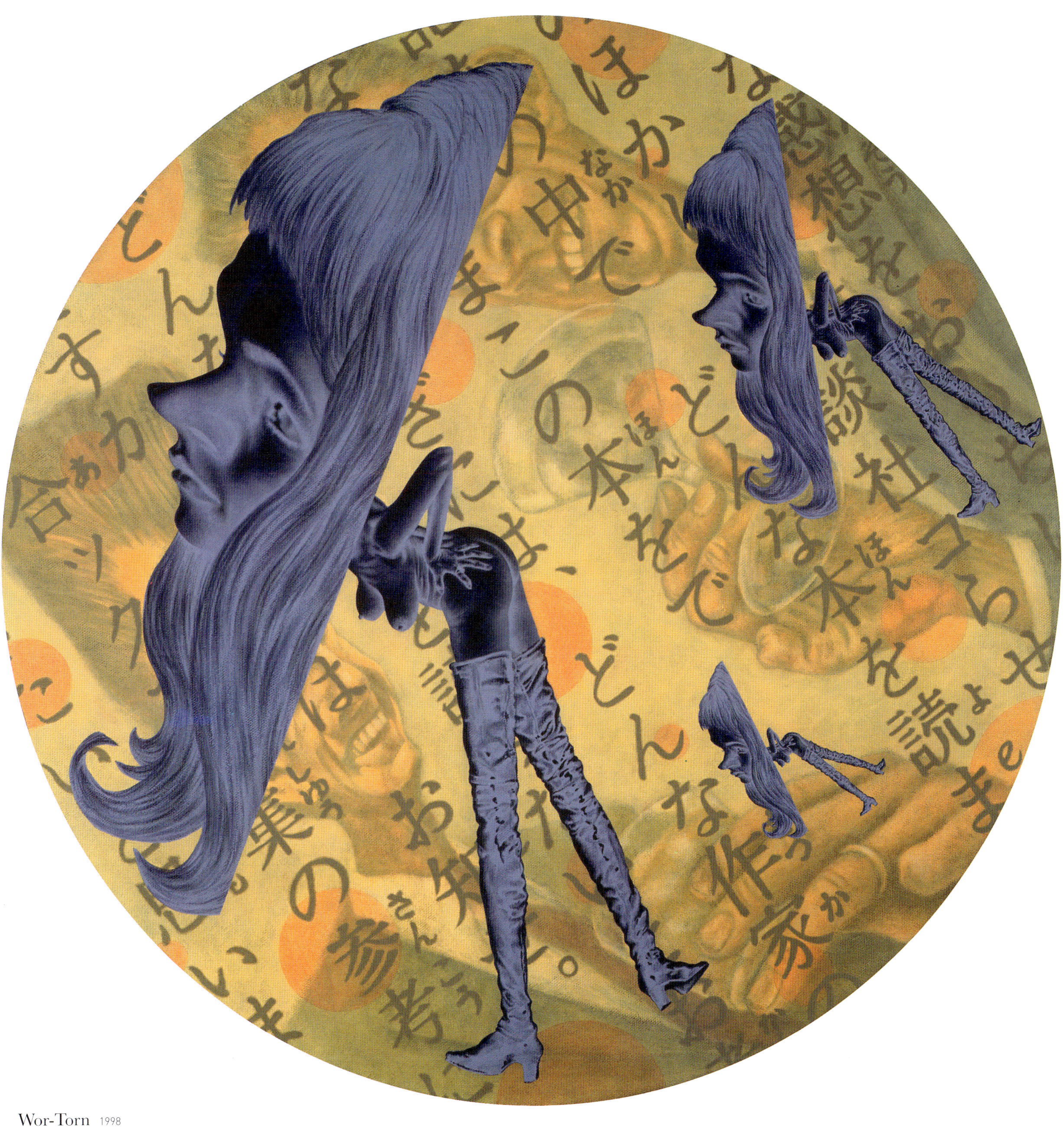

Wor-Torn 1998

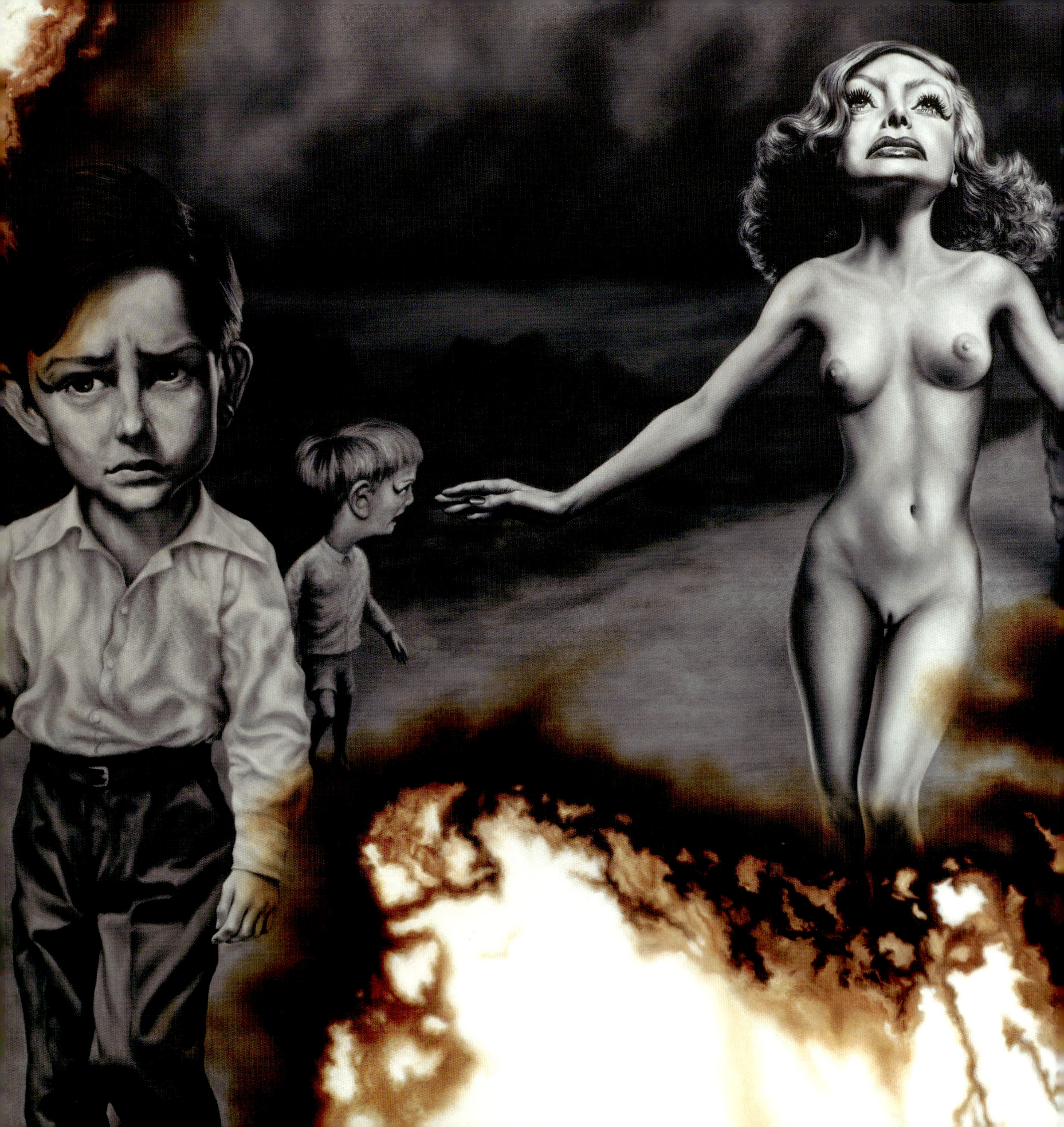

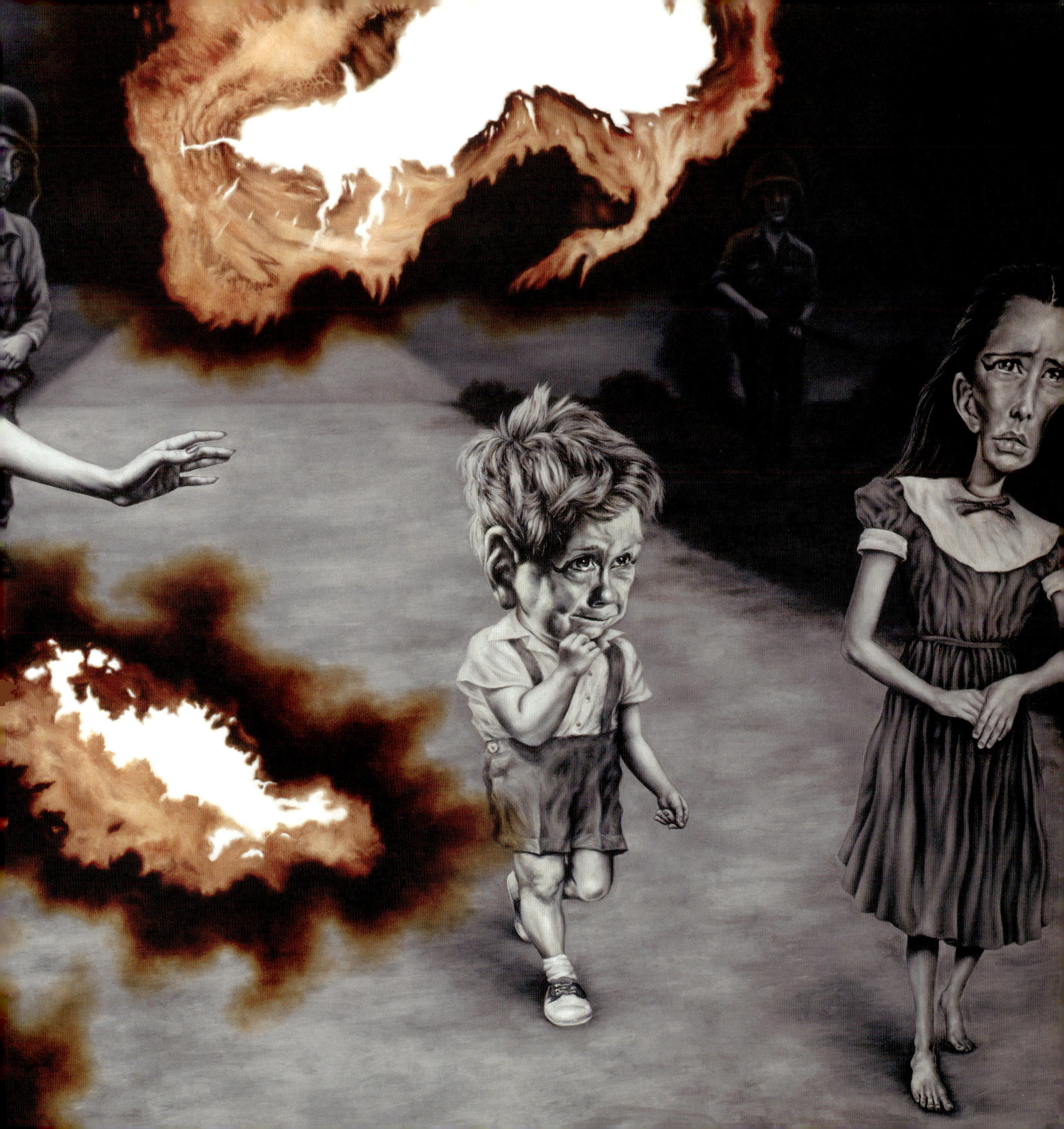

← "Nam!" 1949 an RKO Picture 1999

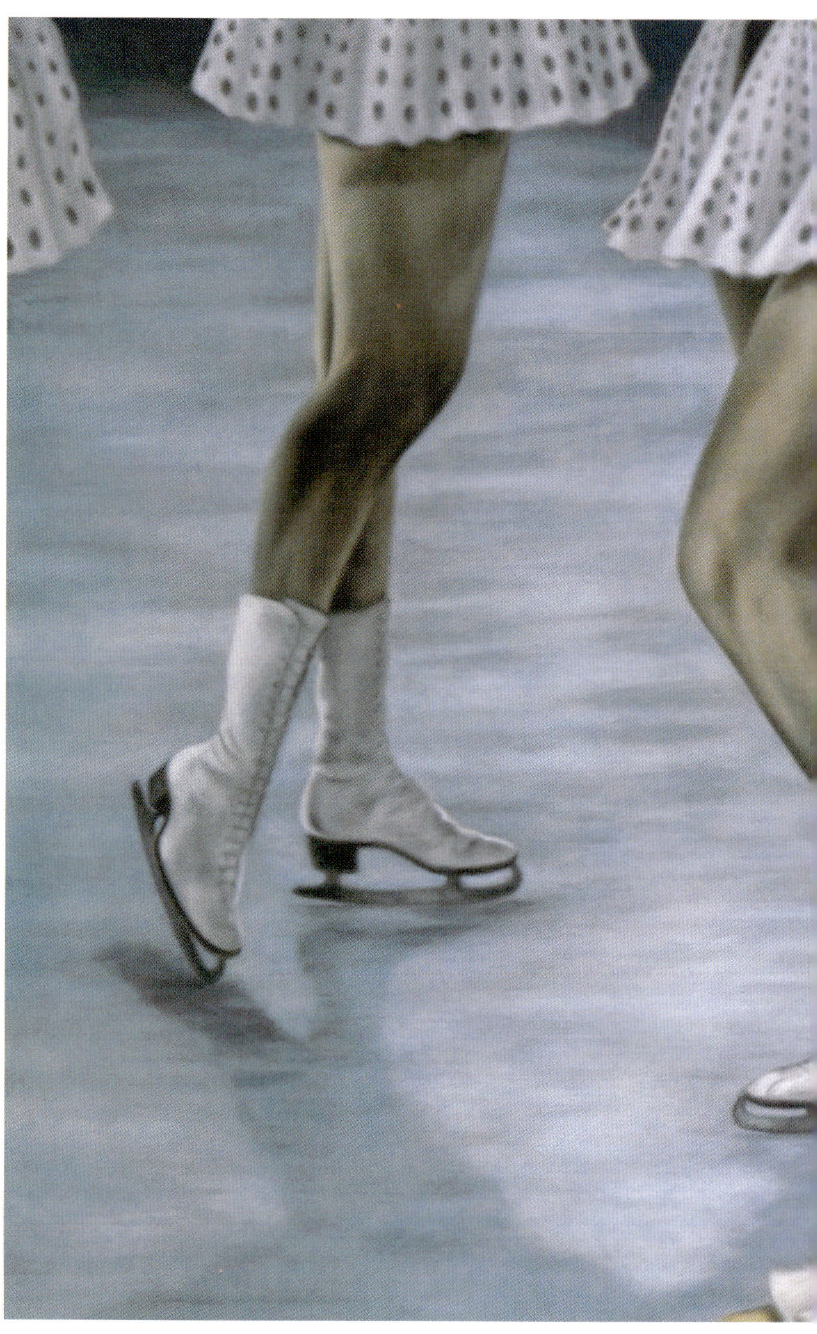

Production Number 1999

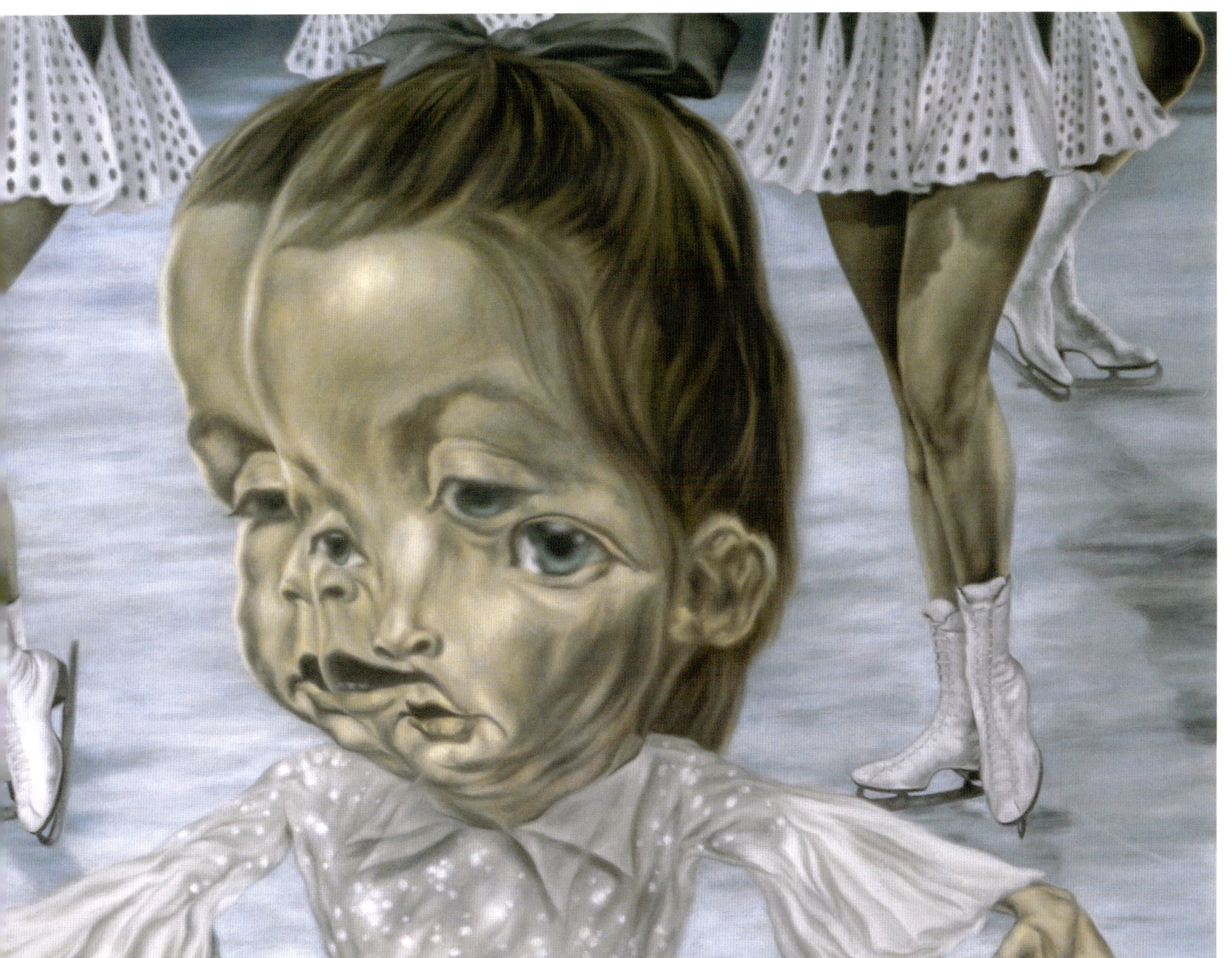

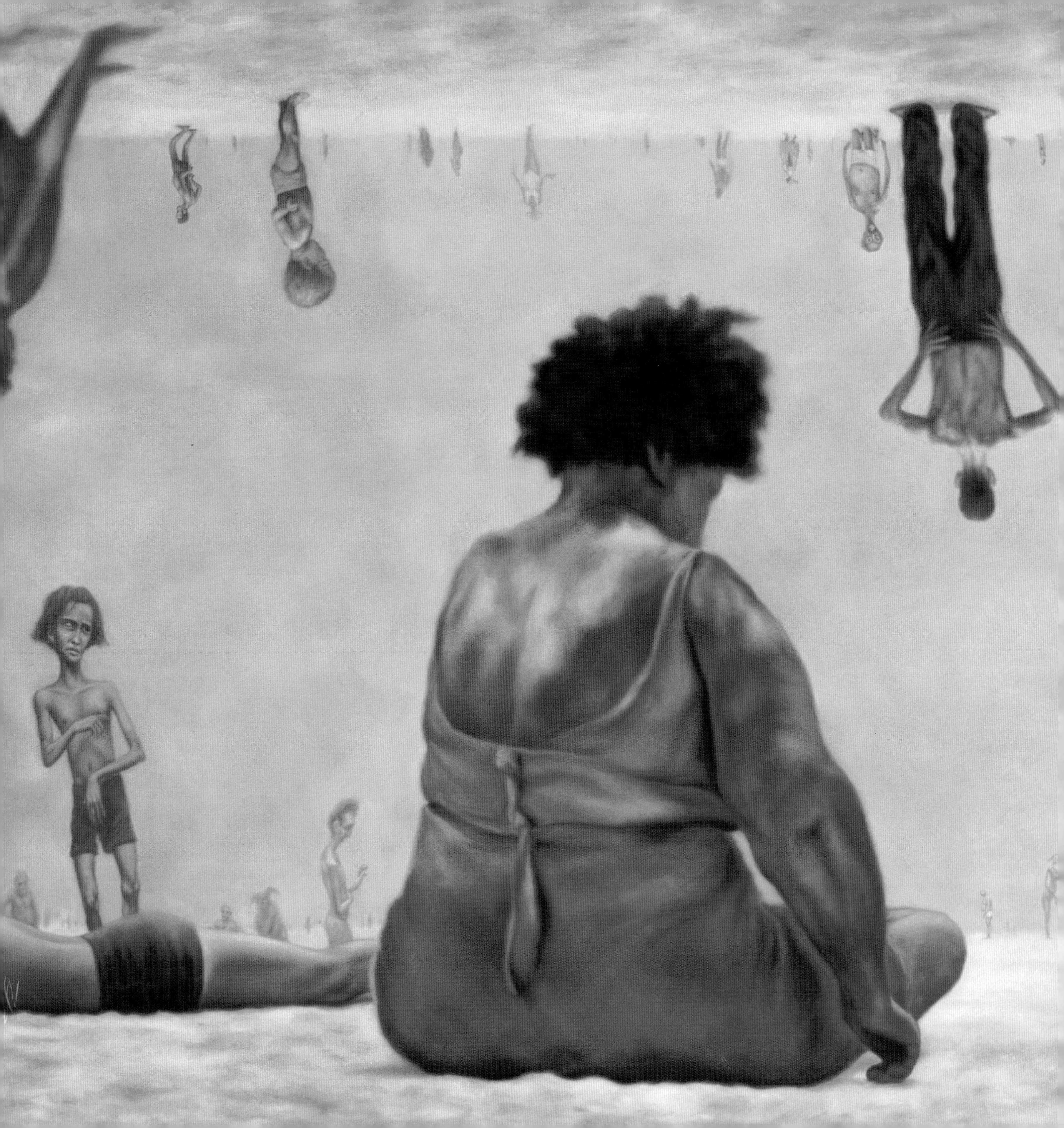

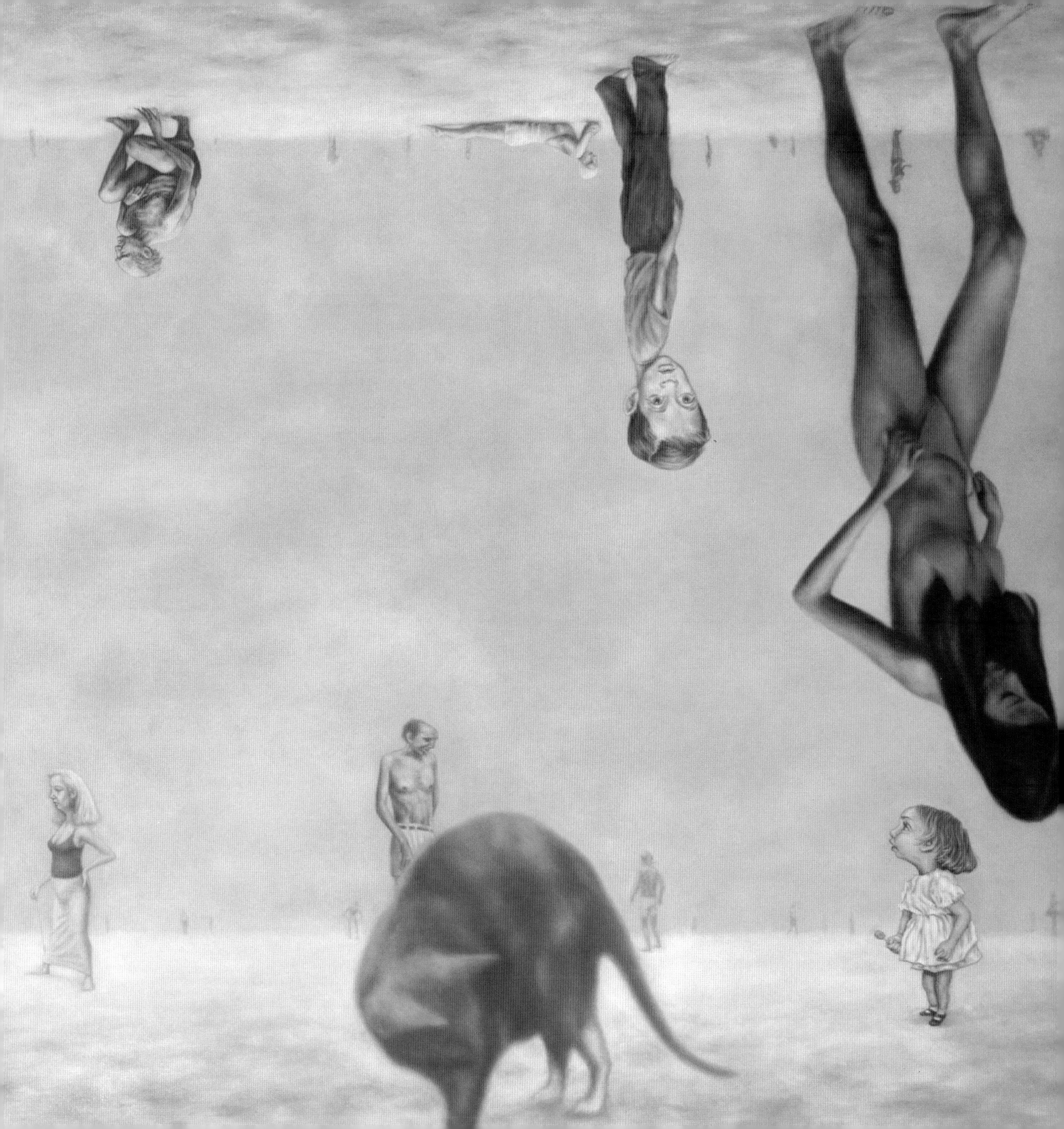

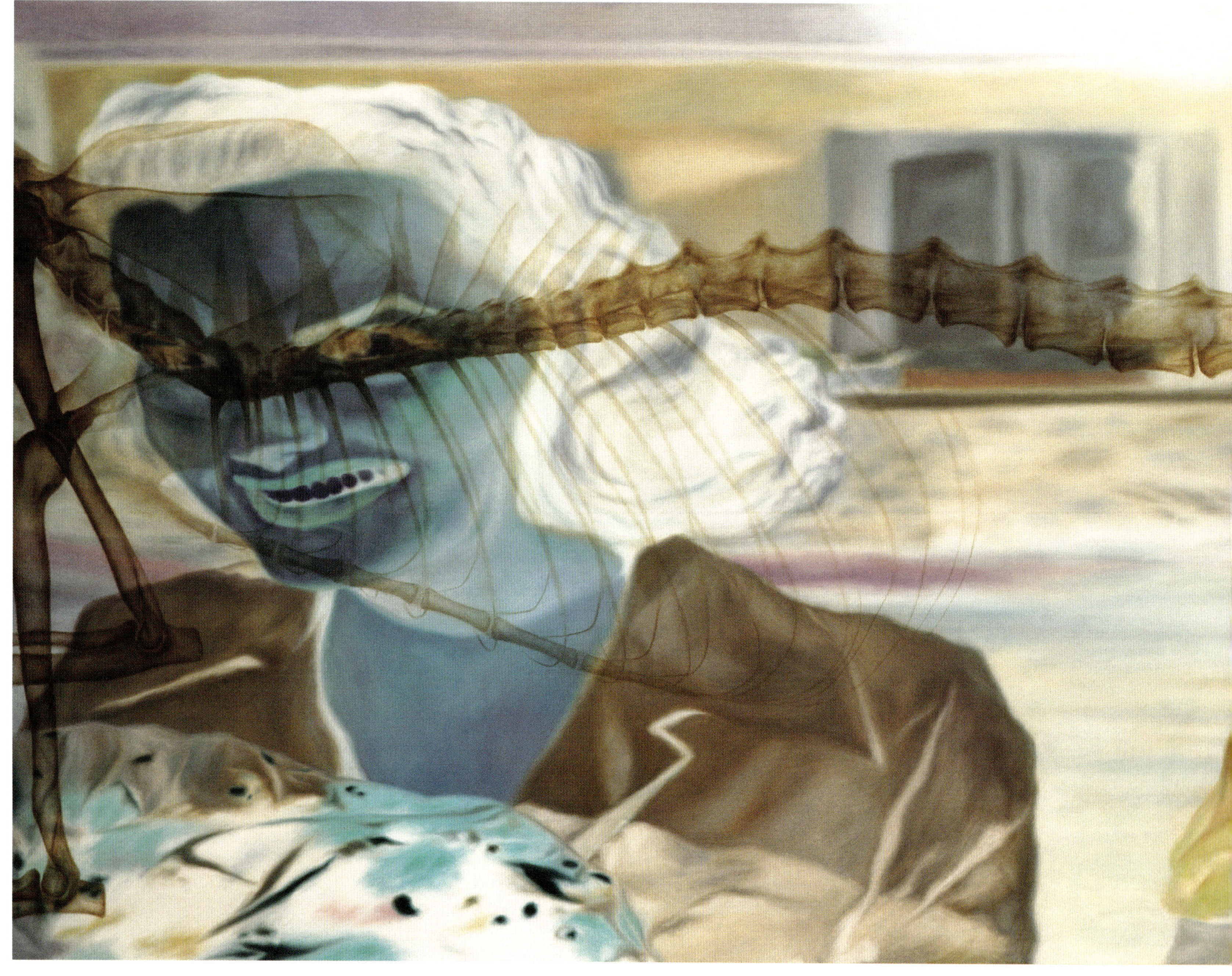

Death Isn't 1999

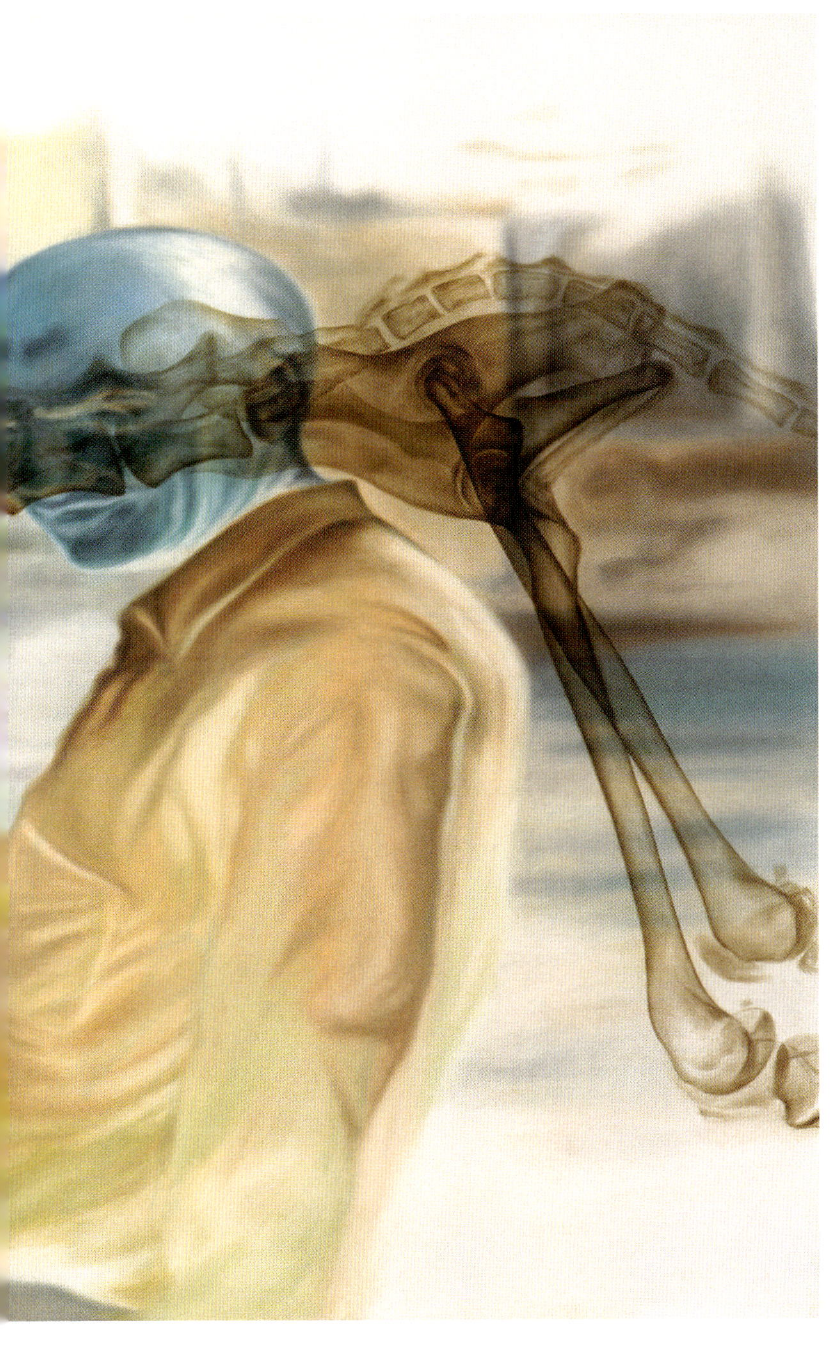

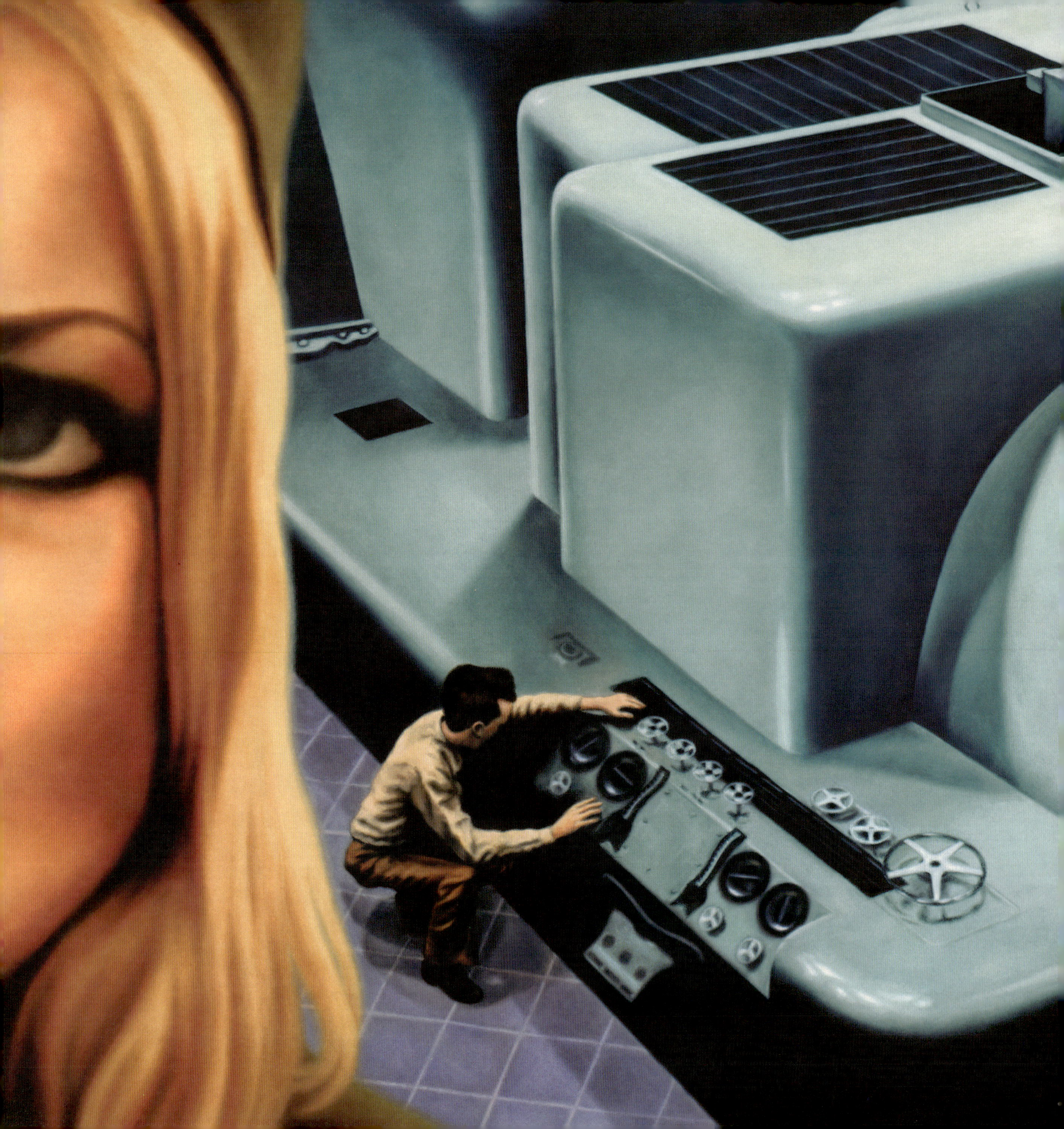

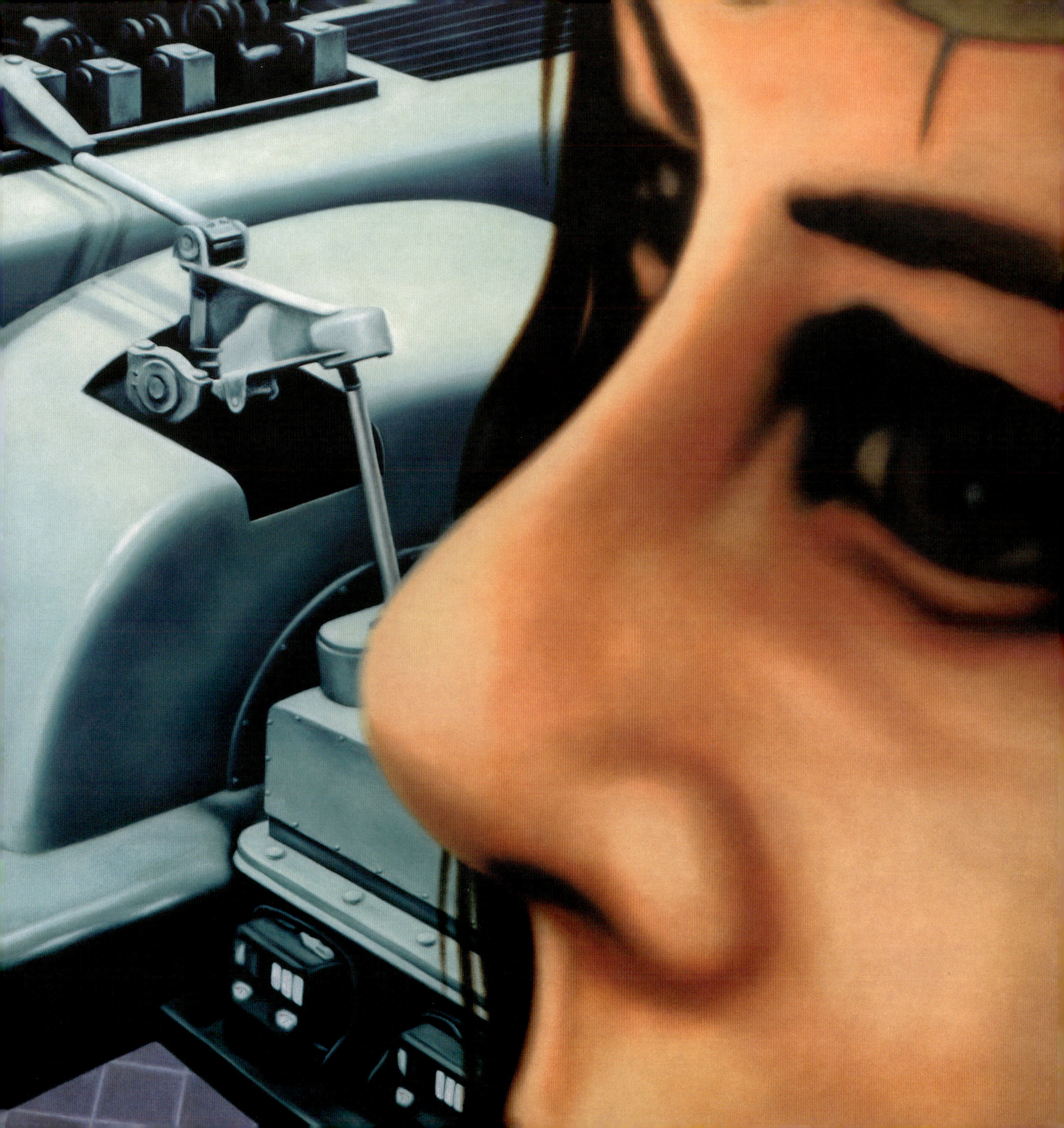

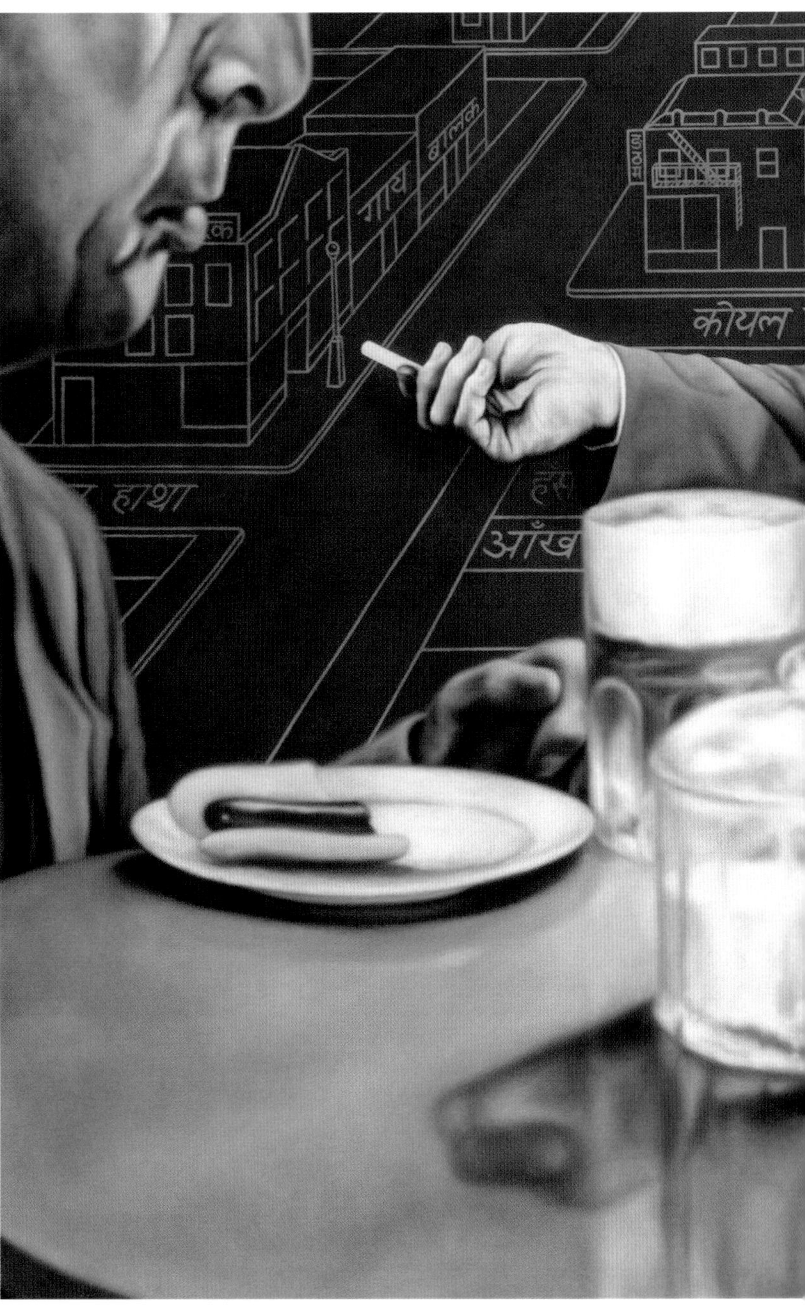

Intermezzo 1999

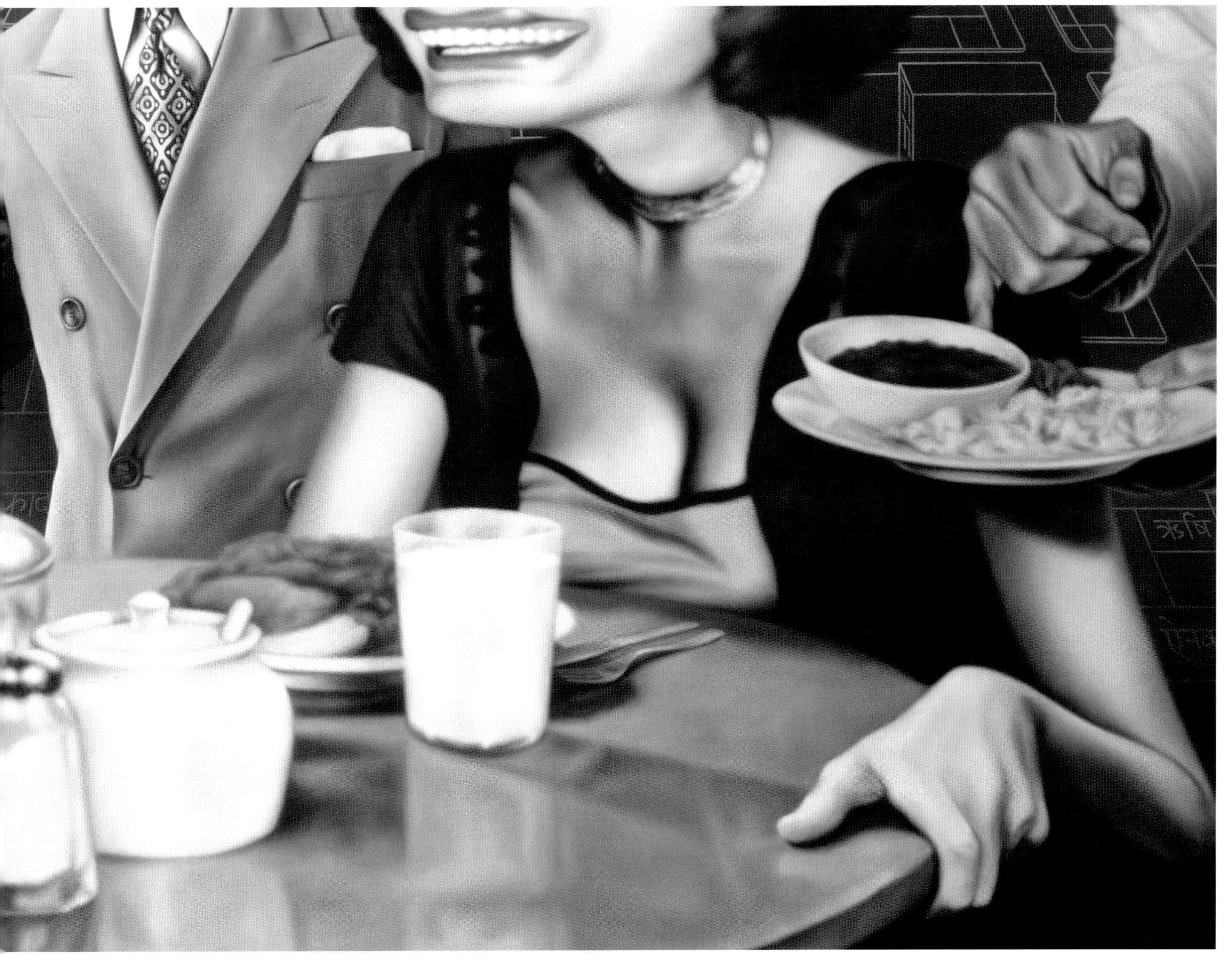

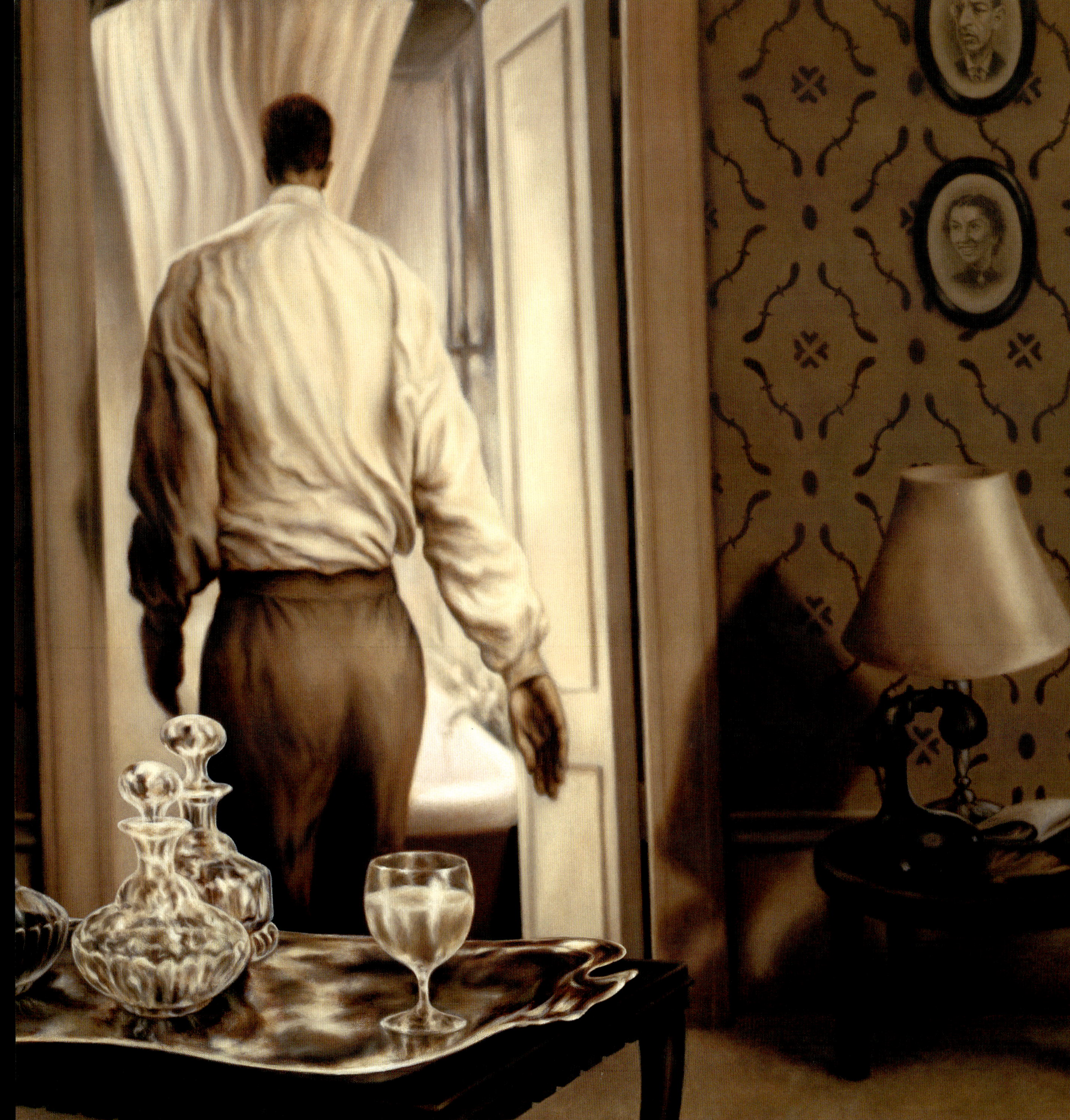

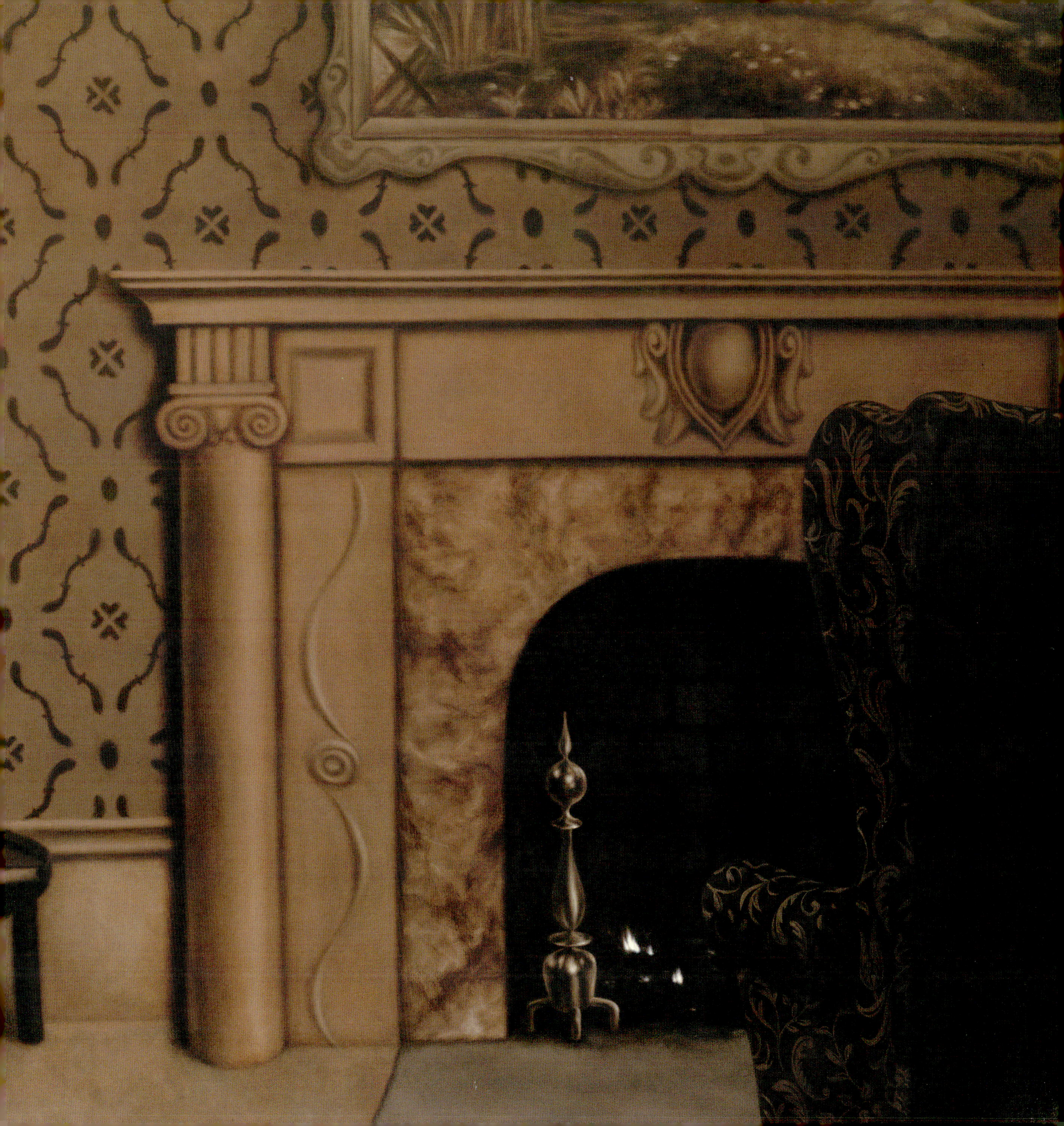

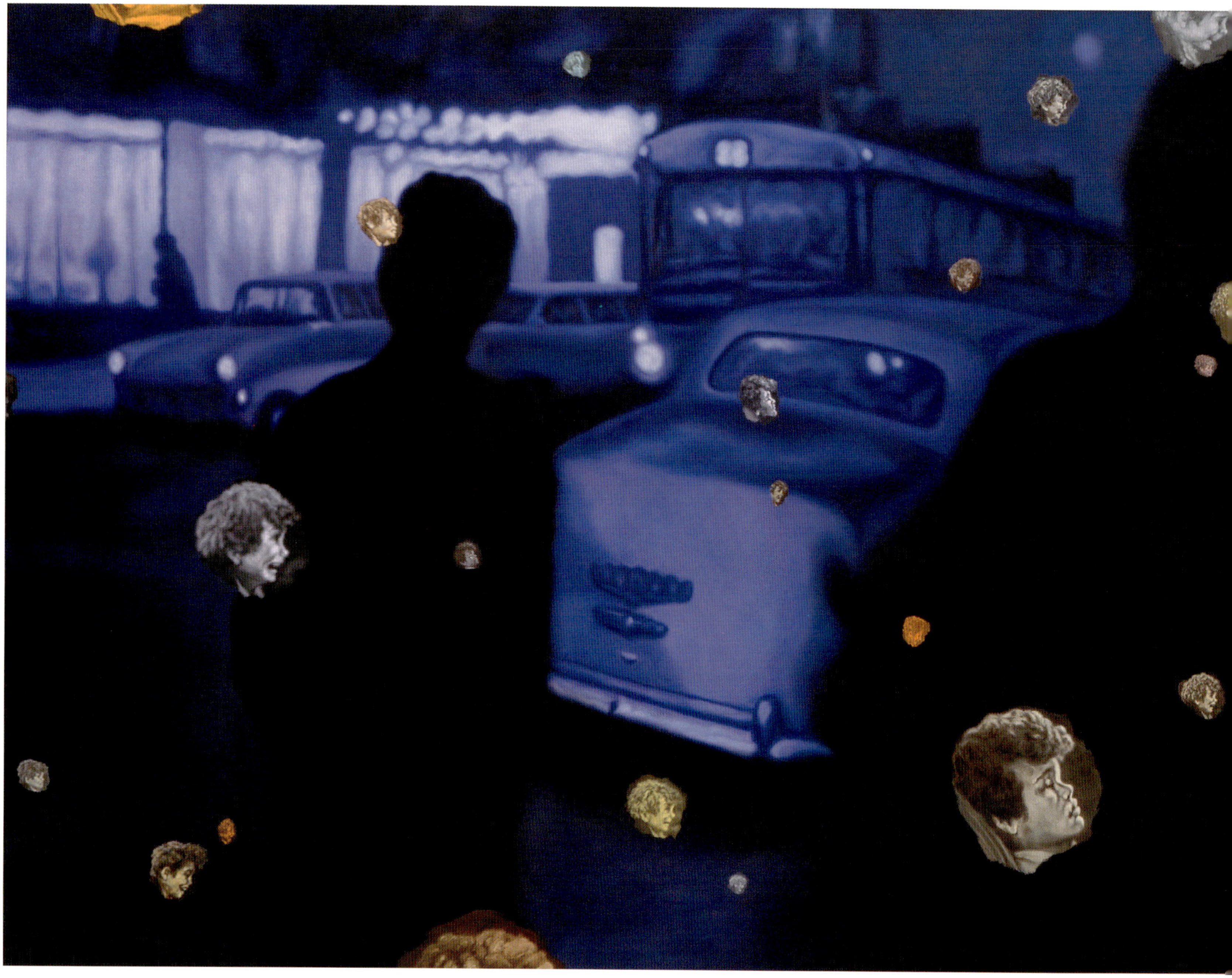

← Untitled 1999

Flurries 1999

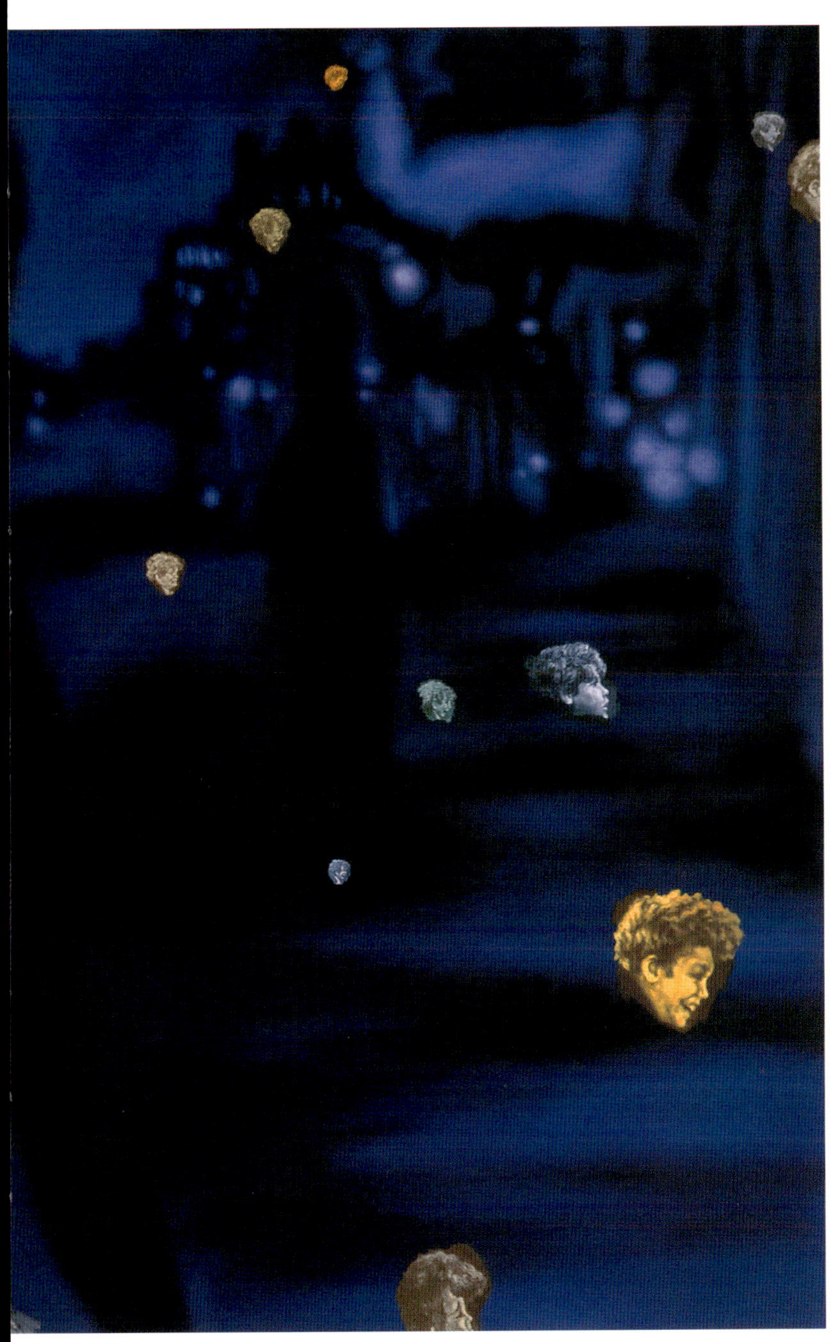

66

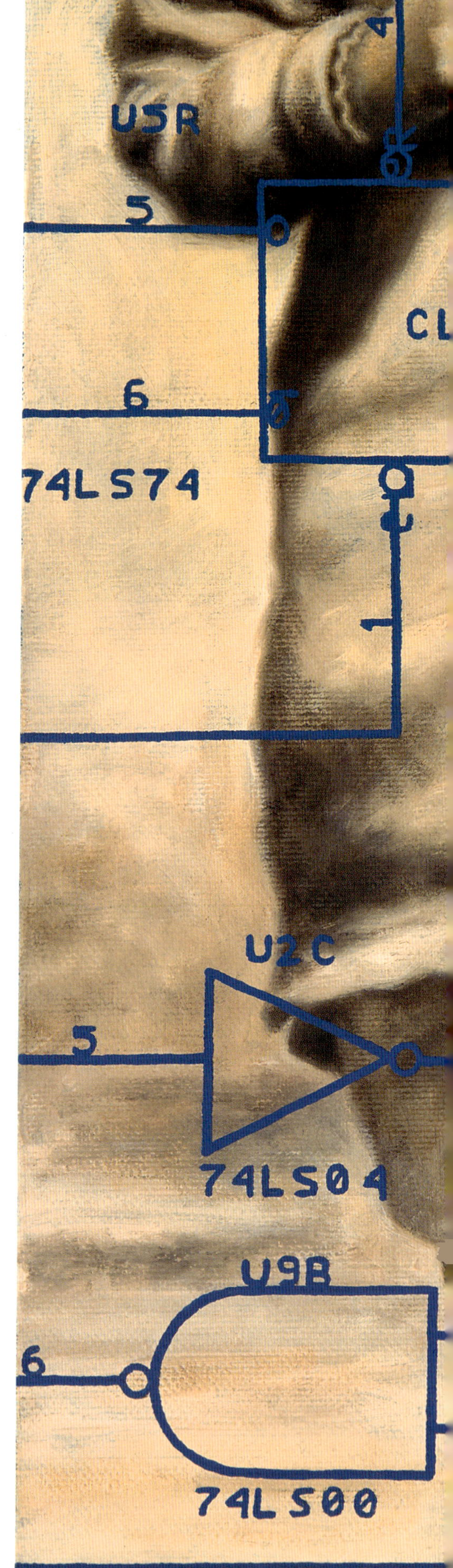

Protocol One 2000

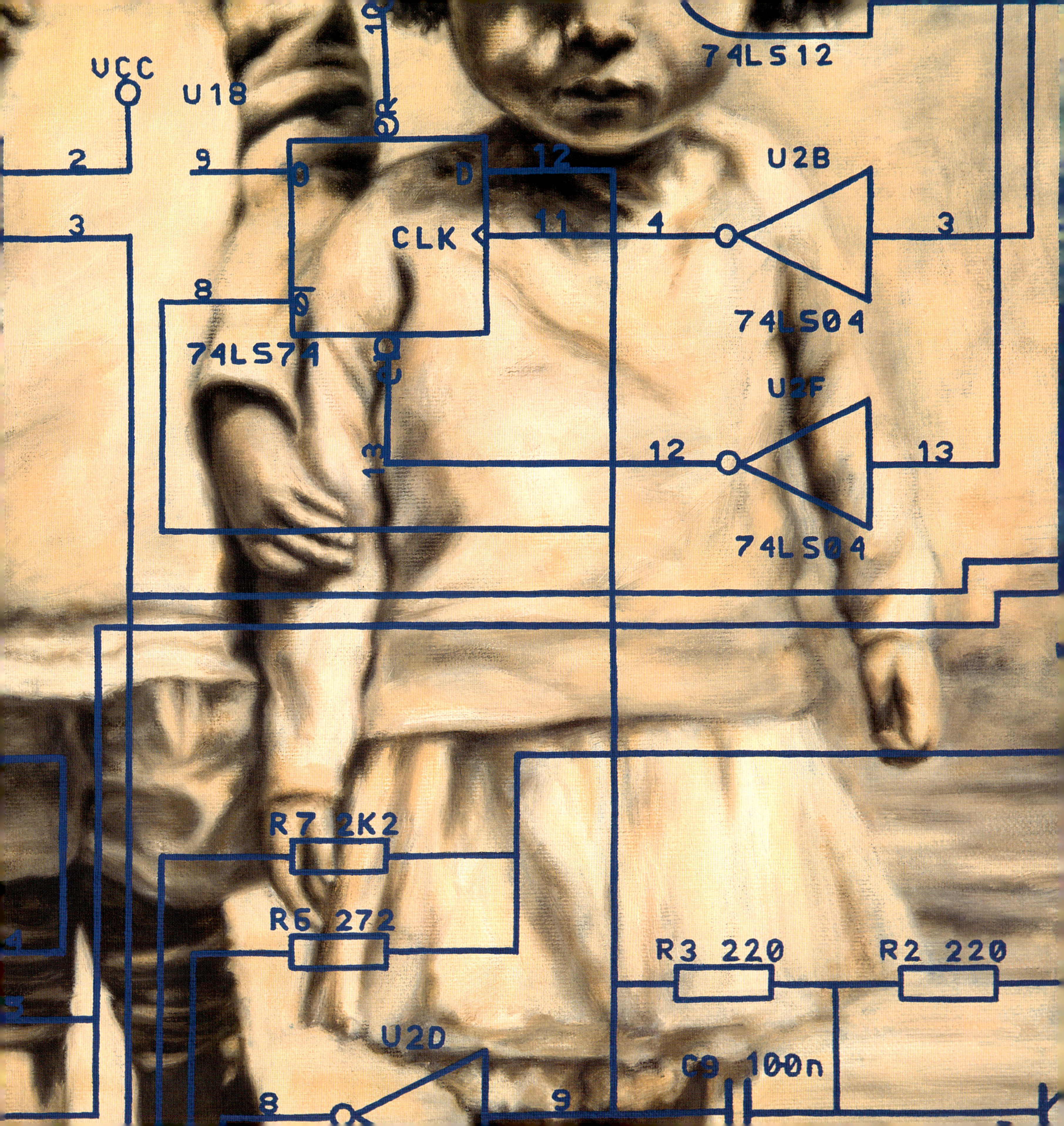
74LS12
VCC
U18
2
9
D
12
CLK
11
4
U2B
3
3
8
74LS04
74LS74
U2F
13
12
13
74LS04
R7 2K2
R6 272
R3 220
R2 220
U2D
C9 100n
8
9

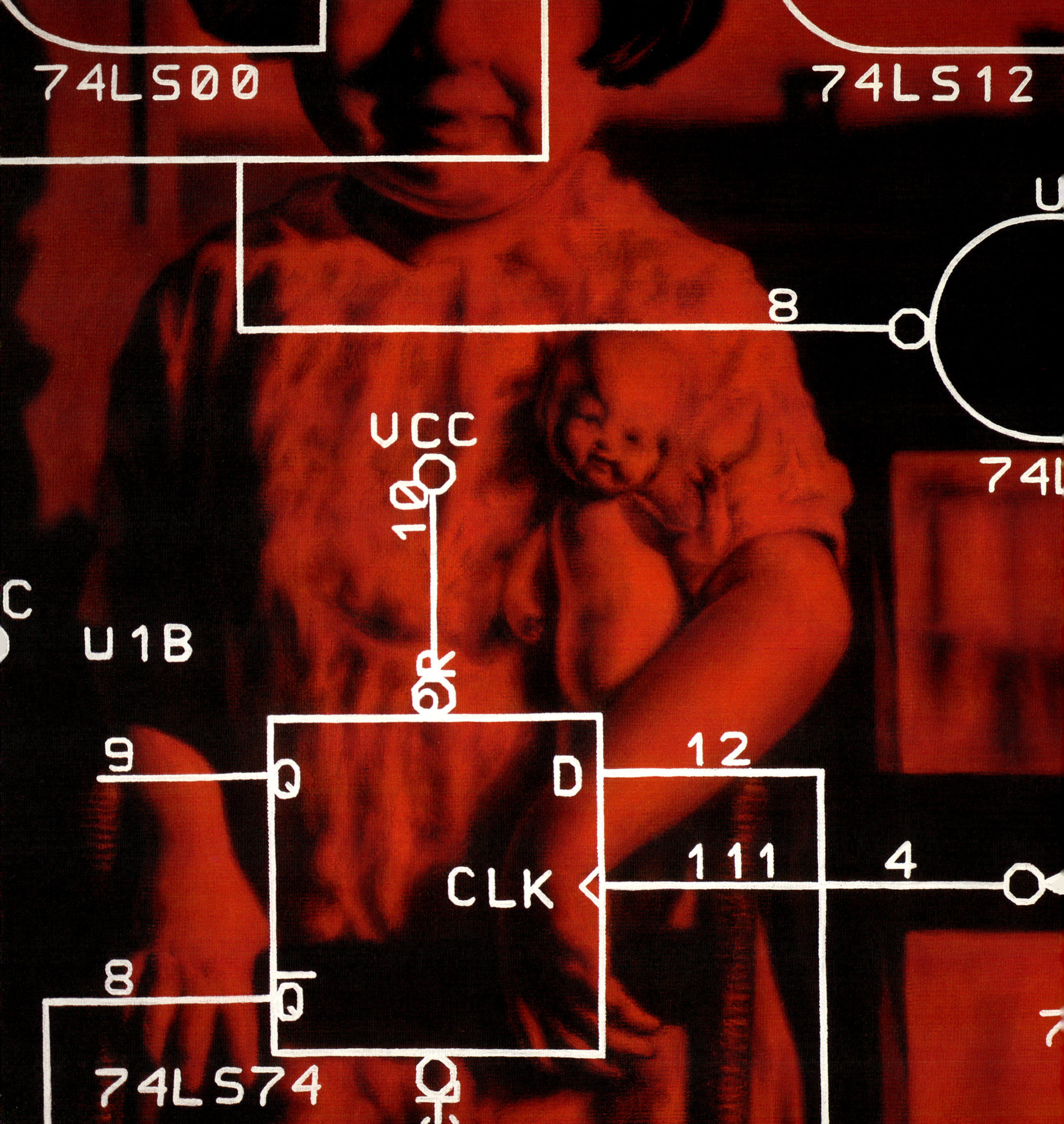
74LS00
74LS12
8
VCC
10
U1B
9
Q
D
12
111
4
CLK
8
Q
74LS74

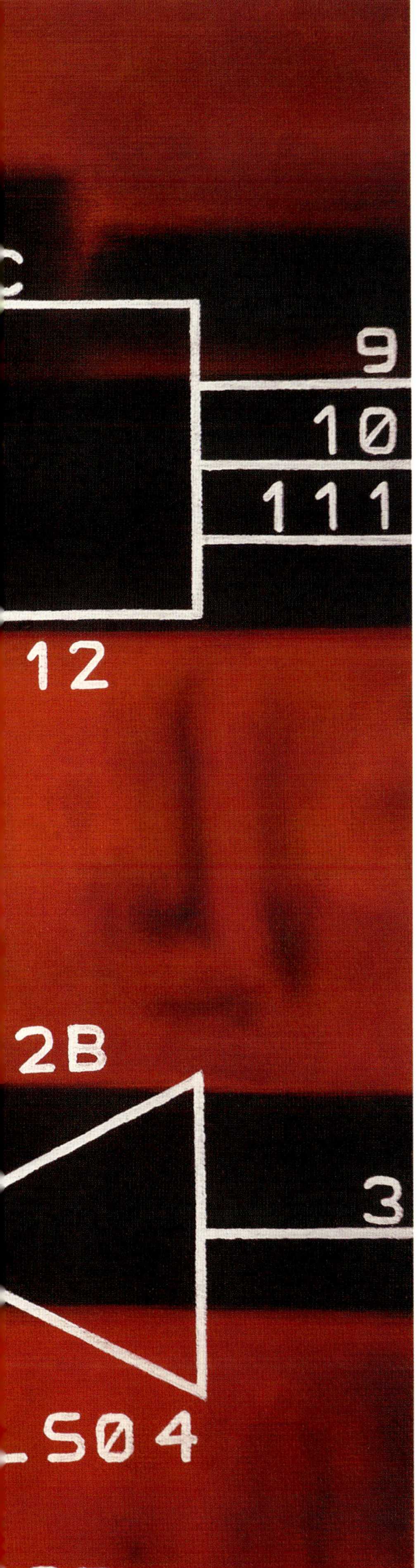

Protocol Two 2000

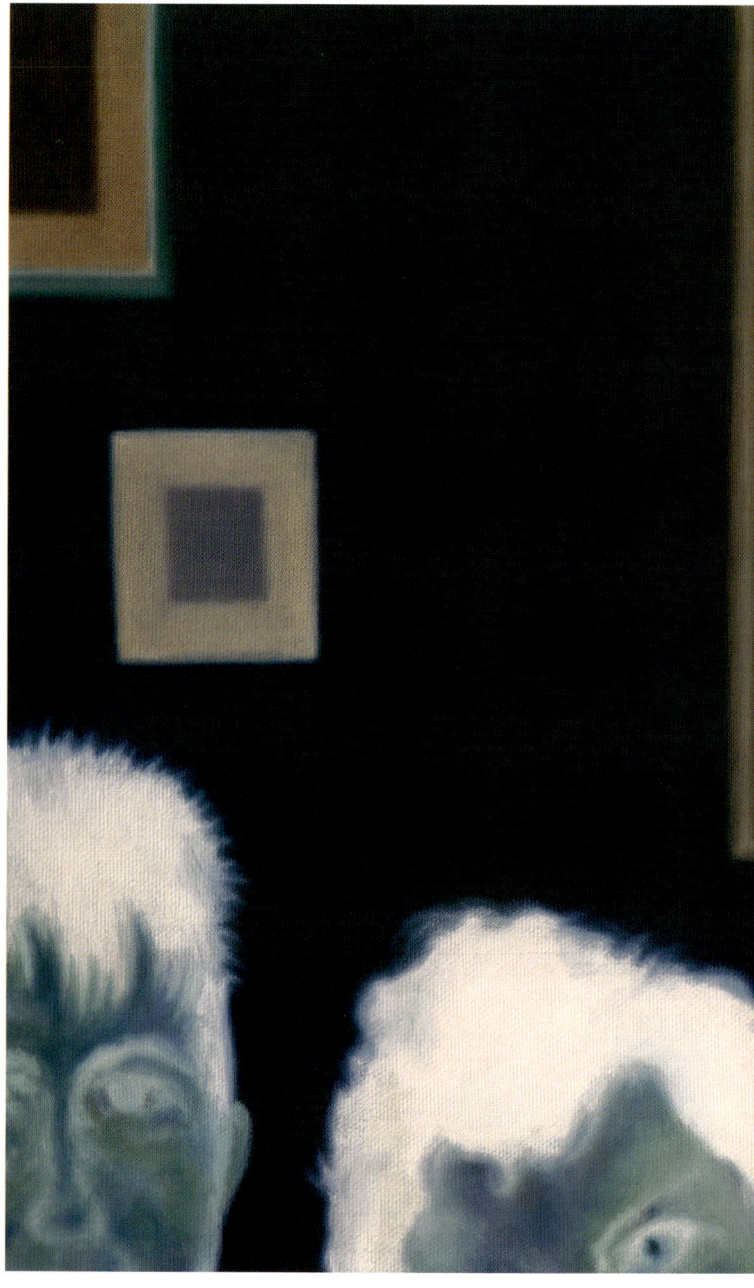

Pelicans 2000

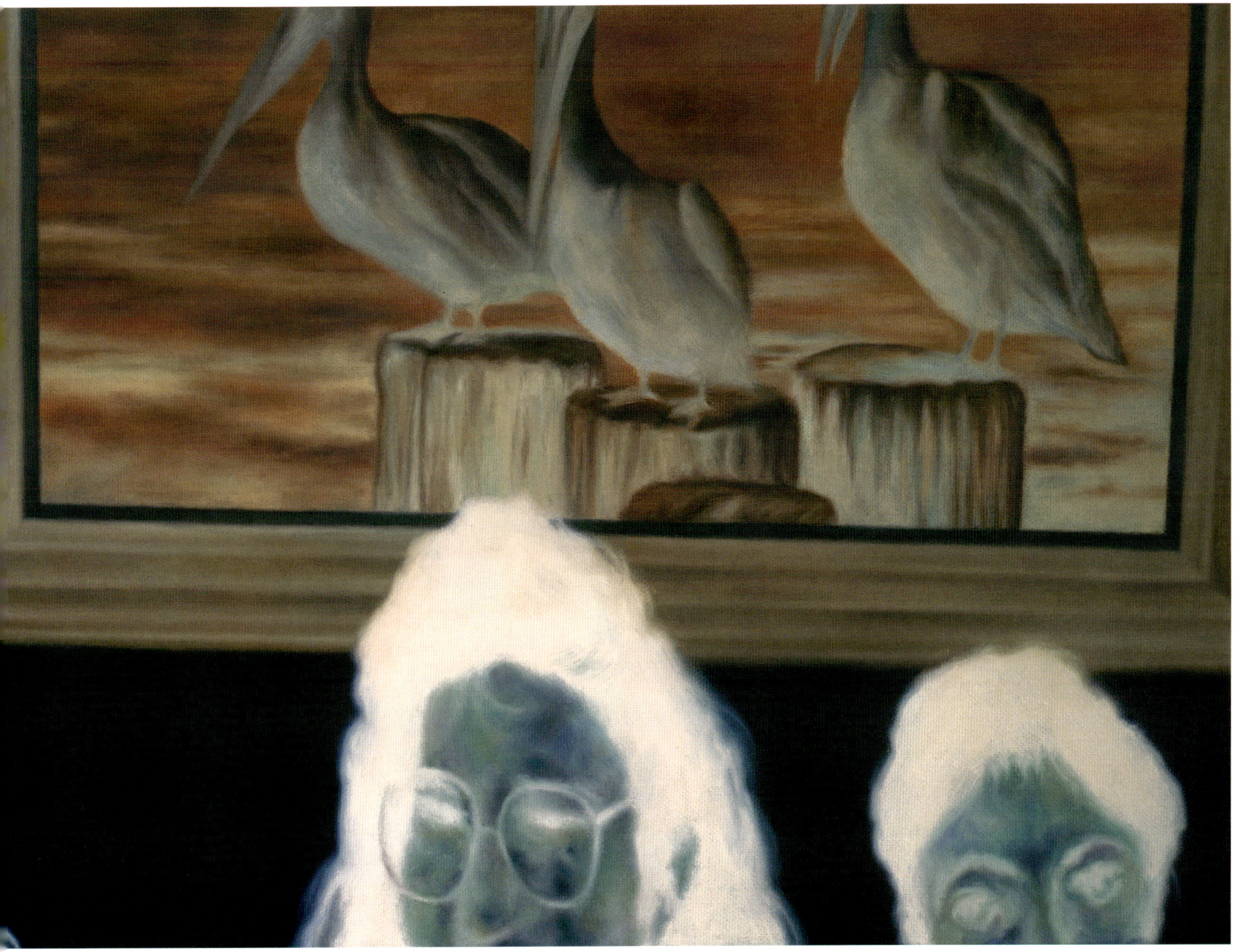

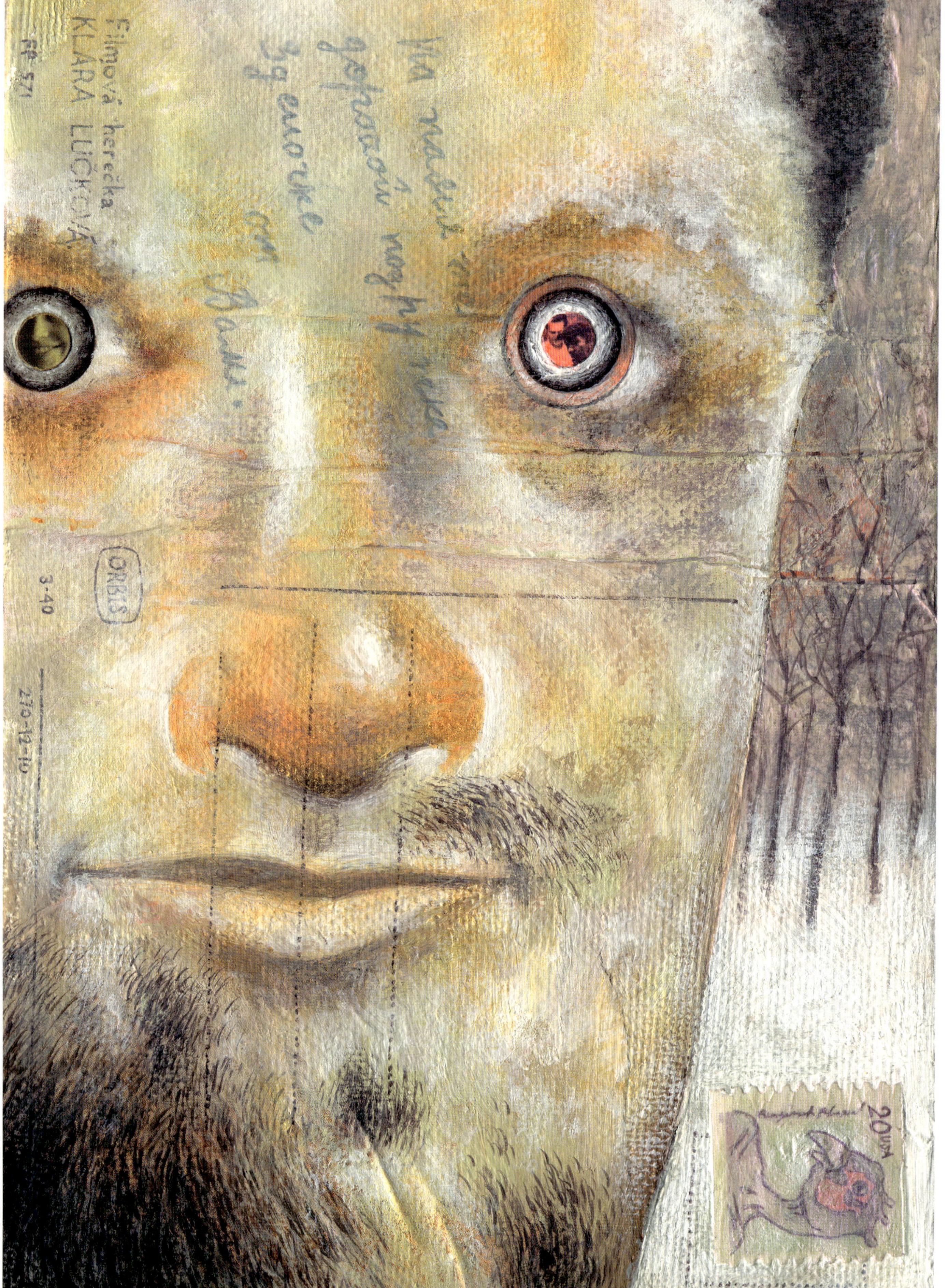

Filmova 2000

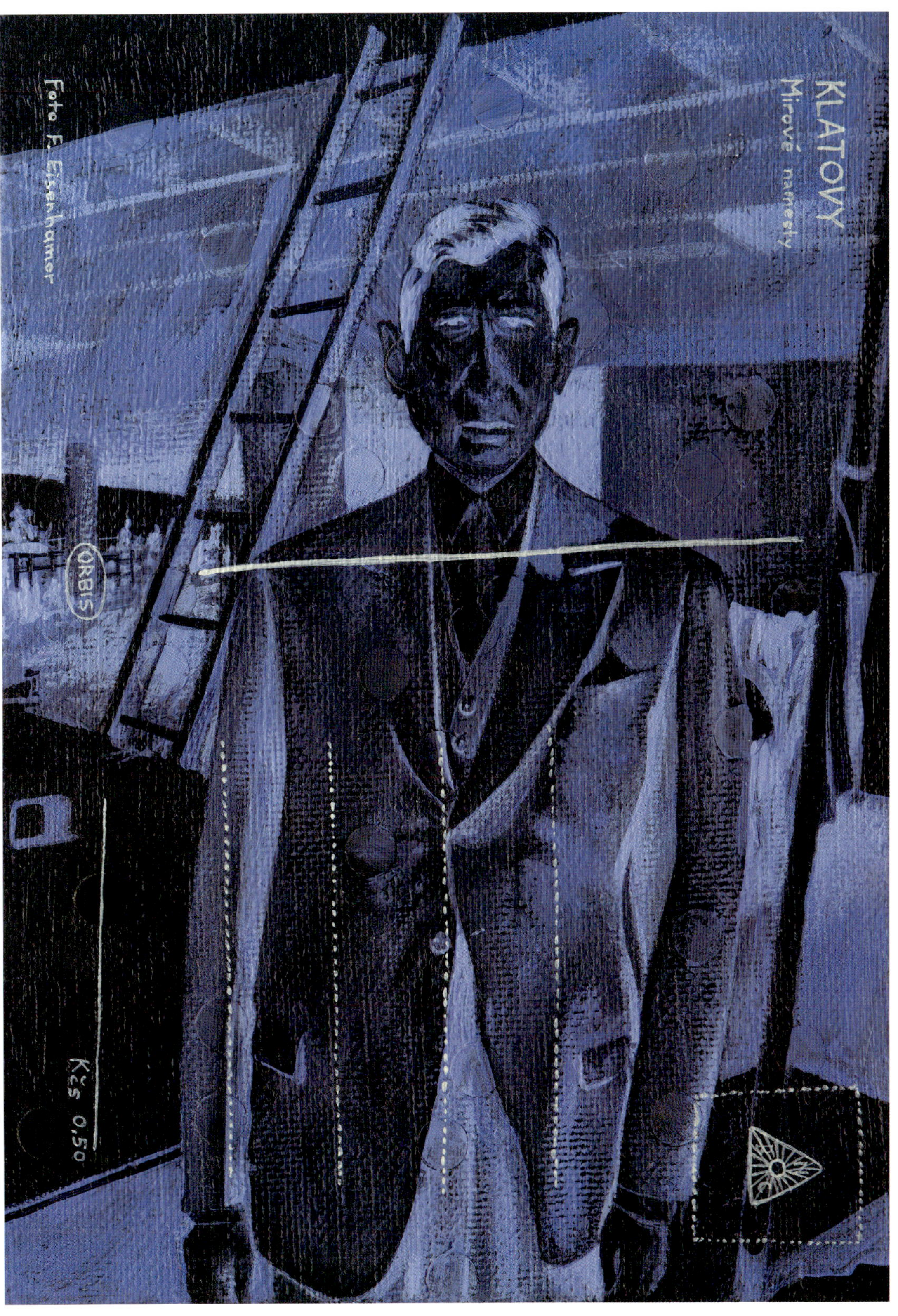

Klatovy 2000

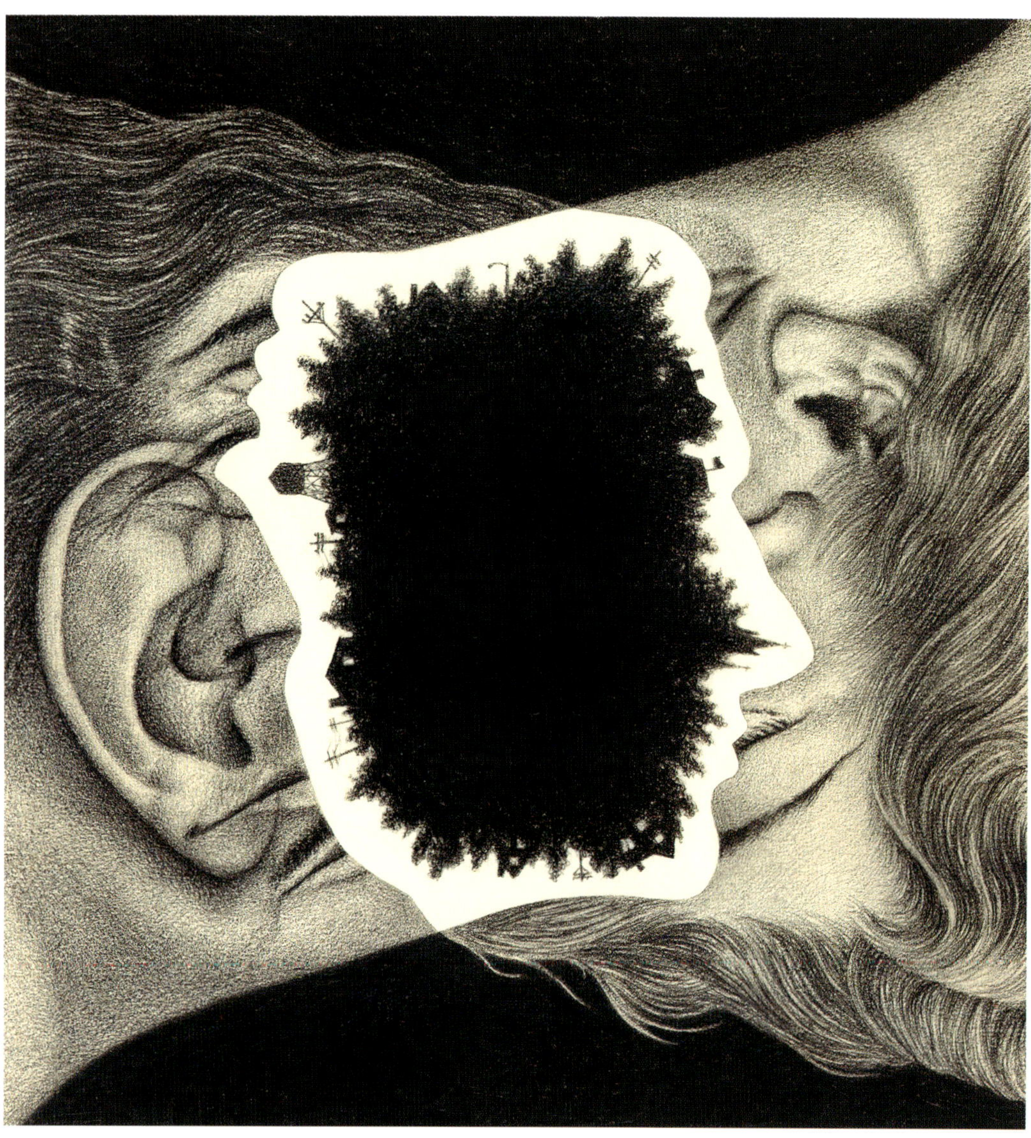

The Ceiling 2001

Let's Celebrate 2001

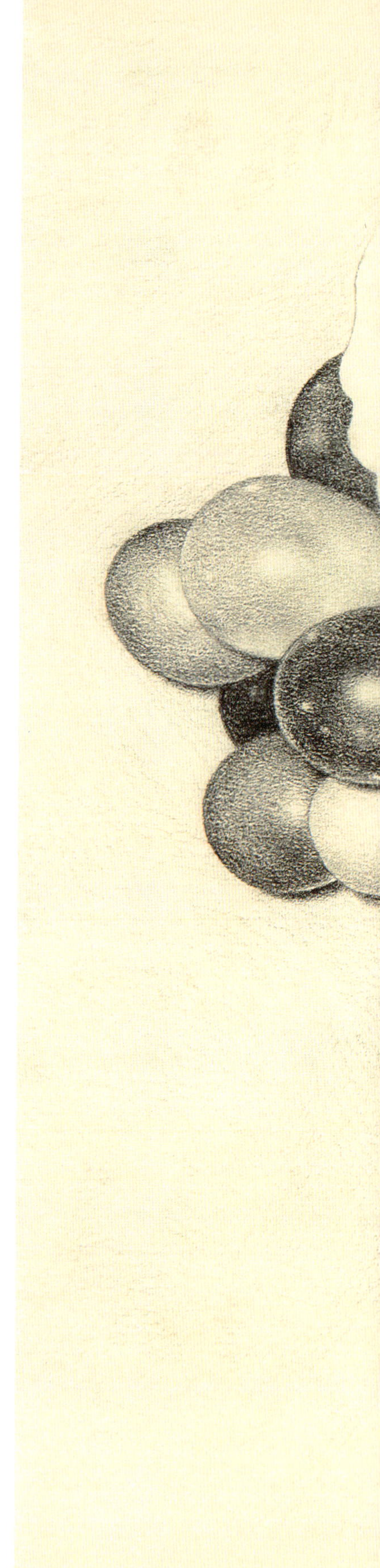

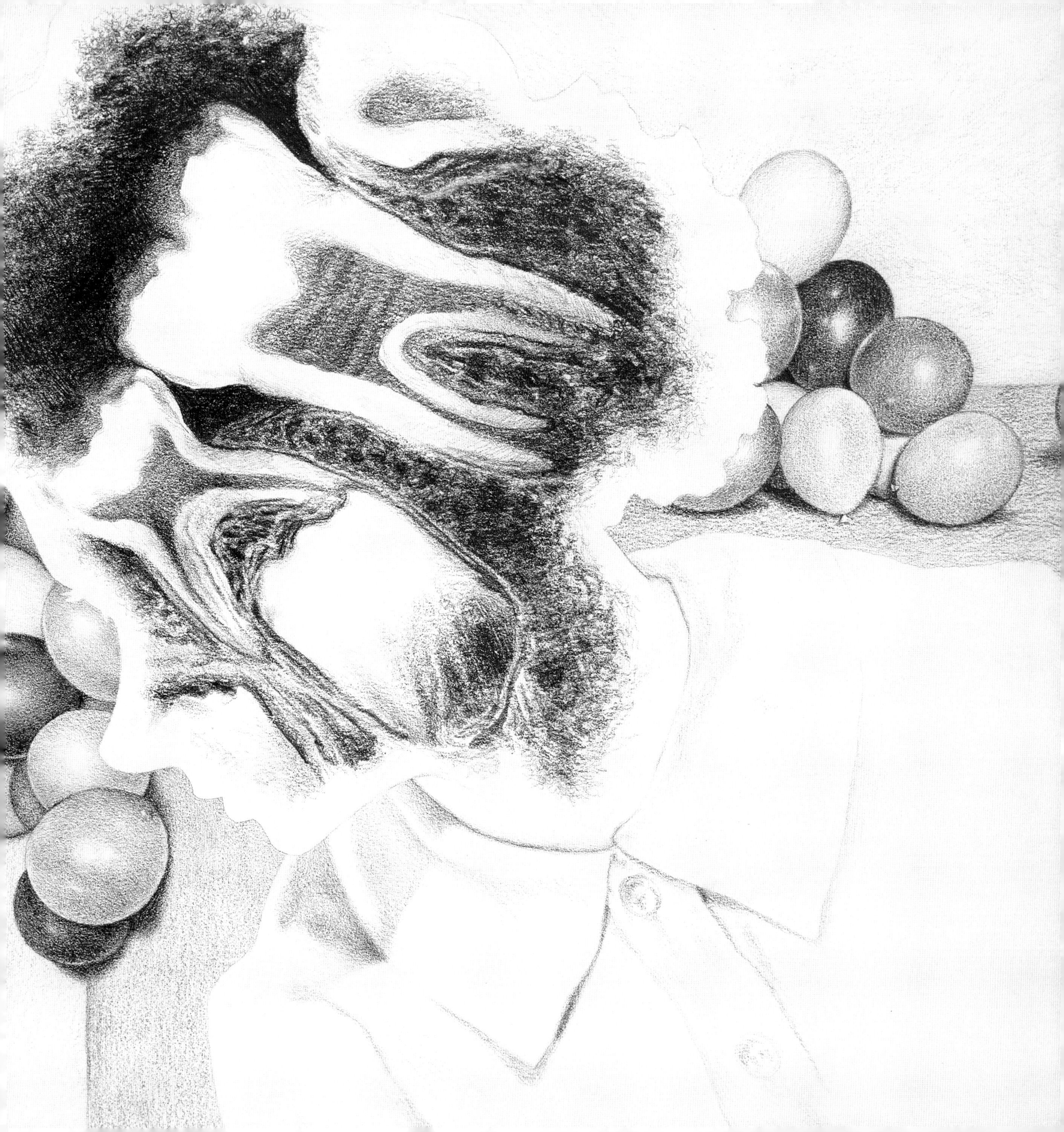

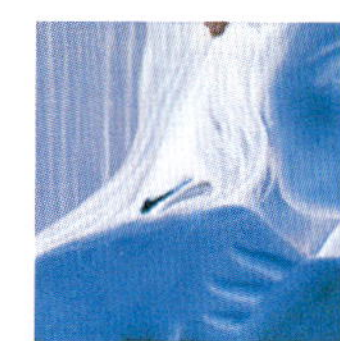
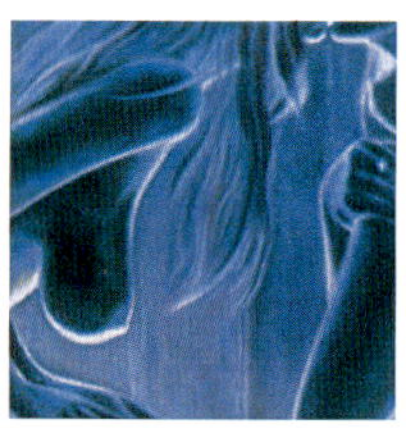
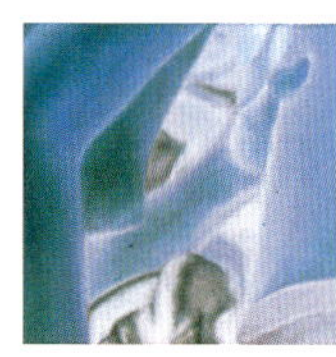
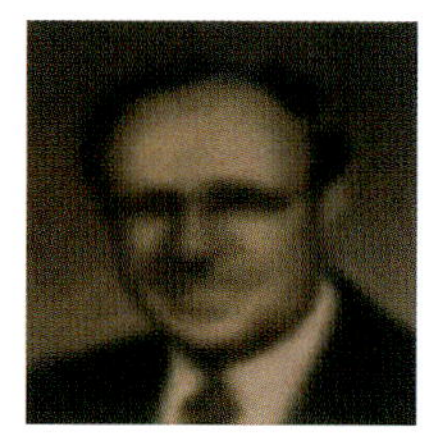
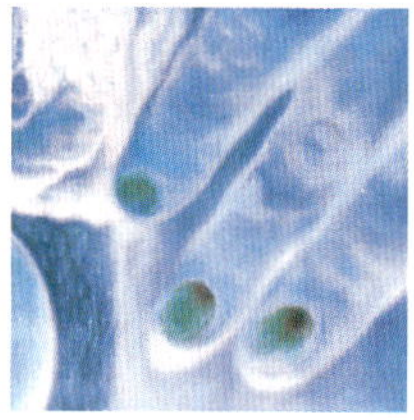
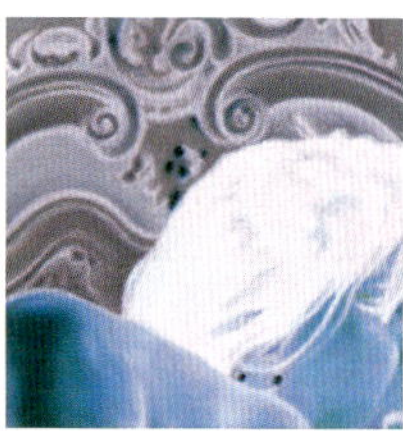
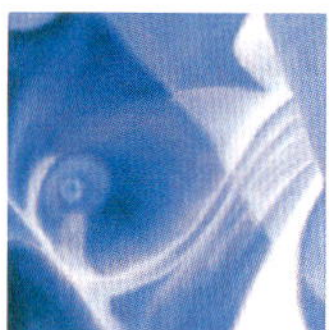
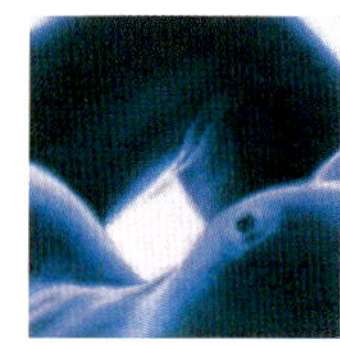
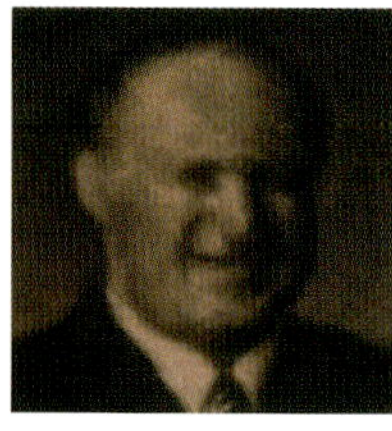
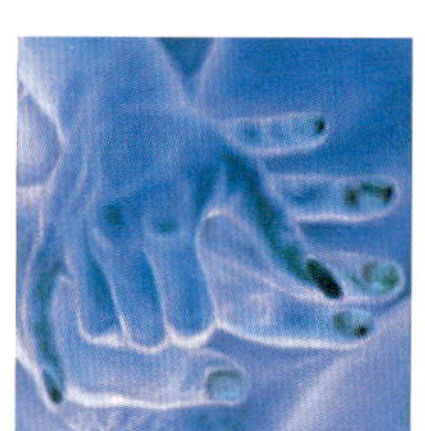
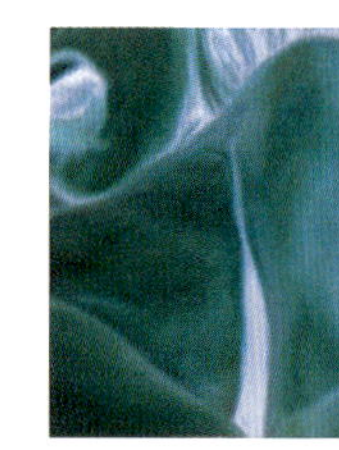
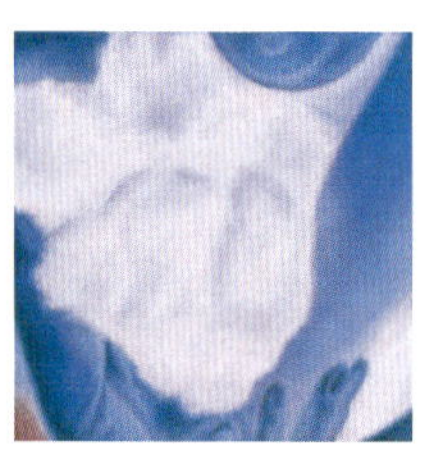
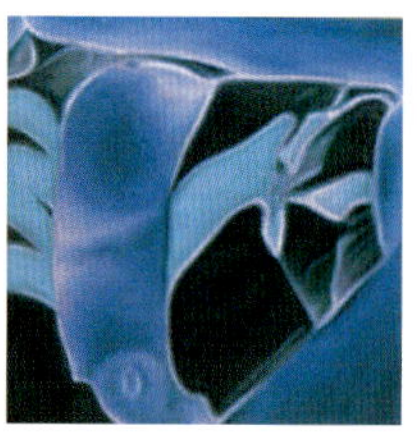
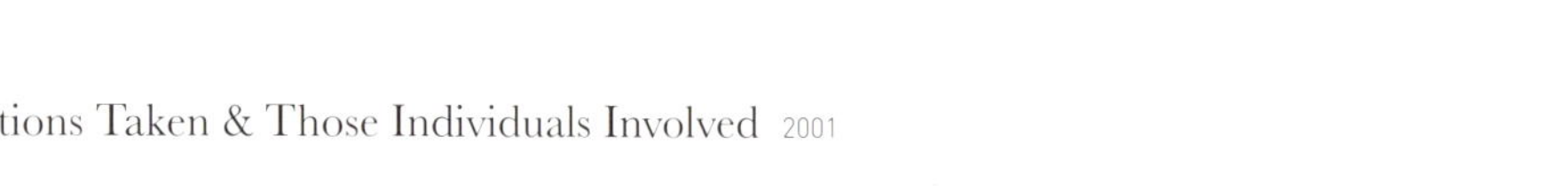

The Actions Taken & Those Individuals Involved 2001

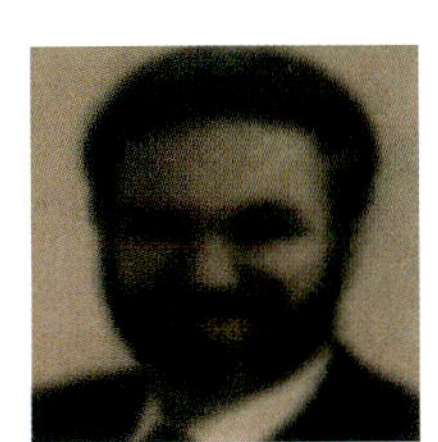

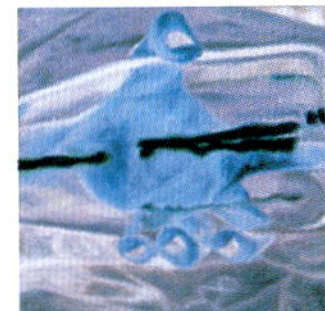

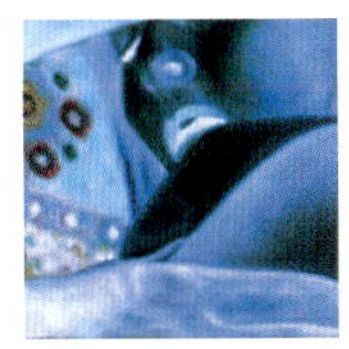

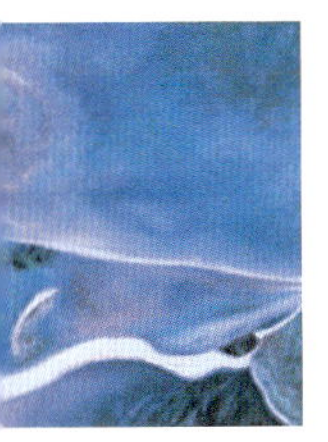

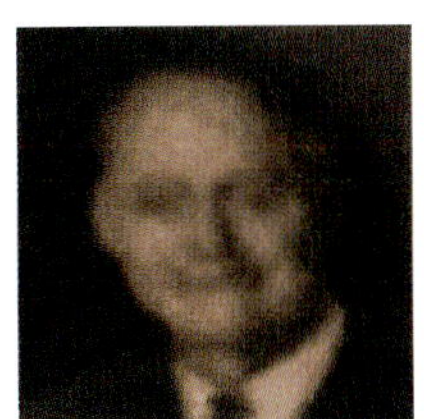

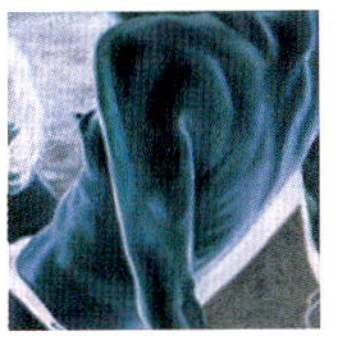

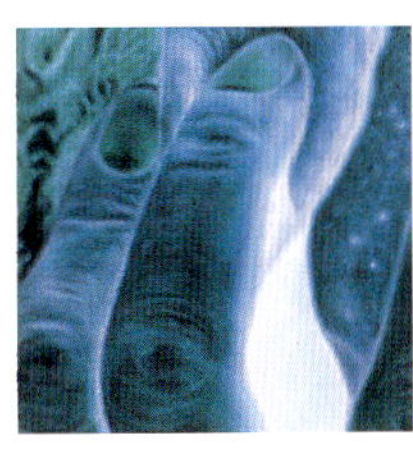

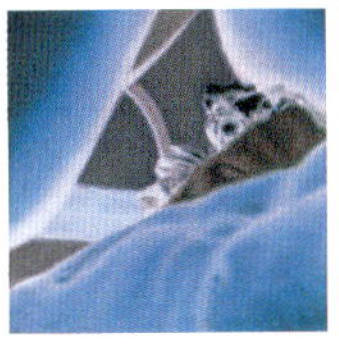

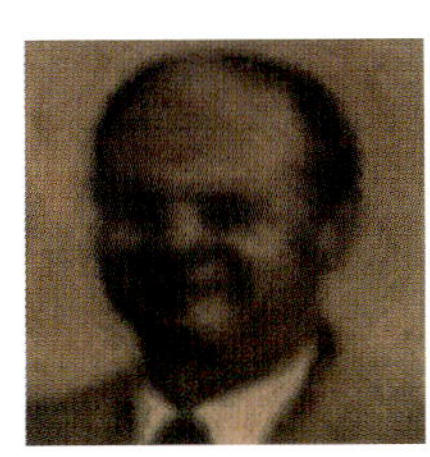

Margo Lefferts 2001

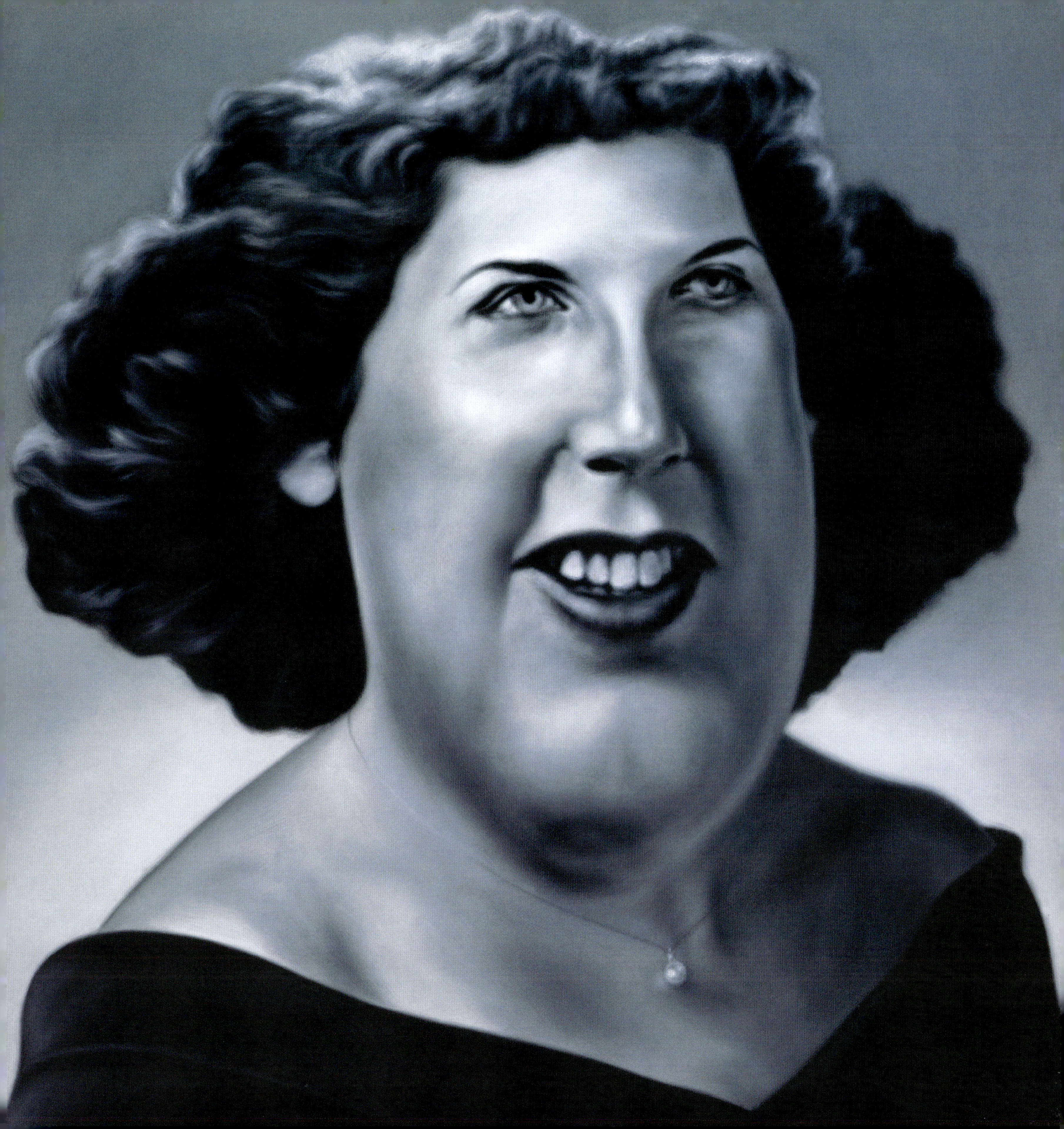

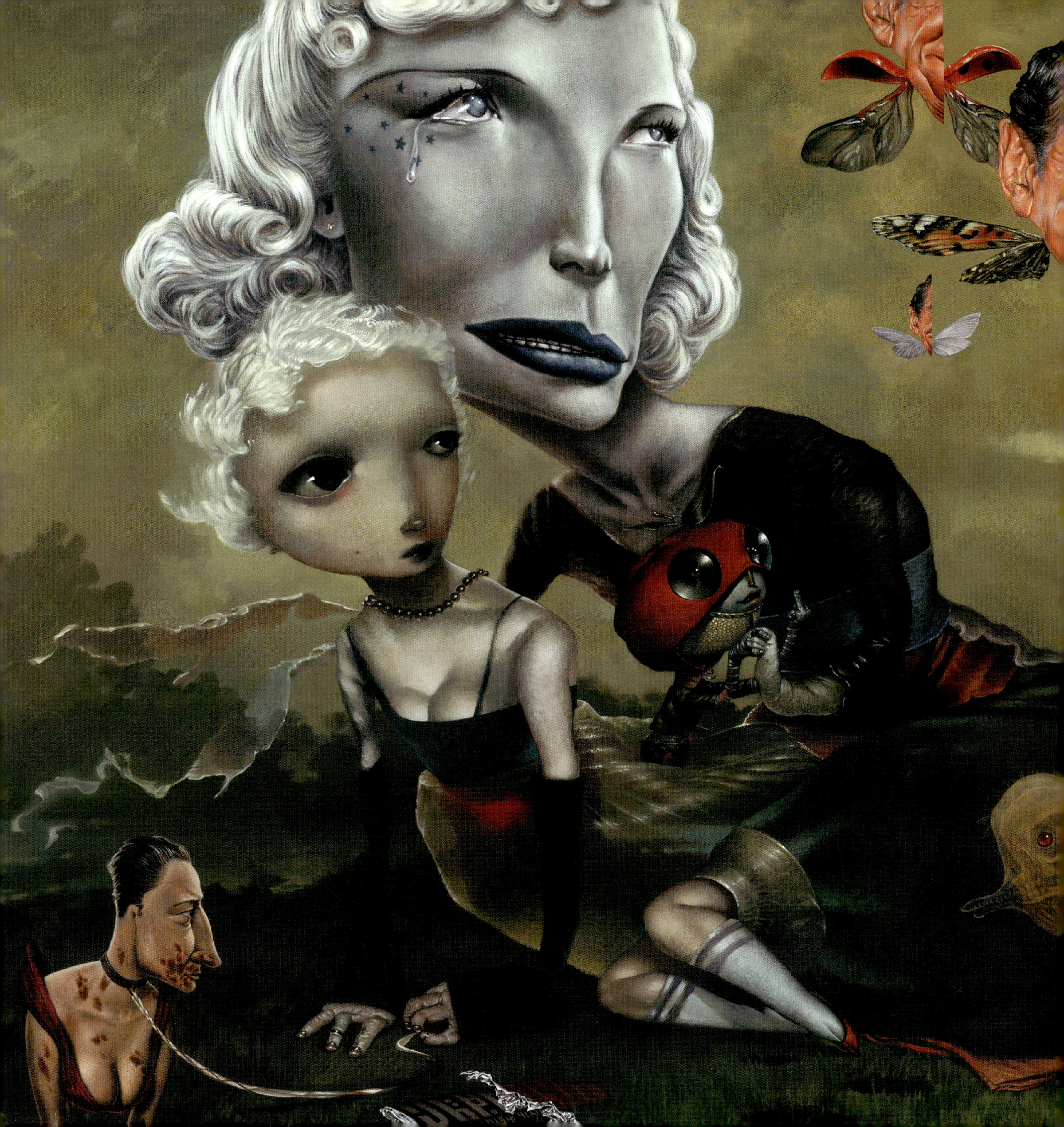

That Which Organizes My Feathers (w/ Joe Sorren) 2001

Golden Moments 200

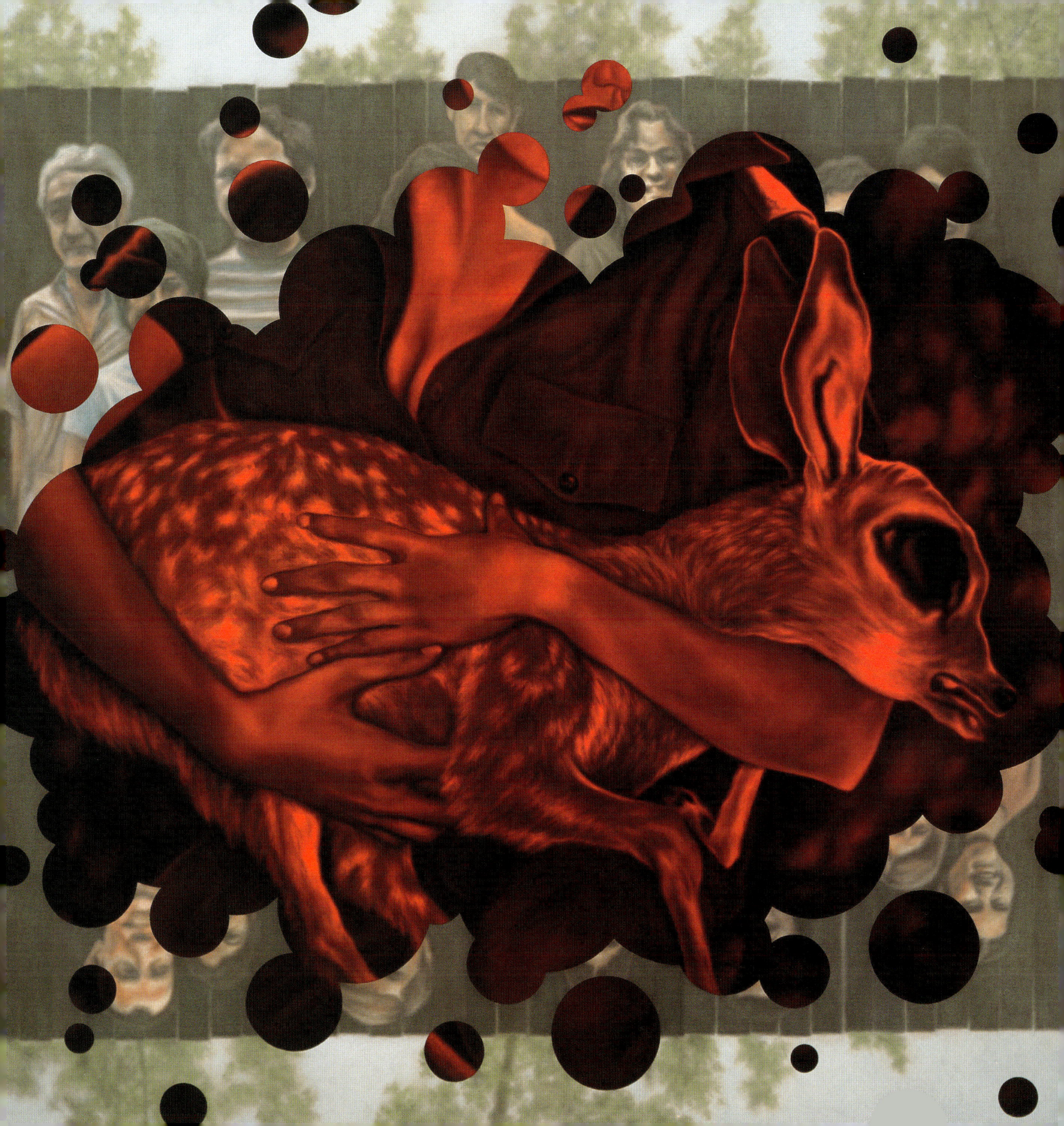

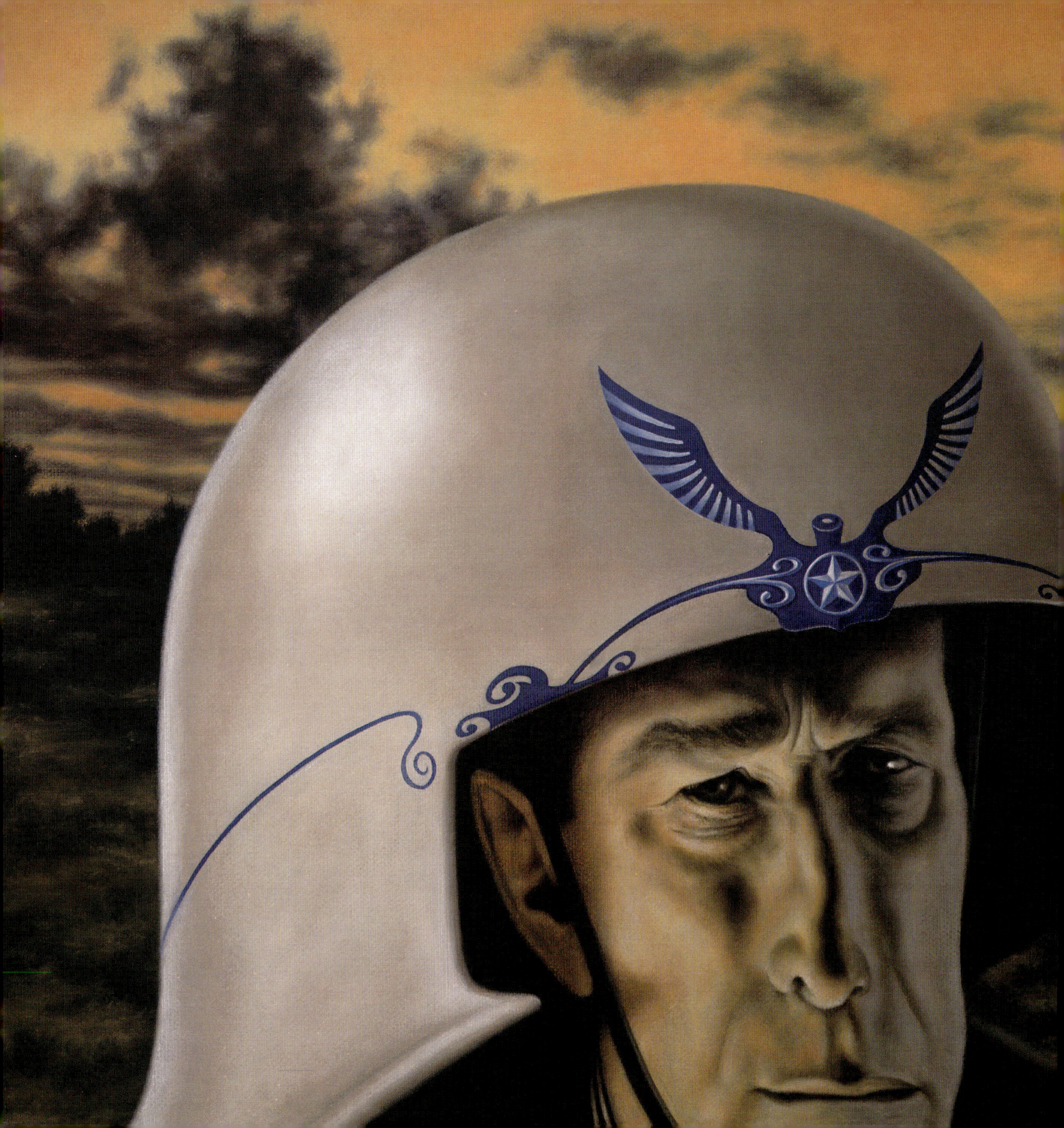

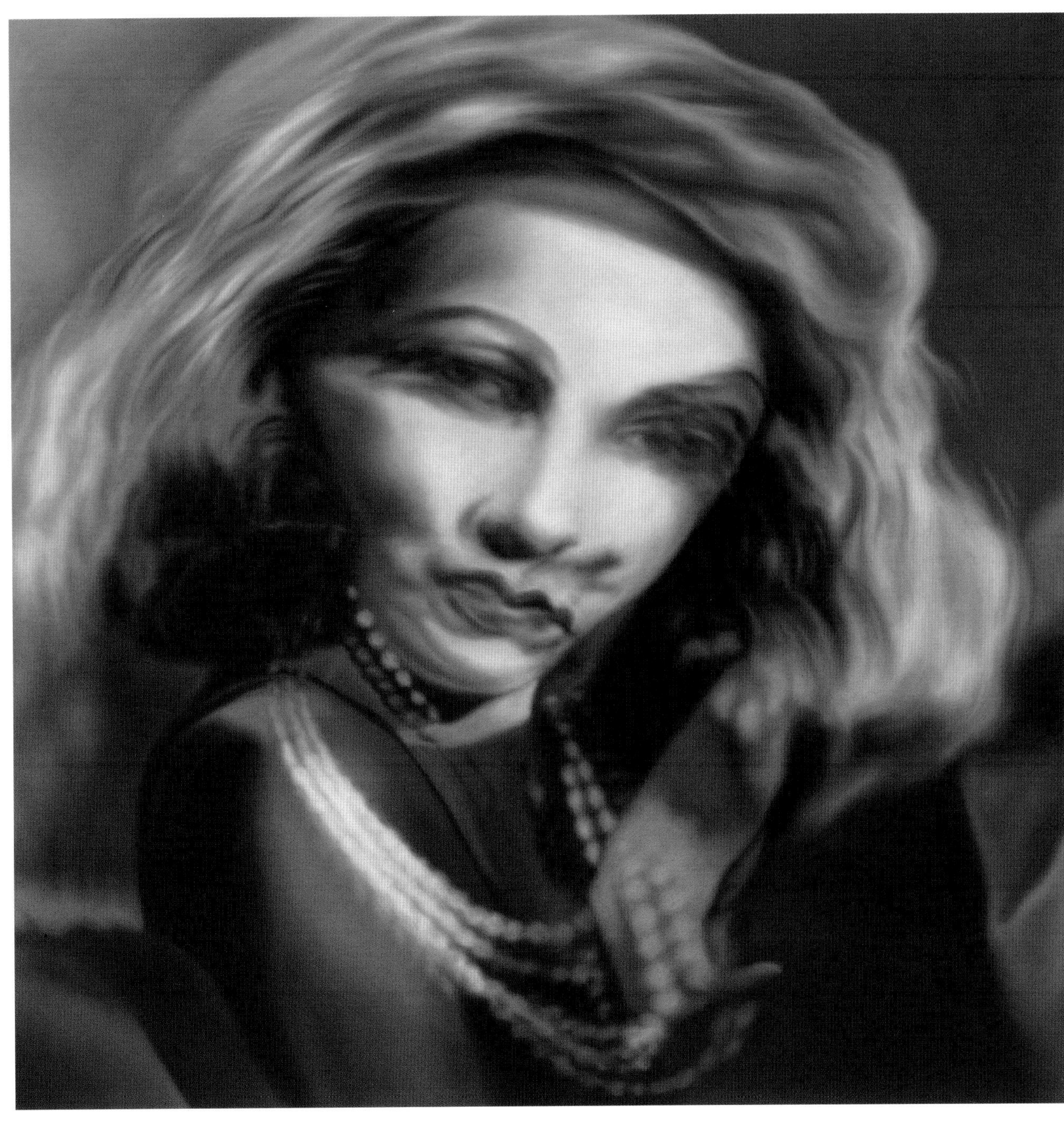

The Sheriff 2001

Starlet 2001

Holy Matron of Ridicule 200[illegible]

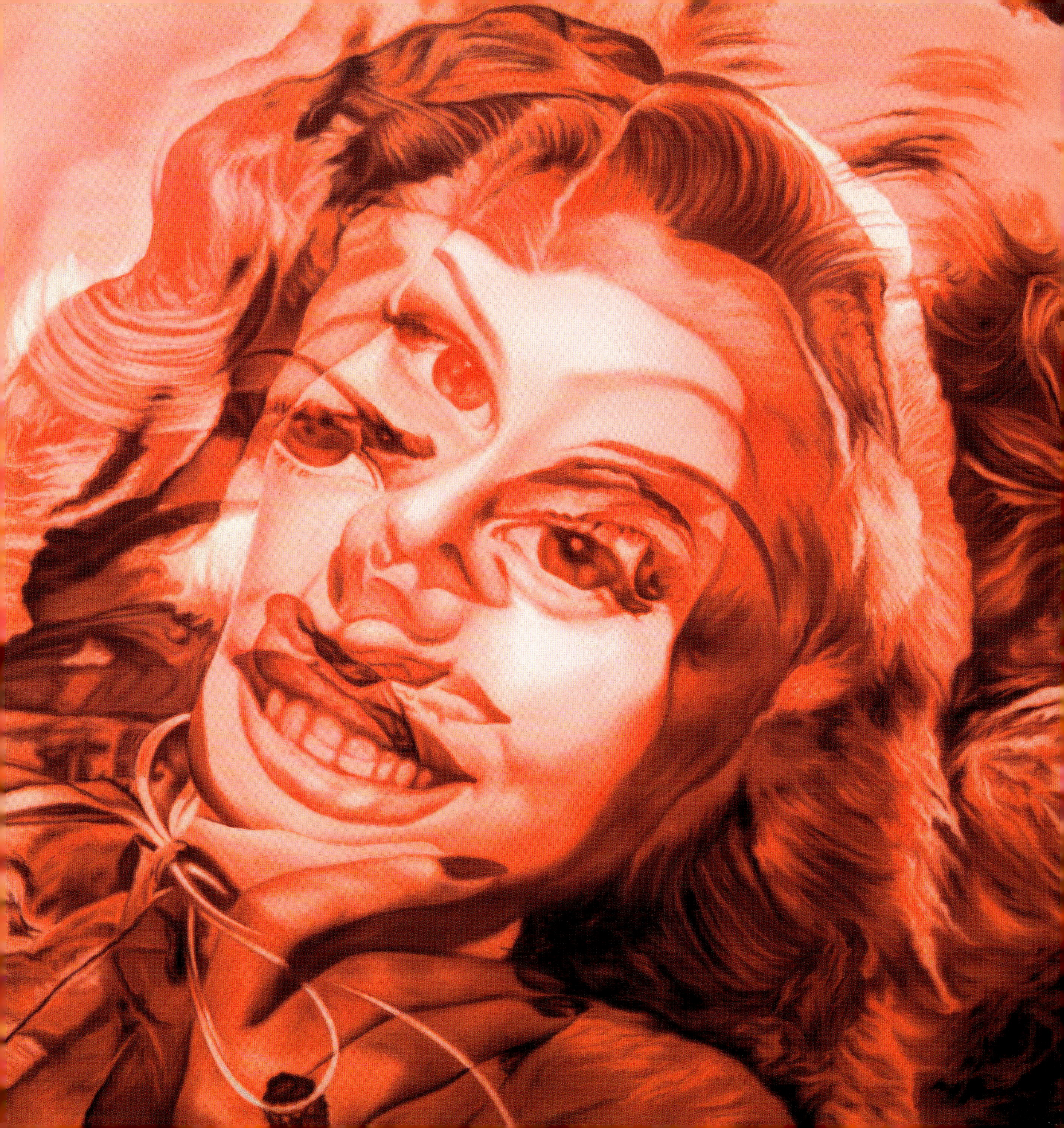

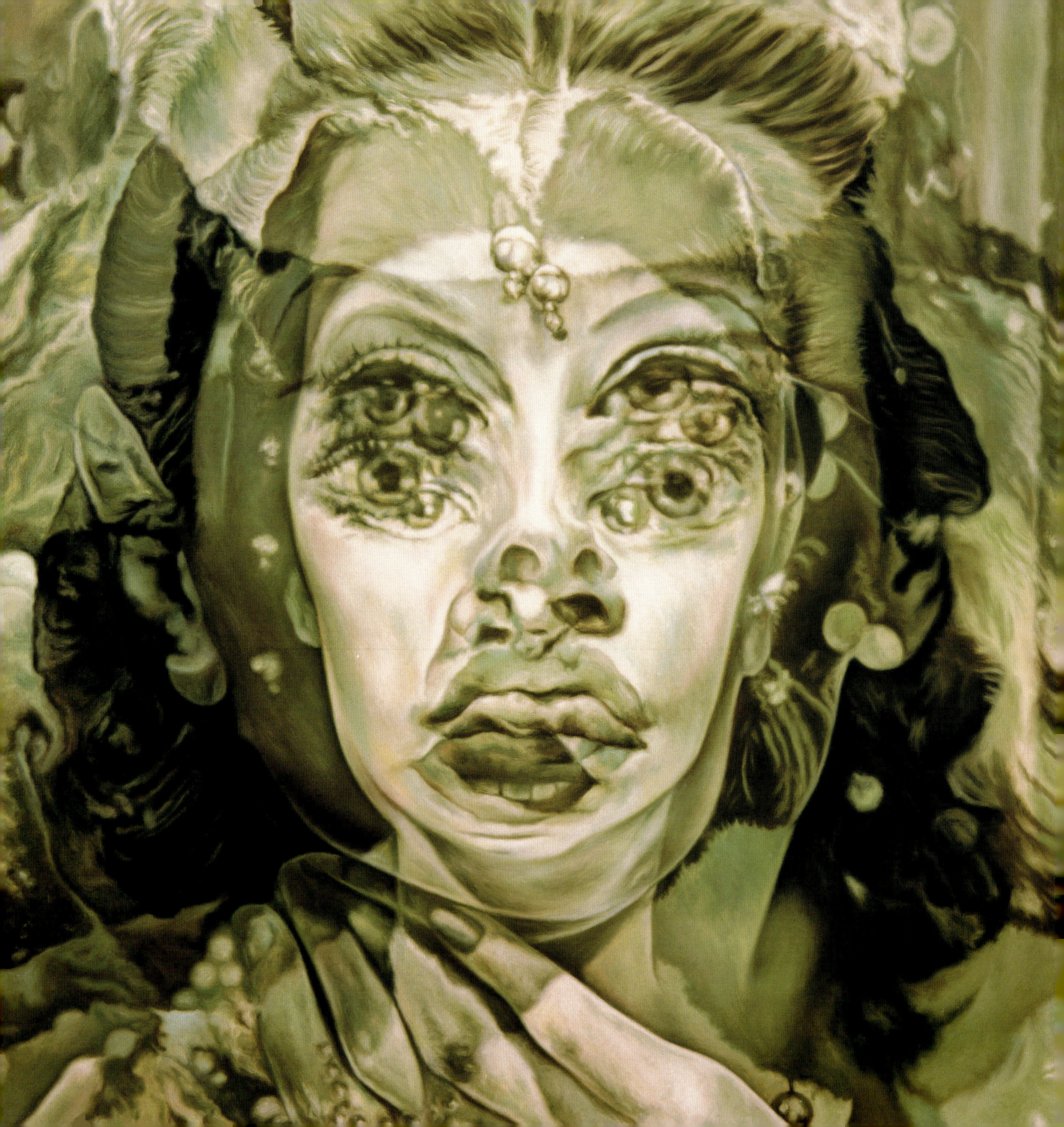

Divine Mother of Guilt 2002

Sacred Lady of Bias 2002

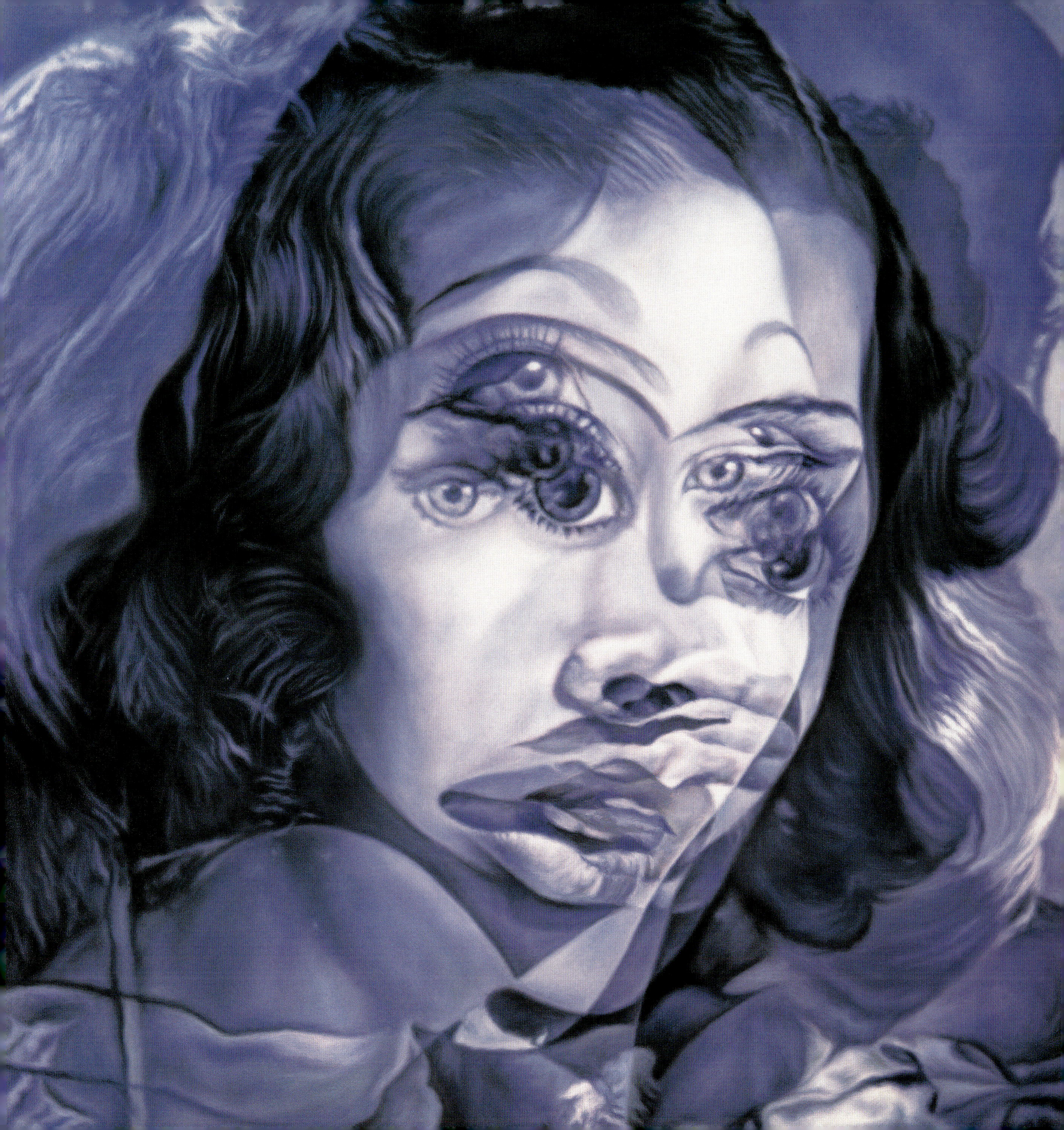

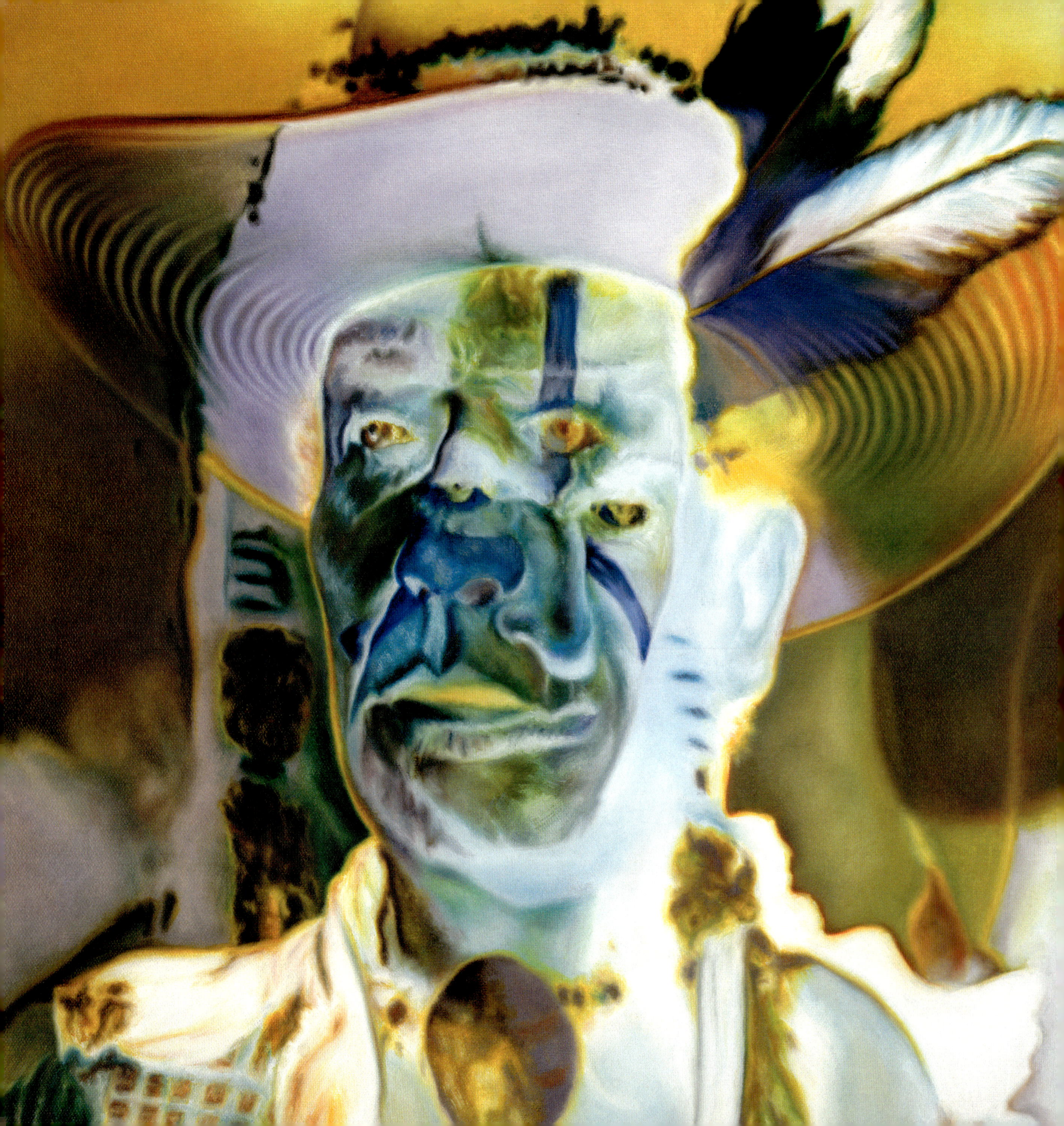

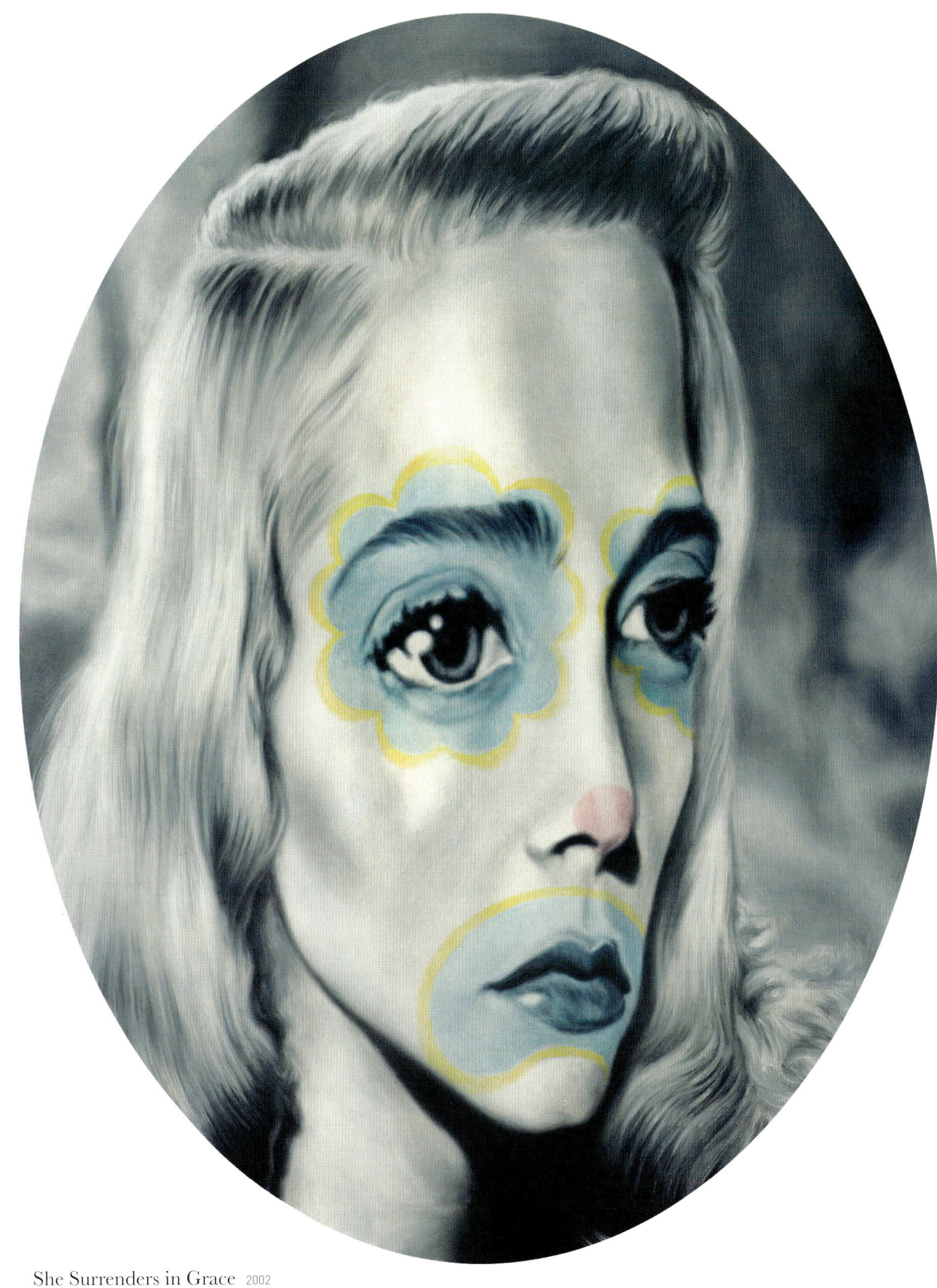

Them or Us 2003

She Surrenders in Grace 2002

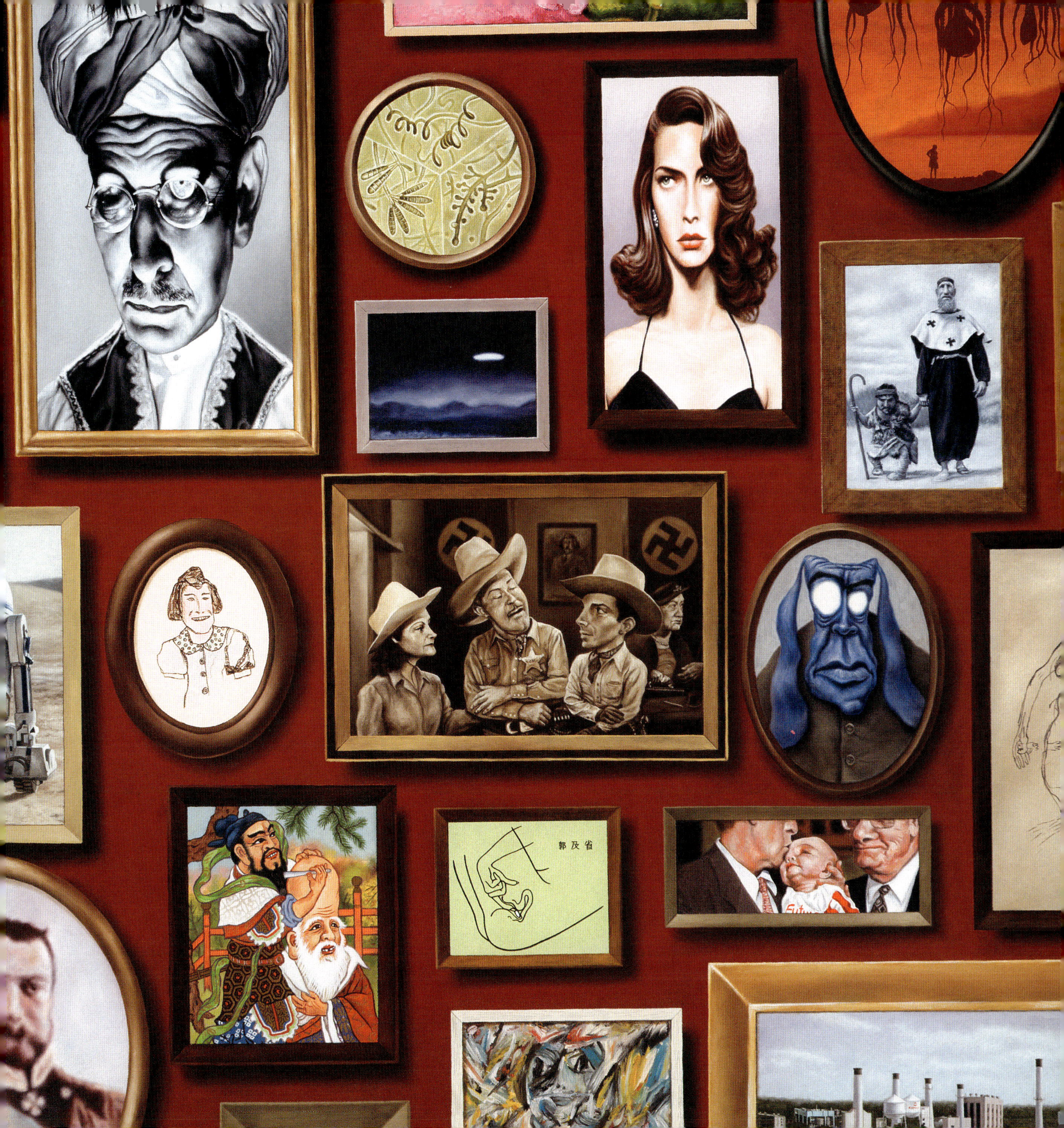
郭及省

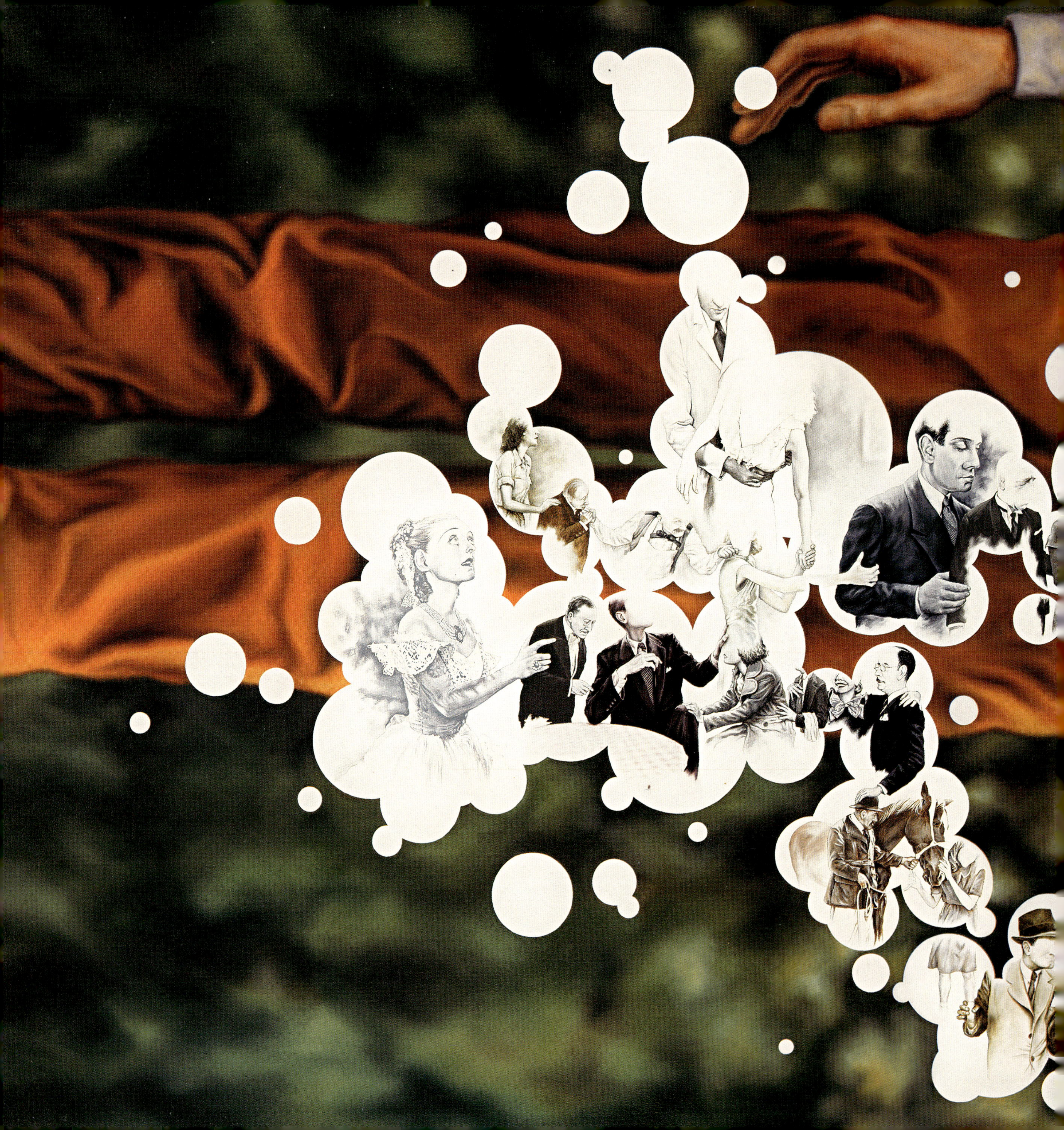

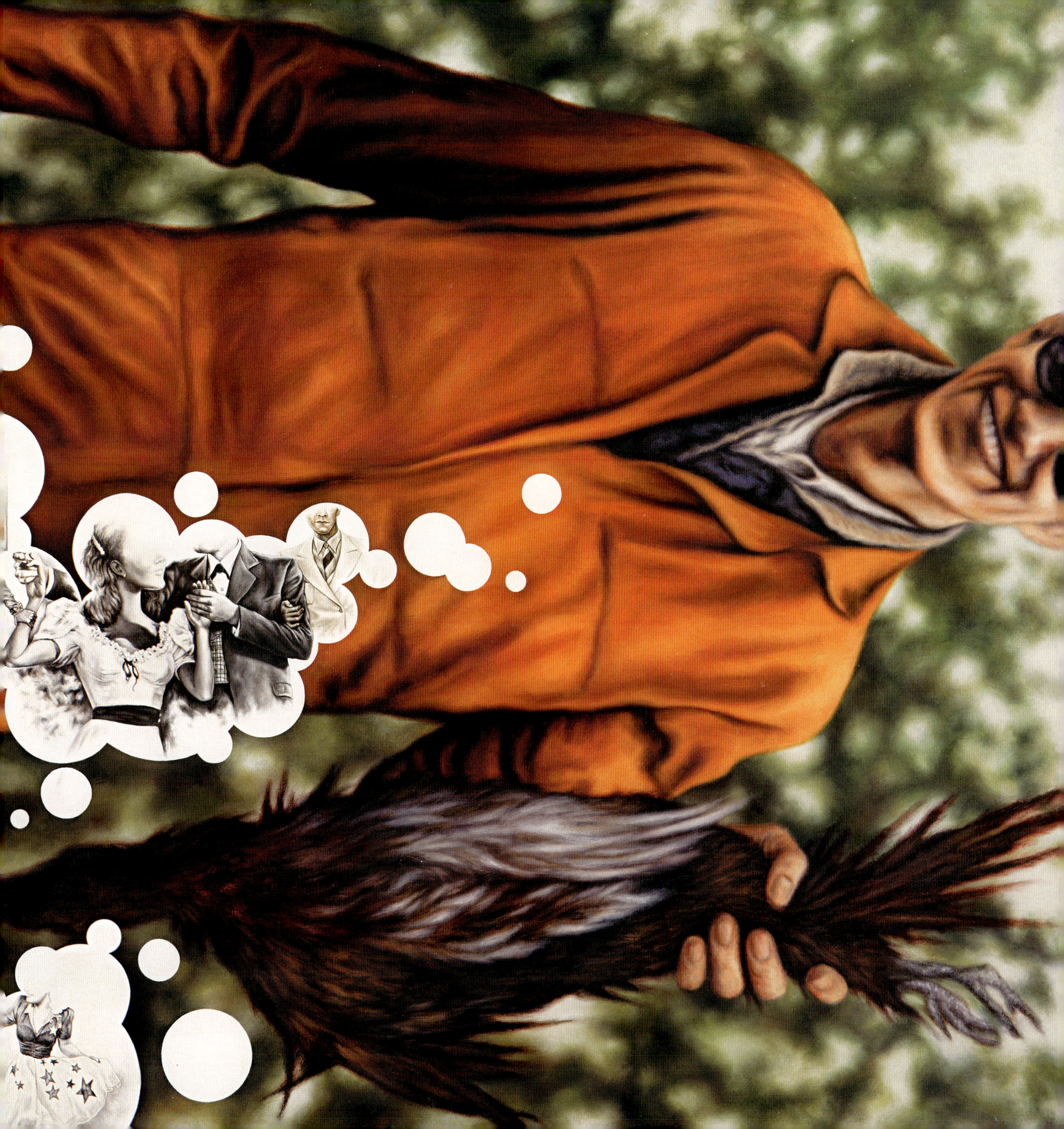

Image Index

64 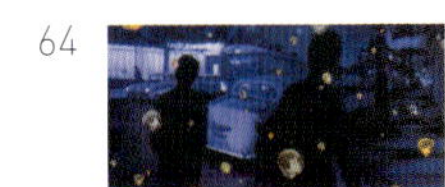

Flurries
1999
Oil on canvas
36 x 72 in.

83 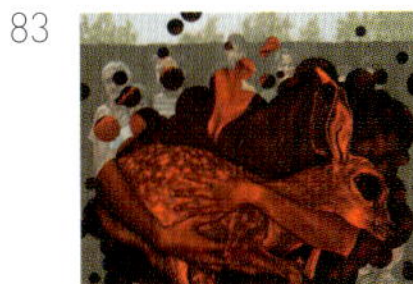

Golden Moments
2001
Oil on canvas
36 x 36 in.
B.J. Miller

38 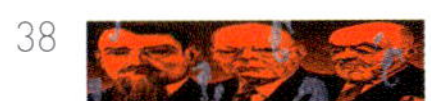

Hats Off to Fission
1998
Acrylic on wood
12 x 48 in.
Chuck Statler

87 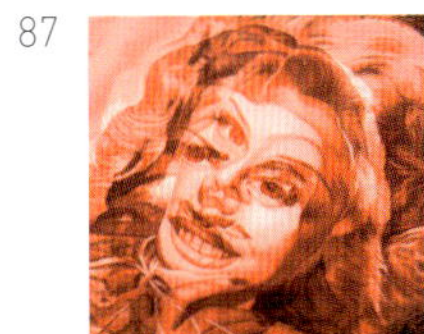

Holy Matron of Ridicule
2003
Oil on canvas
36 x 36 in.

41 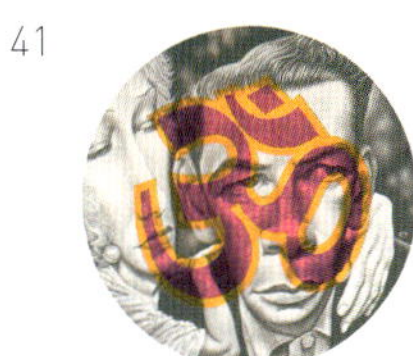

I Am a Fugitive from a Chain Gang: OM
1998
Acrylic on canvas
10 x 10 in.
Robert Roth

41 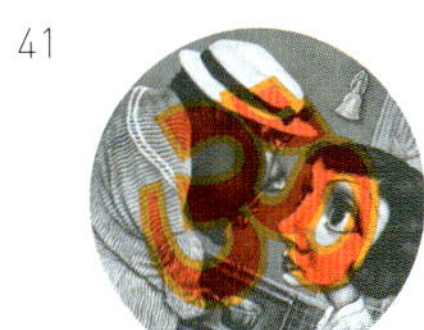

Imitation of Life: OM
1998
Acrylic on canvas
8 x 8 in.
Robert Roth

61 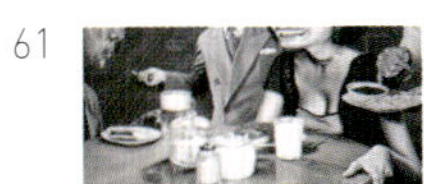

Intermezzo
1999
Oil on canvas
36 x 72 in.
Andrew & Nicole McWhorter

41 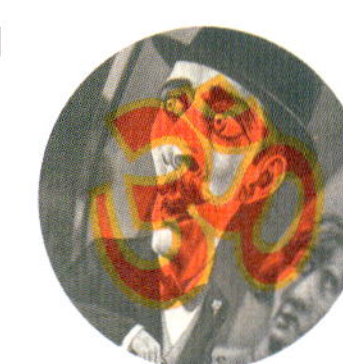

It: OM
1998
Acrylic on canvas
8 x 8 in.
Robert Roth

73 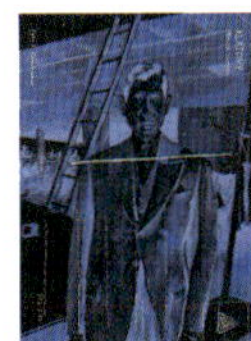

Klatovy
2000
Acrylic and collage on canvas
7 x 5 in.
Craig Scholla

36 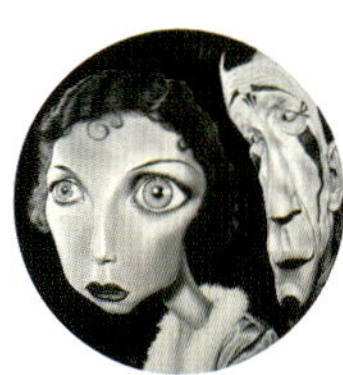

Laugh, Clown, Laugh
1998
Acrylic & pocket pussy on wood
42 x 42 in.
Robert Roth

75 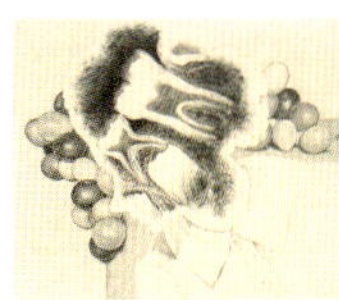

Let's Celebrate
2001
Graphite on paper
8 x 10 in.

79 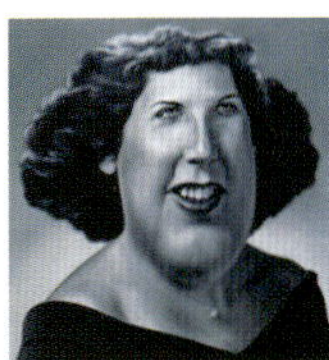

Margo Lefferts
2001
Oil on canvas
24 x 24 in.
David Arquette & Courteney Cox

50 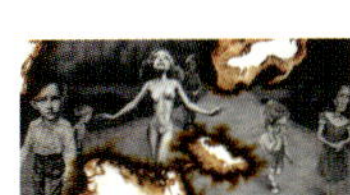

"Nam!" 1949 an RKO Picture
1999
Oil on canvas
36 x 72 in.
Tom Patchett

58 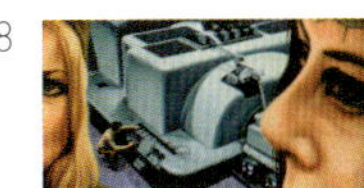

Orientation, The
1999
Oil on canvas
36 x 72 in.
Tom Patchett

96 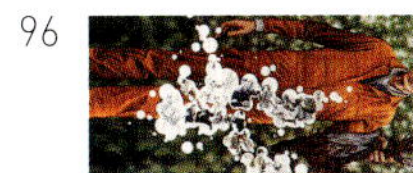

Spores of Today (Anima Rising)
2000-2003
Oil on canvas
35 x 72 in.

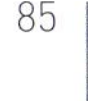
85 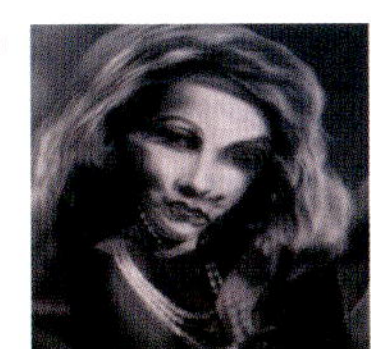

Starlet
2001
Oil on canvas
24 x 24 in.
Norman Fisher-Jones

32 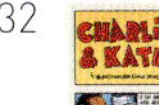 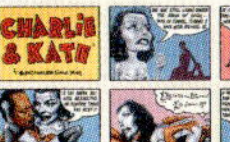

Sunday Funnies, The
1996
Acrylic on canvas
18 x 36 in.
Bart Nagel

54 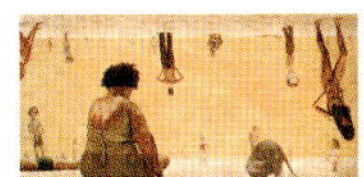

Swims
1999
Oil on canvas
36 x 72 in.
Christopher Washburn

80 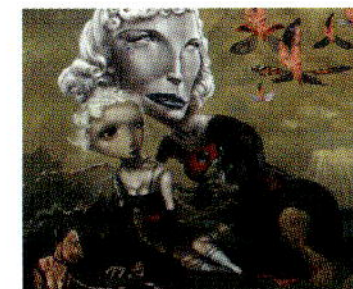

That Which Organizes My Feathers (w/ Joe Sorren)
2001
Acrylic on canvas
30 x 36 in.
Patricia Arquette

92 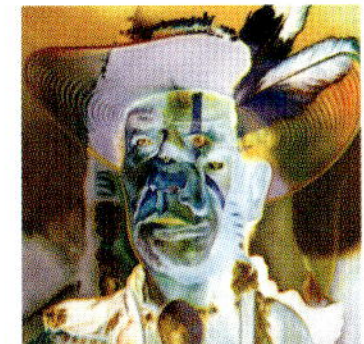

Them or Us
2003
Oil on canvas
18 x 18 in.
Jamie & Linda Stanek

41 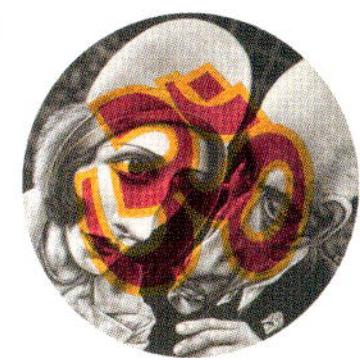

Trial of Mary Dugan: OM, The
1998
Acrylic on canvas
10 x 10 in.
Robert Roth

40 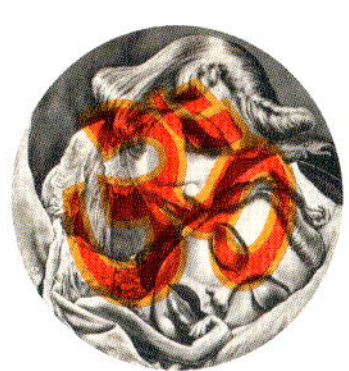

Two Girls and a Sailor: OM
1998
Acrylic on canvas
12 x 12 in.
Robert Roth

62 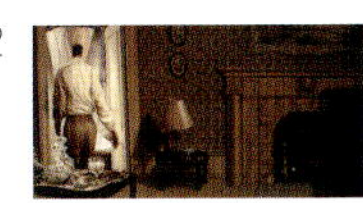

Untitled
1999
Oil on canvas
36 x 72 in.
Viggo Mortensen

49 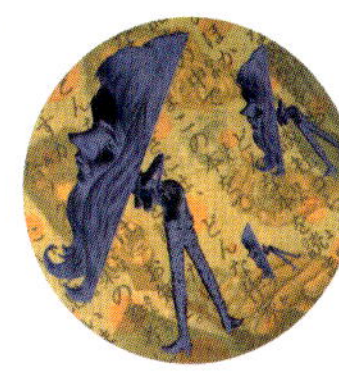

Wor-Torn
1998
Acrylic on canvas
20 x 20 in.
Mike Gosselin

20 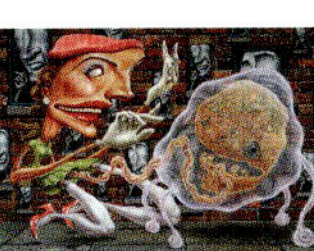

You Add Fresh Eggs
1996
Acrylic on board
20 x 30 in.
Leonardo DiCaprio

42 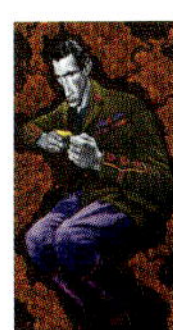

Young Gary Cooper in Termite Mound with Post-It ™
1998
Acrylic on canvas
30 x 15 in.

Biography

1968 Born Gemini, June 3rd in Ann Arbor, Michigan
1986-1990 Attended Rhode Island School of Design, BFA
1990-2000 Worked in San Francisco
Lives and works in New York

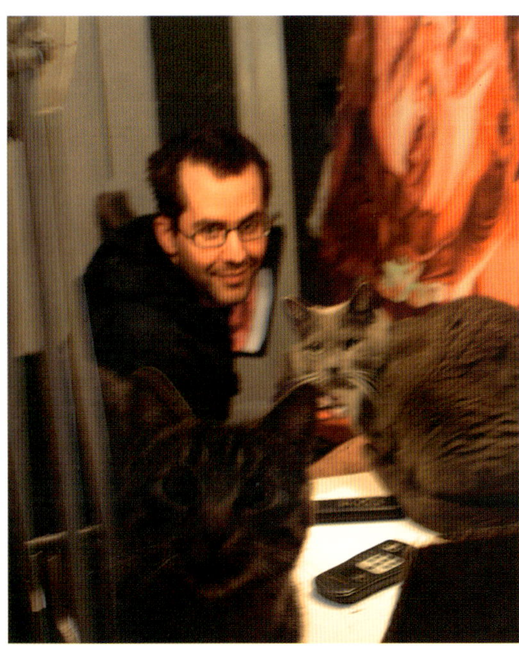

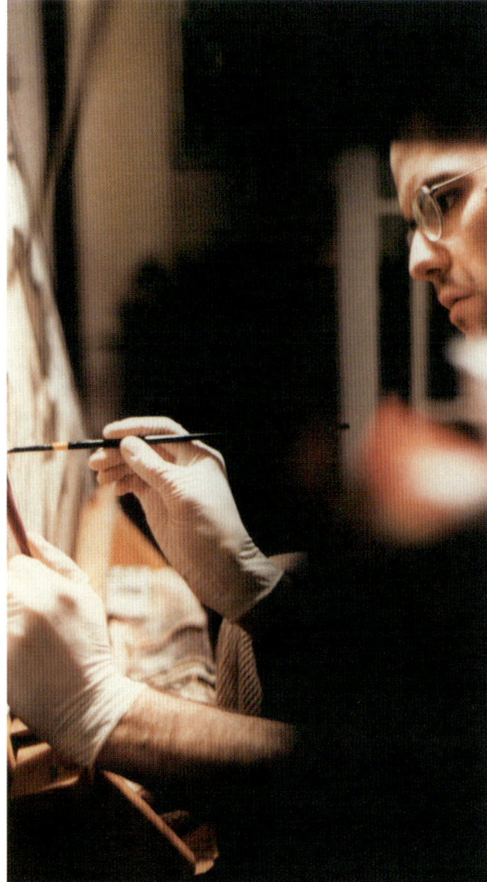

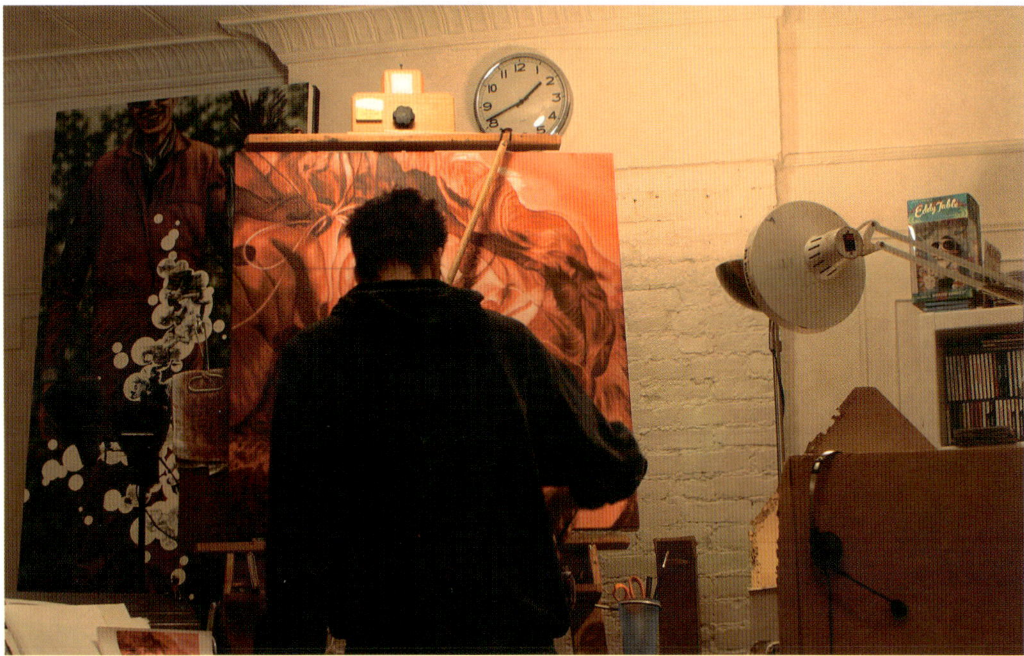

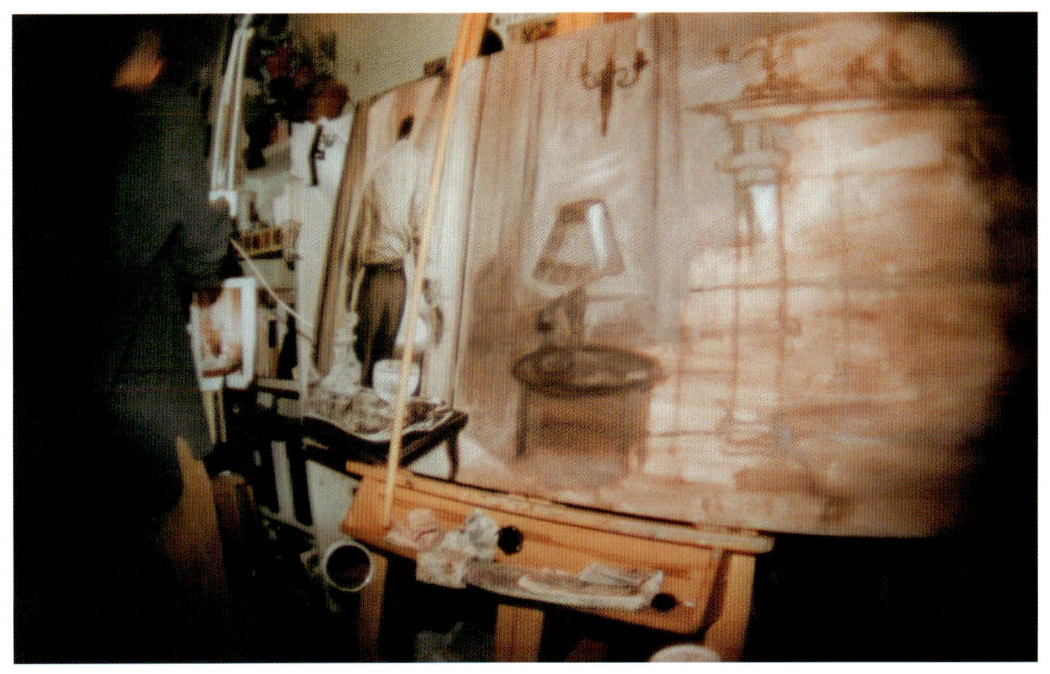

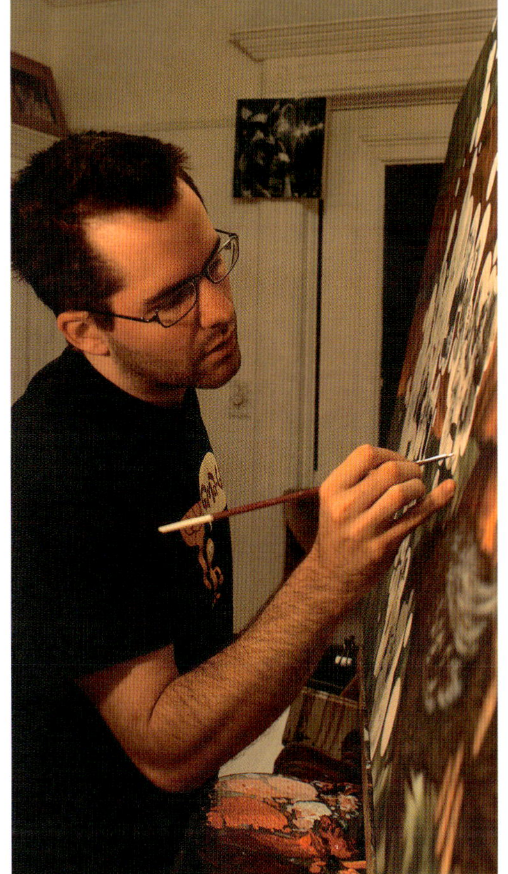

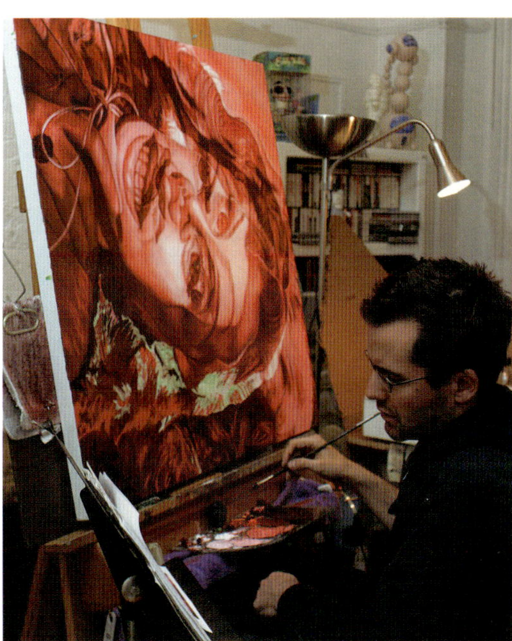

Photos of "Spores" and "Holy Matron" in progress by Ben Wagner 2003
Photos of "Untitled" in progress by Robynne Flynn 1999

Resume

Selected Solo Exhibitions:

2004 “Who Are Parents?” Earl McGrath Gallery, New York
2004 “Lil’ Marbles” Varnish Fine Art, San Francisco
2001 “Pink Bits & The Glory of Autumn” La Luz De Jesus, Los Angeles
2000 “Good/Blanco” 111 Minna Gallery, San Francisco
1999 “Motion Pictures” Track 16 Gallery, Los Angeles
1998 “Birdy Sounds” La Luz De Jesus, Los Angeles
1996 “Contrived Works” La Luz De Jesus, Los Angeles

Selected Group Exhibitions:

2003 “Raising The Brow” Earl McGrath Gallery, New York & Los Angeles
“Dealer’s Choice” 31 Grand, Brooklyn
“Decipher 2.0” NY Arts Gallery, New York
“Move 9: Lead Poisoning” New Image Art, Los Angeles
“Group Exhibition, Gallery Artists” Varnish Fine Art, San Francisco
“A Thousand Clowns” Robert Berman Gallery, Los Angeles
“The Sci-Fi Western” 111 Minna Gallery, San Francisco
“Assembly” The Front Room, Brooklyn
“Invitational VI” La Luz De Jesus, Los Angeles

2002 "High on Life: Transcending Addiction" The American Visionary Art Museum, Baltimore
"Group Exhibition, Gallery Artists" Earl McGrath Gallery, New York
"Look At Me, What Do You See, What Do You See" Gracie Mansion Gallery, New York
"Customized Culture" Rockford Art Museum, Rockford, IL
"Juxtapoz 8th Anniversary Exhibition" Track 16 Gallery, Los Angeles
"Dime Bag" New Image Art, Los Angeles
"Panorama" The Front Room, Brooklyn
"Invitational V" La Luz De Jesus, Los Angeles

2001 "Ten Fold" The ______ Project, New York
"The Exquisite Day Project" Plus Ultra, Brooklyn
"Group Show" Merry Karnowsky Gallery, Los Angeles
"Auction" New Langton Arts, San Francisco
"Yuzen Surf" Moda Politica, Tokyo & Chisou Gallery, Kyoto
"Stranger Than You" New Langton Arts, San Francisco
"Invitational IV" La Luz De Jesus, Los Angeles

2000 "Group Exhibition" Roq La Rue Gallery, Seattle
"Drawing Show" La Luz De Jesus, Los Angeles
"Move 5" Art Works Book Art Space, Bergamot Station, Santa Monica
"Up from the Underground" Art & Culture Center, Hollywood, Florida
"Invitational III" La Luz De Jesus, Los Angeles

1999 "Friends of Tibet Auction" La Luz De Jesus, Los Angeles
"Aieee! The Monster Show!" Roq La Rue Gallery, Seattle
"C Stands For . . . " C-Pop Gallery, Detroit
"Group Show" Revelation Gallery, San Francisco
"Invitational II" La Luz De Jesus, Los Angeles

1998 "Kittens & Kads" Merry Karnowsky Gallery, Los Angeles
"Move 2" New Image Art, Los Angeles
"No Red Ribbons II" Julie Rico Gallery, Santa Monica
"Tribute to Billy Shire" Track 16 Gallery, Santa Monica
"Eight Painters" 111 Minna Gallery, San Francisco (Curator)
"Acme Custom 2" Somar Gallery, San Francisco
"Invitational" La Luz De Jesus, Los Angeles

1997 "Unorthodox" 111 Minna Gallery, San Francisco
"The Narrative Image" CBGB Gallery, New York
"No Red Ribbons I" La Luz De Jesus, Los Angeles

1996 "All California - All Media" Downey Museum of Art, Downey, CA
"Holiday Pop Jamboree" Bess Cutler Gallery, New York

1995 "Dia De Los Muertos" La Luz De Jesus, Los Angeles

Acknowledgments

The following people had a direct hand in the creation of this book. Thank you:

Ron Turner, Gail Zappa, Viggo Mortensen, Carlo McCormick, Alix Sloan, Mark Ryden, Joe Sorren, Billy Shire, Annie Tucker, Bucky Sinister, Kenny Yu, Helena Chow, Elizabeth Kairys, Claudia Brandenburg, Paul Felder, Jordin Rey Isip, Rich Jacobs, Dana Wysocki, Ben Wagner, Gregory Silberman, and Karin Skaggs.

The following is a list of those who have generously provided love, support, encouragement, time, money, humor, and ass-kicking. Each has contributed to my development, creative and otherwise. I thank and love most of them with all and some of them with most of my heart.

All That Is, Terri Tate, Thomas & Laurie White, Justin White, Nancy McGinnis & Georgie Ray, Rupert & Anne Atkin, Gordon & Helen White, Robert White, Gregory Atkin, Valerie Wilkins & family, William Atkin & family, Michael Kubacki & family, Ande & Peter Ferretti, Jeffrey Belanger & family, The Janssens, William B. Dennes, Elizabeth Kairys, Brad Mossman & Lotte Svenningsen, David Fremont, Carol Majewski, Milo & Greta, Jason Porter, Jordin Isip, Melinda Beck & Chloe, Joe Sorren, Jessica, Martha & Henry Sorren, Robin Scovill, Christine Maggiore, Charlie & Eliza Jane, Peter Altenberg & Kalyan, Bernie Jungle, Douglas Piburn, Gayle Pillsbury & Stella, Ellae Elinwood, Peter Bernhardt, Robert & Suzanne Williams, Billy Shire & La Luz De Jesus Gallery, Mark Ryden, Earl McGrath, Alix Sloan, Gail Zappa, Leonardo DiCaprio, George DiCaprio, Jamie O'Shea, Annie "Pal" Tucker & Juxtapoz, Ron Turner & Last Gasp, Gomez Bueno & Mia Sevier, David Weeks, Georgie Stout & Fenner, Eiming Jung & 111 Minna Gallery, Andrew, Nicole & Owen McWhorter, Carlo McCormick, Isabel Samaras, Marcos Sorensen & Nico, Jeff Zimmerman, Gina de la Chesnaye & Athena, Rob Clayton, Christian Clayton, Linda, David & Coco Parrick, Taylor McKimens & Misaki Kawai, Merry Karnowsky, Pilar Perez, Laurie Steelink, Tom Patchett & Track 16 Gallery, Viggo Mortensen, David Arquette & Courteney Cox, Patricia Arquette, Emily Cohen, John Pine & Caleb, Bart Nagel & Bonnie Powell, Elise Cannon, Robert Jess Roth, Moon Unit Zappa, Dweezil, Ahmet & Diva Zappa, Paul Felder, Kevin Thatcher, Michelle Smith, Dale Flattum & Elijah, Michel Chenelle, Long Gone John, Kidada Jones, Jasper Husch, Patrick Callery, Takuji Masuda, Joel Stein, Todd & Kathy Schorr, John & Stephanie Rubeli, Michael Mees, Norman Fisher-Jones, David McWilliam & family, Rob Avsharian, Bobby Roe, Kay Gould-Caskey, Thomas Brophy & family, Richard King, Rich Jacobs, Kevin Ancell, Barbara & Maria Penrod, Jud Bergeron & Varnish Fine Art, Scott Musgrove, Kelly, Cole & Zaida Marquis, Aimee Macauley, Jonathan Davis & Korn, Les Rogers, Alethia Weingarten, Kimberly Schifino, Robynne Flynn, Sarah Trigg, Tara Cullen, Tim Brock, Gabriela Rivera Zuñiga, Carrie Bradley, Christopher Washburn, Paul Fine, Andrew Burrell, Lorenzo Maggiore, Joy & Cleo, Dave Eggers, Doze Green, Brent Roam, Carl Dunn,

Katy Petty, Catarina Correia, Emily Keyishian, Jason Kleinberg, James, Ryan & Casey Gallagher, Calef Brown, Claudia Brandenburg, Stephen, Elizabeth & Hazel Curley, Marc Sutherland, Lisa Leingang, Amro & Rebecca, Bill & Marjorie Fremont, Seymour & Rosalyn Pedinoff, John Copeland, Adam McCauley, Dave Cooper, Corey Porter, Larry Jones, Kevin Beals, Matt Goldman, Ken Grekin & Dan Wood, Glenn Barr, Fred Muench & Jodi Levine, Pamela Hobbs, Todd, Leslie & Oskar, Ben Wagner, Robert Chapel, Fred Dodsworth, Hideki Matsuoka, Eden Palmer, Craig & Mollie, Kim Mazrui, Juan Miguel Avila, Lisa Hammersly, Angelique Quillay, Carina Chocano, The Kairys Family, Saren Sakurai, Andrew Jenkins, Katherine Cohen, Gwen Jansma, Gregge Tiffen, Gus Leinbach & Camp Innisfree, Jo Miles Schuman, Hall & Klein, Pamela Bashir, Jim Corbitt, & Burns Park Elementary, Elaine Headly, Tom Dodd, & Community High School, Mahler Ryder, Fritz Drury, Russell O. Jones, Anthony Russo, Dagmar Frinta, David Porter, Brice Hobbs, & The Rhode Island School of Design, Maslov/Weinberg, Rodger Stevens, Joe Coleman & Whitney Ward, Tony Shafrazi, Tom Patterson, The American Visionary Art Museum, Kenny Schachter, Eric Foss & The Gentlemen of Fuse Gallery, Douglas Nason, Greg Escalante, David Fitschen, Aaron Rose, Marsea Goldberg & New Image Art, Kirsten Anderson & Roq La Rue Gallery, Leslie Napoles, James Bewley, Massimiliano Geraci & Cyberzone, Ikkei Arai, Gracie Mansion, Robert Berman, Debi Jacobsen & L'Imagerie Gallery, Artkrush.com, Jonathan LeVine & Tin Man Alley, Richard E. Stuart, B.J. Miller, Gary Himelfarb, Adeo Ressi, Tom Thewes & C-Pop, Katharine Gates, Gregory & Susan Silberman, Andra Hill, ArtPress, Noah Mass, Bess Cutler, Roberto Parada, Jamie & Linda Stanek, Maria, Juliette, Liane & The Alternative Pick, Dan Leone & Tami Lipsee, Gary Taxali, Barry McGee, Steve Ellis, Mark Heflin, Chris Johanson, Winston Smith & Jana Herzen, Katherine Streeter, Lisa Stefanelli, Matt Stahl, Christine Shields, Scott Stowell, Chris Mars, Dalek & Sarah, Hiroshi Kimura, Gary Panter, Alison Pebworth, E. V. Day, Tom Galbraith & Carolyn Jones, Janice Tuuri, Carla Zizo, Tracy, Jeff & Heather Zmrzlina, Virgil Shaw, Georganne Deen, Daniel Clowes, Siri Margerin, Jeffrey Decoster, Joe, LeAnn & Spinnaker Auer, Ben Long, Shana Dambrot, Lennie Mace, Picture Mechanics, Homer Flynn, Steven Cerio, John Moore, Yuri & Josh, Kaws, Tim Bower, Aaron Smith, Johanna St.Clair, Jeff Hathaway, Ruth Marten, Peter & Jolene, Ben & Becky, Todd Barry, Peter Halley, Anita Kunz, Maya Hayuk, Craig LaRotonda & Kim Maria, Guy Capecelatro III, Ken Anbender, Paul Bright, Brad Johnson, Bill Hunt, Sean Holihan, Nat & Kristen, Jonathon Rosen, Joe & Candice Sloan, Mark Ulriksen, Harvey Bennett Stafford, Callie Scoville, Jeff Quinn, Day Milman, Andy Murdock, Jorge Colombo, Pamelia Kurstin, Dani Freitag, Henrik Drescher, Patton Oswalt, Sarah Nichols, Sara Hsiang & family, Michael Udowitz, Ryan Ring, Paul Philpott, Anthony Ausgang, Chip Wass, Scott Lenhardt, Gene Mollica, Jim Thirlwell, Michael & Andy, Annie Crawford, Liesel Wieneke, Elizabeth Alberda, Kenneth B. Smith, Gary Himelfarb & RAS Records, Bob Schreck, Jennifer Rogers, Mike Gosselin, Will Rostov, Paul Perez, Martin Schenk, Julie Simms, Gary Cifra, Chuck Statler, Jim & Karen Levilee, Phil Goset, Brian Billmeier, Brendan White, Andrew Hulktrans, Taylor Mell, Joshua & Jennifer Davis, Susan Langholz, Marty Moore, Max Henry, Roger Avary, Tim Palen, A.J. Jacobs, Billy Ozone, Rob Weisbach, The Meices, Dr. Barbara Fishelson, Andy Kindler, Vance Ypsilanti, Mitch Altman, Naoto Hattori, Cris Mastellone, Jiri Jacknowitz, Robert Knowles, Matthew Spahr, William Rafuse, James Wood, Jennifer Lovold, Craig Scholla, Kurt Scholla, Christopher Pinkerton, Paul Miller, Jim McCloud, Ron Lim, Jeremy Revell, Gary Pressman, David Littleton, John Purlia, Samuel Hoffberger, Joey Burkhart, Kenley Lamaute, Christopher Brennan, Richard Lau, The Reverend Derek William Palmer, Julie Pacer, Joshua Liner & Lineage Gallery, Ted Mathot, David McMurry, Jon Hanna, Chad Tills, Justin Tuttle, Patricia Abbott, Sean Moloney, Gregory Noppe, Patricia Watson, Reza Assemi, Zev Levy, Brett Hess, Phillip Buchanan, e. a. minters, Barney Firks, Amanda Jane Miller, Clifford Abrams, Jack Jowett, Harry Saylor & Orbit Gallery, Paul Watson, Carl Amt, Keizo Fujimoto, Harry Hollander, Hayden Foreman-Smith, Anyone who was, is, or will be a fan of my work, You, for buying this book, George, Speed, Spike, Bubba, Pooky, Murphy, The Princess, Chelsea, Glorious, Minnesota, Ishi, and especially those who forgive me for inadvertently leaving them off of this list.

Inspiration

This is an incomplete list of individuals, entities, and objects that have impacted my life and art. Many are no longer relevant, some matter much more than others, but all have touched me somewhere, to some degree. I thank them, and I thank those who led me to them.

Francis Vincent Zappa
Howard Zinn
Emiliano Zapata
Lisa Yuskavage
Neil Young
Loretta Young
Yes
X (the band)
Malcolm X
Steven Wright
Stephen Wright
Frank Lloyd Wright
Stevie Wonder
Adolph Wölfli
Flip Wilson
Brian Wilson
Cris Williamson
Tony Williams
Tennessee Williams
Gene Wilder
Oscar Wilde
The Who
Elton & Betty White
Bukka White
Nathaniel West
Tom Wesselmann
Junior Wells
H.G. Wells
Orson Welles
Dr. Andrew Weil
Johnny Guitar Watson
Muddy Waters
John W. Waterhouse
Grover Washington, Jr.
Warm Wires
Andy Warhol
Chris Ware
Neal Donald Walsh
Thomas Fats Waller
Rufus Wainwright
Loudon Wainwright III
Édouard Vuillard
Kurt Vonnegut, Jr.
Don van Vliet
Bill Viola
Thomas Vinterberg
Villa Alegre
Gore Vidal
Jan Vermeer
Velázquez
Edgard Varèse
Alida Valli
Uz Jsme Doma
Nick Ut
Kool Keith & Ultramags
Ui
U.S. Maple
Cy Twombly
Mark Twain
Luc Tuymans
Harriet Tubman
François Truffaut
Trouble Funk
Tripping Daisy
Lars von Trier
1976 Toyota Corolla (x2)
John Kennedy Toole
Eckhart Tolle
J.R.R. Tolkien
Lou Whitaker & The 1984 Detroit Tigers
Gene Tierney
Three Day Stubble
Hunter S. Thompson
Marlo Thomas & Friends
Wayne Thiebaud
Thinking Fellers Union Local 282
Leon Theremin
Nikola Tesla
Television (the band)
James Taylor
Elizabeth Taylor
Cecil Taylor
Yves Tanguy
Rufino Tamayo
David Byrne & Talking Heads
Sun Ra
Supergrass
Whitley Streiber
Igor Stravinsky
Sly Stone
Dean Stockwell
James Stewart
Stereolab
Frank Stella
John Steinbeck
Steely Dan
Steel Pulse
Steel Pole Bathtub
Ralph Steadman
Harry Dean Stanton
U Srinivas
Spot 1019
Sir Stanley Spencer
Alexander Skip Spence
The Specials
Sparklehorse
Sissy Spacek
Souled American
Sonic Youth
Son House
Robert Wyatt & The Soft Machine
Phoebe Snow
The Smiths
Harry Smith
Elliott Smith
Bessie Smith
Slint
Vilgot Sjöman
Sitting Bull
Douglas Sirk
David Alfaro Siqueiros
Frank Sinatra
Paul Simon & Art Garfunkel
Shel Silverstein
Sarah Silverman
Wayne Shorter
Cindy Sherman
George Bernard Shaw
Gary Shandling
Shakey Jake
The Shaggs
Dr. Seuss
Georges Seurat
Seth
Maurice Sendak
Peter Sellers
Colin Self
David & Amy Sedaris
Sesame Street
The Sea and Cake
Lizabeth Scott
George C. Scott
Charles Schulz
Schoolhouse Rock
Egon Schiele
Cal Schenkel
Christian Schad
Richard Scary
Saturday Night Live (1975-80)
Erik Satie
Swami Satchidananda
Sasquatch
Jean-Paul Sartre
David Salle
Jerome David Salinger
Niki de Saint Phalle
SCTV
Ken Russell
Ed Ruscha
Run-DMC
Gena Rowlands
Mark Rothko
Alexander Ross
James Rosenquist
Esther Rolle
Mr. Fred Rogers
Nicolas Roeg
Auguste Rodin
Jane Roberts & Robert Butts
Tom Robbins
Diego Rivera
Gerhard Richter
Paul Reubens
The Residents
Rembrandt
Wilhelm Reich
Paula Rego
Ishmael Reed
Nicholas Ray
Wilson Rawls
Robert Rauschenberg
Rankin-Bass
Ella Raines
Gilda Radner
Radiohead
R.E.M.
Thomas Pynchon
Public Enemy
Richard Pryor
Sergei Prokofiev
Prince
Vincent Price
Archer Prewitt
Elvis Presley
William Powell
Sidney Poitier
Iggy Pop
Polvo
The Police
Roman Polanski
Pixies
Dr. Pitcairn
Pink Floyd
Pablo Picasso
The Philly Fanatic
Regis Philbin
The Pharcyde
Juster, Feiffer & The Phantom Tollbooth
Paul Pfeiffer
Raymond Pettibon
Penthouse Magazine (circa 1980)
Leonard Peltier
Eldred Gregory Peck
Stephen Malkmus & Pavement
Jaco Pastorious
Ed Paschke
George Clinton & Parliament/ Funkadelic
Charlie Parker
Outkast
Tony Oursler
George Orwell
Joe Orton
José Clemente Orozco
Orange Julius
Yoko Ono
Will Oldham
Claes Oldenburg
Bob Odenkirk
Eugene O'Neill
Margaret O'Brien
Don Novello
Irving Norman
Nirvana
Anaïs Nin
Harry Nilsson
Randy Newman
Paul Newman
The New Zoo Revue
Willie Nelson
Negativland
Conlon Nancarrow
Vladimir Nabokov
My Bloody Valentine
Muddy Waters
Alphonse Mucha
W.A. Mozart
Berry Gordy & Motown
The Mothers of Invention
Victor Moscoso
Michael Moore
Henry Moore
Monty Python
Thelonious Sphere Monk
Piet Mondrian
Amedeo Modigliani
Joni Mitchell
Minutemen
Minor Threat
Mink Lungs
Charles Mingus
Henry Miller
Milk Cult
Joan Miró
Mercury Rev
The MEGO Spiderman
Meat Puppets
Blind Willie McTell
John McLaughlin
Robert McChesney
MC5
George McGovern
Paul McCartney
Cory McAbee
Archie Mayo
Curtis Mayfield
Matta
Henri Matisse
Massive Attack
The Marx Brothers
Don Martin
Robert Nesta Marley
Marisol
Édouard Manet
Man Ray
Norman Mailer
René Magritte
Magic Sam
William M. Gaines & Mad Magazine
David Lynch
George Lucas (pre-1999)
Myrna Loy
H.P. Lovecraft
Los Lobos
Looney Tunes
The Little Rascals
Little My
Booker Little
Richard Lindner
Lincoln Logs
Abbey Lincoln
Fang Lijun
Lightnin' Hopkins
György Ligeti
Roy Lichtenstein
David Letterman
Dom Leone
Leonardo da Vinci
John Lennon
Jack Lemon
Vivian Leigh
Mike Leigh
Tom Lehrer
LEGO
Fernand Leger
Stan Lee
Harper Lee

Ang Lee
Led Zeppelin
Timothy Leary
Leadbelly
Jacob Lawrence
Stan Laurel & Oliver Hardy
Gary Larson
Fritz Lang
Hedy Lamarr
Veronica Lake
Yayoi Kusama
Stanley Kubrick
Kruder & Dorfmeister
John Kricfalusi
Mark Kozelek
Ernie Kovacs
Jack Kornfield
Willem de Kooning
Don Knotts
Gustav Klimt
B. Kliban
Paul Klee
R.B. Kitaj
Ray Davies & The Kinks
Stephen King
Martin Luther King, Jr.
Carole King
Krzysztof Kieslowski
Søren Kierkegaard
Ken Kesey
Jack Kerouac
Grace Kelly
Edward & Nancy Kienholz
Kenner
Buster Keaton
Steve Keane
Elia Kazan
Charlie Kaufman
Wassily Kandinsky
Frida Kahlo
Franz Kafka
James Joyce
Joy Division
Louis Jordan
Allen Jones
Robert Johnson
Ray Johnson
Lonnie Johnson
Jasper Johns
Elton John
Jethro Tull
The Jerky Boys
Thomas Jefferson
Keith Jarrett
Jim Jarmusch
Al Jaffee
Michael Jackson
Ishi (the last Yahi)
Ingres
Aldous Huxley
Shemp, Moe & Curly Howard & Larry Fine
Edward Hopper
John Lee Hooker
Billie Holiday
Hans Holbein
David Hockney
Christopher Hitchens (re: Kissinger)
Alfred Hitchcock
Bill Hicks
Werner Herzog
Kristen Hersh

Herbie The Love Bug
Katherine Hepburn
Audrey Hepburn
Jim Henson
Doug Henning
Jimi Hendrix
Ernest Hemingway
Joseph L. Heller
Martin Heidegger
Rita Hayworth
Todd Haynes
Sterling Hayden
Louise Hay
Donny Hathaway
P. J. Harvey
Ray Harryhausen
George Harrison
Harm Farm
The Harlem Globetrotters
Duane Hanson
Barry Hannah
Herbie Hancock
Richard Hamilton
Neil Hamburger
Buddy Guy
Woody & Arlo Guthrie
Philip Guston
George Grosz
Bertram Myron Gross
Matt Groening
David Grisman
D.W. Griffith
The Reverend Al Green
El Greco
Grant Lee Buffalo
Cary Grant
Granfaloon Bus
Grandaddy
Glenn Gould
Arshile Gorky
Edward Gorey
Michel Gondry
Leon Golub
Andy Goldsworthy
William Gerald Golding
Rube Goldberg
Vincent van Gogh
Jean-Luc Godard
Crispin Glover
Allen Ginsburg
Gilbert & George
The Ghoul
Sir Graves Ghastly
Mahatma Ghandi
George & Ira Gershwin
Geronimo
Ben Gazzara
Marvin Gaye
Paul Gauguin
Antonio Gaudi
Greta Garbo
Gang Starr
Gang Of Four
Vincent Gallo
Robert Pollard & GBV
Buckminster Fuller
Fugazi
John Frusciante
Edith Frost
The Friendly Giant
Lucian Freud
Tom Friedman
Anitra Frazier
Aretha Franklin

Redd Foxx
Fly Ashtray
The Fleetwood Diner
The Flaming Lips
Ella Fitzgerald
Robert Fisk
Fisher-Price
The Fisher 500-C
Fishbone
W.C. Fields
María Félix
Fela Anikulapo-Kuti
FedEx
William Faulkner
The Fat Boys
R.W. Fassbinder
John Fante
Mark E. Smith & The Fall
Peter Falk
Jan van Eyck
Richard Estes
Inka Essenhigh
Max Ernst
Werner Erhard
James Ensor
Brian Eno
Rodegast, Stanton & Emmanuel
Ed Emberly
E.K. Duke Ellington
The Electric Company
Dwight D. Eisenhower
Albert Einstein
Betty Edwards
Ed's Redeeming Qualities
Earth Wind & Fire
Charles & Ray Eames
Thomas Eakins
Bob Dylan
Shelly Duvall
Robert Duvall
George Duke
Marcel Duchamp
Jean Dubuffet
Nick Drake
Robert Downey, Sr. & Jr.
Arthur Dove
Frederick Douglass
Domino's Pizza World Headquarters
Eric Dolphy
Willie Dixon
Otto Dix
Thomas M. Disch
Charles Dickens
Philip K. Dick
Devo
Don DeLillo
Dolores del Rio
Desmond Dekker
Jack DeJohnette
Claude Debussy
James Dean
De La Soul
Stuart Davis
Miles Davis
Bette Davis
Ram Dass
Bhagavan Das
Danielson Familie
Salvador Dalí
Roald Dahl
Edward S. Curtis

John Currin
The Cure
Walter Cunningham
e.e. cummings
Robert Crumb
David Cross
Mort Crim
Joan Crawford
Henry Cowell
Elvis Costello
Bill Cosby
Francis Ford Coppola
Gary Cooper
Tim Conway
Bobby Conn
Richard Condon
John Coltrane
Alice Coltrane
Ornette Coleman
Nat King Cole
The Coen Brothers
Daniel Clowes
Montgomery Clift
Francesco Clemente
The Clash
Noam Chomsky
Julia Child
Chief Joseph
Vic Chesnutt
Ray Charles
Charles Chaplin
Lon Chaney
Paul Cézanne
Edgar Cayce
Cat Power
Carlos Castaneda
Seymour Cassel
John Cassavetes
Mary Cassatt
George Washington Carver
Ron Carter
Jimmy Carter
Ray Carney
George Carlin
Carravagio
Captain Beefheart
Cantinflas
Joseph Campbell
Cab Calloway
Alexander Calder
Paul Cadmus
Sebastian Cabot
Butthole Surfers
William S. Burroughs
Charles Burns
Carol Burnett
Anthony Burgess
Burger Chef
Luis Buñuel
Charles Bukowski
LTJ Bukem
Built to Spill
Jeff Buckley
Shelby Bryant
Lenny Bruce
James Brown
Mel Brooks
Wilfred Brimley's Double
André Breton
The Breeders
Richard Brautigan
Marlon Brando
Brainiac
Ray Bradbury

David Bowie
Pierre Boulez
Fernando Botero
Hieronymus Bosch
Betty Boop
KRS One & Boogie Down Productions
Pierre Bonnard
Humphrey Bogart
Blur
Judy Blume
The Blues Brothers
Mel Blanc
William Blake
Peter Blake
Black Sabbath
Biz Markie
Bill Bixby
Simon Bisley
Big Star
Bruce Bickford
Ashley Bickerton
Joseph Beuys
Benji
Saul Bellow
Hans Bellmer
Ludwig van Beethoven
Max Beckmann
Beck Hansen
The Beatles
The Beastie Boys
Jean-Michel Basquiat
Georg Baselitz
Bella Bartok
John Barrymore
Syd Barrett
Matthew Barney
Jamey Barnard
Brigitte Bardot
Devendra Banhart
Nikhil Banerjee
Anne Bancroft
Balthus
J.G. Ballard
John Baldessari
Ralph Bakshi
Chet Baker
Ben H. Bagdikian
The Bad News Bears
Francis Bacon
J.S. Bach
Lauren Bacall
The Atari 2600
Hal Ashby
Richard Artschwager
Art Ensemble of Chicago
Louis Armstrong
The Arboretum
Sergio Aragones
Steve Jobs & Apple
Aphex Twin
Michelangelo Antonioni
Wes Anderson
P.T. Anderson
Lindsay Anderson
Robert Altman
Michael Almereyda
Woody Allen
Muhammad Ali
Ivan Albright
Josef Albers
Aesop Rock
Adobe Systems
Acetone
A Tribe Called Quest

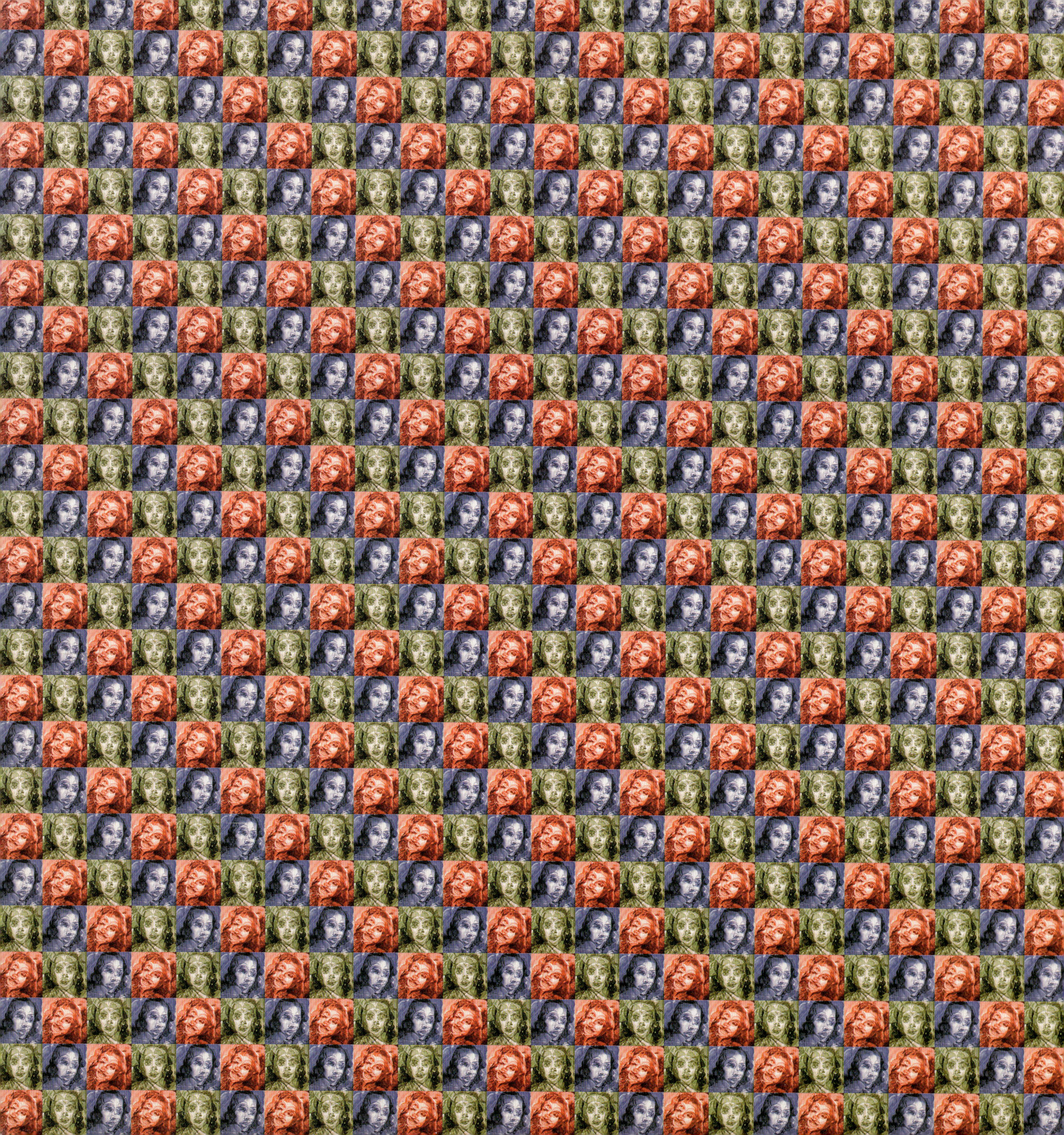